**"GREAT DETAIL . . . SURPRISING
TWISTS . . . A PERFECT PITCH."**
—*Virginia Pilot and Ledger Star*

Sportswriter Joe Tinker had to fight not to
play dumb when he left his baseball beat to
hunt a killer in New York's smart set. Among
the suspects were a Broadway producer who
put actors rather than actresses on his casting
couch . . . a handsome gigolo who gave good
value for the high prices that his female companions paid . . . a ravishing divorcée who
used her penthouse in the sky for her version
of heavenly sex . . . an ambitious thespian
willing to play a variety of roles in bed to win
a job on the stage. And shadowing them all
is the memory of the maddeningly beautiful,
sensually uninhibited, and savagely vengeful
young heiress whose death made the front
page of every paper in the city—and threatens
to end the career of an all-time great ballplayer
before it has begun.

Joe Tinker knew all about pennant races. But
this was different. It was a race against time
and terror in an arena of foul play where it
was hard to keep track of the victims and the
victimizers without a scorecard.

LAST MAN OUT

LAST MAN OUT

Donald Honig

A SIGNET BOOK

SIGNET
Published by the Penguin Group
Penguin Books USA Inc., 375 Hudson Street,
New York, New York 10014, U.S.A.
Penguin Books Ltd, 27 Wrights Lane,
London W8 5TZ, England
Penguin Books Australia Ltd, Ringwood,
Victoria, Australia
Penguin Books Canada Ltd, 10 Alcorn Avenue,
Toronto, Ontario, Canada M4V 3B2
Penguin Books (N.Z.) Ltd, 182–190 Wairau Road,
Auckland 10, New Zealand

Penguin Books Ltd, Registered Offices:
Harmondsworth, Middlesex, England

Published by Signet, an imprint of Dutton Signet,
a division of Penguin Books USA Inc.
Previously published in a Dutton edition.

First Signet Printing, July, 1994
10 9 8 7 6 5 4 3 2 1

Ⓢ REGISTERED TRADEMARK—MARCA REGISTRADA

Printed in the United States of America

PUBLISHER'S NOTE
This is a work of fiction. Names, characters, places, and incidents either
are the products of the author's imagination or are used fictitiously, and
any resemblance to actual persons, living or dead, events, or locales is
entirely coincidental.

For my daughter, Cathy

1

She had been living alone, except for a live-in maid, at the two-storied East Fiftieth Street townhouse for nearly six months. Before that her father had also been in residence there, but he had moved out just about the time the war had ended. There had been, the neighbors recalled, a noisy commotion concerning a young G.I. the father had brought home one night. What had annoyed them more than anything else, the neighbors said, was the father's lack of discretion, his parading young men, mostly servicemen, in and out of the place night and morning, until the day the police were called and pulled the irate, disheveled G.I. from the house while the trembling father stood in the doorway at the head of the high brownstone stoop and watched. A few days later a moving van came and collected the father's belongings, and he was gone. But things didn't change all that much. You see, one of the neighbors said, she wasn't any better than her father.

Her name was Gloria Manley, and the joke among those who knew her was that she was most inaptly named, for she was extraordinarily womanly, sleekly feminine, with a pride of step and carriage that exuded wealth and breeding, and a sensuality that seemed ripened beyond her twenty years, the image burnished by the cool self-confidence of one who knew she was being admired.

And yet there was a duality, for there were times when friends and neighbors saw the teenager that had not yet totally abandoned the woman's full-blown body, when she appeared in a baggy sweater, plaid skirt, bobby sox, and flat-heeled shoes, blonde hair pulled back into a ponytail secured with a brightly colored ribbon. Some of her friends said that at times they sensed a certain sadness in her, like a regret for having grown up too fast, while at other times there was a whimsical detachment about it all, as if being young and beautiful and wealthy and without inhibition or responsibility was too enthralling to think about, a bowl of sweets to gorge oneself upon.

She could have been two different people, the neighbors said: the one engulfed in furs and sparkling with jewelry, the other like a Hollywood idealization of the girl next door. The haughty one would erupt from taxicabs at 4:00 A.M. accompanied by companions still in noisy revelry—men in tuxedos with white silk scarves around their necks and women in fur wraps and evening gowns—laughing loudly on the empty sidewalks, sometimes singing. Like they were the only ones in the city, one neighbor said, while another remembered a top-hatted reveler paying the cabbie by throwing a handful of bills through the window and telling him to take what he needed and burn the rest. Another remembered being awakened from sleep by the 4:00 A.M. hubbub of Gloria's arrival and going to the window and there she was: "Dancing in the middle of the street like she was on an MGM sound stage, whirling in and out of the street light, in her stockinged feet, looking very delicate and graceful and mysterious, her white gown floating around her as she spun about. I think she was drunk. I think they all were drunk. But her friends just stood on the curb and watched and never said a word. When she was finished they extended their hands and she reached out rather regally and then they all went into the house."

Occasionally the other one—the child side of Gloria Manley—would appear at their doors, the neighbors said, offering an apology if her friends had disturbed them the night before. They had been celebrating this birthday or that anniversary, she would explain, at this or that club. The apology, offered with a rueful smile, generally succeeded in placating offended sensibilities. She even, one neighbor recalled, told us we were welcome to come in and join the party next time it happened, as if we were all up and idling at four o'clock in the morning.

Yes, a neighbor said, she'd come to the door the next day like some kid trying to sell you a subscription to the *Saturday Evening Post* and make that apology and it sounded sincere enough, but at the same time you could see her eyes were bloodshot and had smudgy circles under them, and you couldn't help but wonder what she was going to look like at the age of thirty.

But she didn't make it to thirty, nor twenty-five either, nor even twenty-one. She was never given the time to look worse, or better, to change her direction, or to just go on dancing in the night.

2

Tinker could not remember the last time he had woken up on the floor. Not only was he on the floor, but it was one that was covered with linoleum and this was the middle of February, always a blunt, inhospitable month in New York. For Tinker, wall-to-wall carpeting was the height of affluence; someday he would have it.

Not only was the linoleum cold, but it offered small relief from the hard floor it thinly covered. Did I collapse here when I came in? he wondered. Had he been sitting on the edge of the bed and in the act of unlacing his shoes toppled over and landed here? At least he'd had the good sense to cover himself with his jacket, which was sprawled emptily across his chest.

He stared balefully at the ceiling, as if warning it not to make judgments. He knew what was going to happen the moment he moved any limb so much as a quarter of an inch—pain, the wretched bruising stiffness that settles insidiously into the bones of anyone who spends the night on a hard surface and which like a poised cobra does not strike until there is movement. Nevertheless, he reassured himself, this was still preferable to some of the billeting he had endured the past few years—stifling troopships on seventeen-day voyages across the Pacific; foxholes, where the fetal position was often the best you could do for yourself; bug-ridden pup tents on malarial islands in a climate torrid enough to make the sun perspire.

So, convinced that misery was relative, Tinker moved, wincing at the shooting pain that punished his back and neck. He sat up, holding his jacket backward against his chest, the collar rubbing against the stubble along his chin. His lips felt as though they would crack under the merest smile. Fortunately, there was nothing to smile about. He resolved not to look into a mirror until he had showered. The one good thing, he thought, rising to one knee and helping himself up by flattening one hand on the seat of a chair and pushing down, was that he wouldn't have to make the bed.

As he slowly undid his tie knot and looked around the apartment—a modest place that could be seen all at once: one room and a kitchenette and a bathroom with cranky pipes and a toilet tank that always sounded like it was breathing—he was too weary and hung over to notice that there was no heat. It all seemed part of the general misery. Aching bones, parched lips, a scratchy throat, and a sodden head tended to dull all perceptions.

For Tinker, life began this day when he stepped tall and naked into his bathtub and turned the shower knob that read HOT and was instantly machine-gunned by a sadistic rush of ice-cold water that forced him to leap to safety. Spinning about, he grabbed for the steampipe to secure his balance. As his fingers embraced the gray pipe that ran from floor to ceiling like a miniature fireman's pole, he realized that it was cold, that the entire apartment was cold. Suddenly fully and shiveringly alert, with an expression of furious revelation in his face, he raised a clenched fist and, shaking it at the gods of adversity, shouted, "Indignities! Fucking indignities!"

Later, sobered, chastened, still tingling from the cold shower he had been forced to endure, Tinker was turning the key in the door of his third-floor walkup. At the same moment his neighbor, Arthur Chiscomb, a portly, well-groomed young professor of literature at New York University, was also leaving his apartment, briefcase in hand.

"Good morning, Joe," Chiscomb said.

"What time is it?" Tinker asked.

"Don't you know?"

"My clock stopped and I don't trust my watch."

Noting Tinker's bloodshot eyes and querulous expression, Chiscomb said, "Do you often start your days this way?"

"Arthur, I started my life this way."

Together they headed for the stairs.

"It's eleven o'clock," Chiscomb said. "A.M."

"The A.M. part I figured out."

"I take it you don't have any heat or hot water either."

"You take it correctly," Tinker said.

"I called the super," Chiscomb said as they began descending the stairs, "and he told me to go fuck myself. I think he was drunk. So I told him to go fuck himself. So there we were, a Ph.D. in English literature and a semiliterate Lithuanian super telling each other to go fuck themselves."

"So much for your Ph.D.," Tinker said.

"I had to boil water to shave with."

"Jesus, I never thought of that," Tinker said, gingerly touching the raw, tiny nicks on his chin.

"It's barbaric."

"You're going to work now?"

"I have an eleven-thirty tutorial," Chiscomb said. "Listen, I quoted you in class the other day."

"No kidding?" Tinker seemed pleased.

They emerged from the building onto West Sixteenth Street and began heading toward Sixth Avenue. Except for a small 6:00 A.M. to midnight grocery store, the kind that still put baskets of fruit and vegetables out front in the summer, it was entirely a residential block, of five- and six-story buildings that had gone up after World War I and that were beginning to lose what modest gentility they had originally possessed. Once upon a time —for many people the words usually meant "before the war"—there had been a doorman for Tinker's building, and the super (a sober one) had had two porters assisting in maintenance. Not anymore.

The aging buildings seemed even gloomier in the gray overcast. Tinker squinted at the cold, cloud-thickened sky and bent into the chill February wind that was blowing scraps of paper along the middle of the street. He was tall, an inch over six feet, sandy haired, rangily built. When he traveled with the ball club he was often mistaken for a player and asked for his autograph. When he informed the fan that he was not a ballplayer but a sportswriter and the fan turned away, it was a case of dual disappointment—Tinker would have enjoyed signing autographs.

Tinker's was clearly an urban face, open, alert, delineated with mischievous guile and practical know-how. His were eyes that were accustomed to staring at crowds of people, tall buildings, ceaseless traffic, panoramas of light. He was a man who flourished nocturnally and diurnally both, motivated by the raucous energy around him. Hobnobbing with celebrities had given him an ease of step and a self-confidence jaunty in display. Tinker drank with athletes, entertainers, politicians, gangsters, policemen, and those suave Broadway characters who lived well on no identifiable income. In the Marine Corps, tossed into a great anonymous pot of strangers, his shrewd self-assurance was immediately recognized for what it was and he was called "Slicker" even before his origins were known. And when he won a Silver Star for heroism on Iwo Jima (exactly one year ago), his buddies facetiously called him a "show-off city boy."

"I was illustrating the difference between journalism and literature," Chiscomb said, "and I decided to use one of your *Daily News* pieces as an example of journalism."

"I'm not sure I want to hear this," Tinker said.

"It was that story you wrote about the Dodgers the other day, where you balanced the team's strengths and weaknesses. I pointed out the unembroidered directness of journalism vis-à-vis the allowed rotundity and stylistic complexities of the novel."

"Like Hemingway, for instance?"

"Hemingway is more complex than you think," Chiscomb said stiffly. "Anyway, I don't teach Hemingway."

"Then who?"

"I was comparing you to Proust."

"For Christ's sake," Tinker said, "I'm a goddamned sportswriter. I'm not even a journalist."

"Don't demean it, Joe. You have great skills as a sportswriter."

"It's basically bullshit."

"Don't tell me you're one of these newspaper-men who's got half a novel lurking in the drawer."

"No. But if you want to compare newspaper work with serious literature—a dubious idea to begin with—you shouldn't use a sportswriter as an example. We're the fun part of the paper; we don't cover anything gripping or momentous."

"Not even something that gets fifty thousand people to their feet screaming?"

"They scream their heads off for a few minutes and then they go home and have a beer and forget the whole thing. Then the show starts right back up again the next day. So what?"

"That's a curious attitude," Chiscomb said. "But anyway, I enjoyed that piece about the Dodgers. You really think they can win this year?"

"I said so to two million readers."

"I hesitate to argue with an expert, but the Brooks are weak on the mound, behind the plate, and at first base. And I'm not so sure about Lavagetto at third, whether he can come back from the service and pick up where he left off. I'd say they're secure only with Reiser in center, Reese at short, Walker in right, and Herman at second, although those last two have got some age on them. Frankly, Joe, I can't see this club beating out the Cardinals."

"There's something you don't know about, pal," Tinker said as they stopped at the corner of Sixth and Fourteenth, Chiscomb prepared to continue walking downtown to NYU, Tinker to take the subway uptown.

"What's that?"

"The Dodgers have a secret weapon."

"With the war over," Chiscomb said, "I would have thought that phrase had become passé."

"They've got a rookie coming up who's as good as Reiser, maybe as good as DiMaggio."

"You're kidding," Chiscomb said with an expectant smile, like a man waiting for a punch line.

"I'm not."

"You didn't mention him in the story."

"I didn't think it would be fair to put that kind of pressure on him. He's just a kid, only twenty-one. He was in the Navy and played on some service teams. The big leaguers who played against him all said he had as much talent as anybody and that he was ready right now."

"Tell me more," Chiscomb said with a foolish grin.

"You'll be late for your tutorial."

"This is more interesting."

"The Yankees offered $100,000 and four players for him but the Dodgers said no. And anytime Branch Rickey turns down that kind of money you know he's got something like the Hope Diamond."

"Who the hell is this kid?"

"He's from some little town in Connecticut. Rickey signed him in '43, just before the kid joined up. He got out of the Navy last summer and the Dodgers sent him to Montreal to finish out the season. Do you know what he batted in about forty games? *Four thirty-one.*"

"Jesus," Chiscomb said.

"He's a right-handed hitter with incredible power. He'll make mincemeat out of that left field in Ebbets. He can run like a deer and he's got an arm like a howitzer. I tell you, this kid was designed in heaven to be a ballplayer. When you see him play you'll think the game was invented just for him. And he's all personality, in a simple, homespun way. The fans are going to love him."

"A noble savage, eh, Joe?"

"They're going to write ballads about this kid."

"What does he play?"

"Outfield; but he can play anywhere—third, first, anywhere."

"And you're going to be reporting it all," Chiscomb said, the envy plain in his face. "When will you be heading out of this dreary climate for spring training?"

"In a couple of weeks."

"Lucky bastard. Six weeks in the sun, getting paid to watch baseball, while we're up here freezing off the best parts of our anatomy. I don't want to hear any further disparaging of sportswriting."

"Plusses and minuses, Arthur," Tinker said. "Plusses and minuses."

They had taken a few steps in parting when Chiscomb turned and over the roar of a departing bus called out to Tinker, "Joe. By the way. What's this golden boy's name?"

"Tippen," Tinker said. "Harvey Tippen. Mark it down."

3

At about the same time that Tinker was standing on the corner of Sixth Avenue and Fourteenth Street informing his neighbor of the glories of Harvey Tippen, Warwick Manley was mounting the brownstone stoop leading to his daughter's front door. Manley was wearing a double-breasted chesterfield topcoat over his dark suit, a slightly angled black homburg, and carried a metal-tipped walking stick in his white-gloved hand. His full white mustache had been carefully groomed. With his poised, preoccupied air, he resembled a casting director's idea of a British cabinet minister.

Lunches with his daughter were prized occasions for Manley, infrequency being one of the reasons. He could not remember the last time they had dined together, sometime in early December. These days the occasions were, to her increasing exasperation, always by her initiative. The telephone would ring and there she would be, demanding to know why he never called her, why it was left to her. He would mumble through some implausible explanation, which she always accepted without comment, though they both knew the truth.

The two hours or so they spent in the restaurant together would be, he knew, almost wordless; but that was all right, for he just wanted to see her, be with her. He enjoyed staring at her when she was looking down at her plate, but the moment she made eye contact with him he turned away, usually with a brief, uncomfortable clearing of his throat.

He knew that she understood him, and her lack of recrimination for some reason filled him with shame, as though it were humiliating for a child to so acutely and compassionately know a parent, and forgive.

So it was with subtly ambivalent feelings that Warwick Manley mounted the front steps of the townhouse that gray-toned February morning. The blinds in every window were pulled shut, and Manley wondered if his daughter had risen yet. He wouldn't have been surprised if she hadn't, despite her having said she was looking forward to seeing him. He knew about the wild and un-clocked life she led; if the stories didn't come to him from mutual friends, then sometimes he would read them in the Broadway columns, where she was variously known as "The Night Club Princess," "The Hare-Brained Heiress," and "The Naughty Bawdy Gloria." An irate Sherman Billingsley had had her thrown out of the Stork Club for dancing on a table; the stone-faced bouncers at the Copa had escorted her and her party out to the sidewalk after she threw coins onto the stage while the headline singer was performing; Gloria and a tuxedoed friend had been arrested for pour-ing a box of soap powder into the Plaza fountain, causing a river of bubbly foam to pour out onto Fifth Avenue.

Manley rang the bell over and over. He could hear it sounding inside. He knew that Gloria could very well be asleep upstairs, but there was no reason why the maid should not answer.

After several frustrating minutes of unanswered ringing, Manley reached into his pocket for his key ring. When he had moved out all those months ago he told her he would keep a key, and she laughed and said, "Why not? Everyone else has one." It was unfortunately true; she gave keys, he knew, to current lovers and to friends and to God knew who else, a practice he disapproved of but could do nothing about. People came and went at all hours of the night; they stayed there when she was away. It seemed to him sometimes that she was bent upon turning the place into a fraternity house.

He turned the key in the lock and pushed the tall, curtained door aside. Shutting it behind him, he silenced the almost rhythmic street noises—on East Fiftieth they sounded comparatively sedate—and walked through the small entrance foyer that gave out into the hallway, where the staircase with its lush red carpeting looked gaudily terraced. After leaving his stick in the umbrella stand near the door, he took several steps forward and stopped, gazing inquiringly up to the head of the stairs. The second-floor corridor was in shadows, as was the living room to his left, where the draperies were drawn shut over the windows. The fact that he could so clearly hear the grandfather clock ticking at the end of the hallway for some reason made him uneasy.

Manley stood at the foot of the stairs and called out his daughter's name. Then he removed his hat, as though somehow this might help, make him more appealing, deserving, and called out again, not loud, his voice sounding inquisitive.

Now he whirled his hat in his hand nervously for a moment. He wondered what he ought to do. Evidently she was still in bed, alone or otherwise. He wished he could go upstairs, but inhibitions, his, prevented that. It would not have bothered her in the least to have her father walk in and find her in bed with a man, nor probably would it have bothered any man in the set she ran with. Whatever his predilections, however, Manley still regarded himself a proper gentleman.

There was no choice, he told himself, but to leave and go home and sit and wait for the phone call, the apology. As he turned to head for the front door something in the darkened living room caught his eye. Frowning, he moved cautiously forward, soundless on the heavy carpeting.

It was as though she were materializing limb by limb before his dilating, incredulous eyes, becoming larger and more graphic as he came forward with small, tentative steps, like a trespasser in a shrine, hat held tightly in both hands, fingers unwittingly crushing the brim.

She was lying on her back, her long white evening gown draping her body sensuously. One arm was stretched back over her head; the other lay at her side. Her head was turned to one side in a rather grotesque way, her hair tossed brokenly across her face. Coming closer, he could see her staring eyes. She looked ice cold, and as he kneeled and extended one trembling hand toward her, he knew she would be.

Manley rose and began backing away. He returned to the hallway and sat down at the foot of the stairs. He covered his face with his hands and his grief suddenly overflowed with body-wracking

sobs, with grief for his daughter and with the beginning of endless censure and pity for himself.
Then he rose and, with one hand raised before
him like a man groping in the dark, he went to
the telephone.

4

When Tinker walked into the *News* sports department just after noon, the large room was deserted except for an office boy posted there to man the telephones. The sports editor, however, had not yet gone to lunch and from behind his desk in his glass-walled office he waved Tinker to him. The young sports hawk removed his topcoat and laid it across the back of his chair. He glanced at the half dozen letters on his desk; from what he could see of them they were all addressed by hand, some even in pencil, and he knew there would not be anything of great interest there. He winked at the office boy and headed in to see his boss.

"I'm sorry I'm late, Scotty," Tinker said, entering the office. He took a seat on a straight-backed wooden chair across the desk from Scott. Tinker's apology was genuine because he liked and respected his boss. The fortyish, stockily built sports editor had a shrewd, understated way of handling his writers. He saw everything and said little, which meant, Tinker knew, that when Scott did speak you paid attention. The word in the department was that the boss was henpecked, which Tinker had found hard to believe until he'd met

Mrs. Scott at the recent office Christmas party and found an overly mannered woman of faded ingénue looks, perfectly turned out and adamantly self-centered, a person who seemed to regard her noninterest in sports as some sort of virtue.

"Joe," Scott said, "I have no complaints about your work; as a matter of fact, I keep hearing it complimented, from people both inside and outside of the paper. But this pattern of late arrivals just won't do."

"I know. I'm trying to fight it off."

"Fight what off?"

"The sense of having no direction."

"In ten years you're going to be the top sportswriter in New York City, possibly in the whole country. That's quite a direction."

"So why do I feel uninspired and irresponsible?"

Scott pulled the cellophane off of a ten-cent White Owl, twirled the cigar thoughtfully in his fingers for a moment, then slipped it into the corner of his mouth. A moment later he struck a match to it and exhaled a haze of gray smoke.

"Joe, you've been out of the service for how long now?"

"Since August."

"Six months. Shouldn't that be long enough to adjust?"

"I know guys who adjusted the next day," Tinker said, crossing his legs and folding his hands over his raised knee.

"Of course, you went through a lot. Christ, a list of your campaigns reads like a history of the war in the Pacific."

"Look, it's not as if I'm turning to splinters or having nightmares or anything like that. It's just that I feel . . . what's that French word?"

"Ennui?"

"No, the other one."

"Malaise."

"That's it."

"A condition of unfocused feelings of mental uneasiness or discomfort," Scott said, as if making a classroom recitation.

"You studied French?"

"My wife knows some phrases," Scott said, adding dryly, "and uses them." He tilted his head up for a moment and exhaled some cigar smoke with what sounded like a sigh.

"I'm finding it tougher and tougher to crank up interest in what I'm writing about," Tinker said.

"It doesn't show."

"It will eventually."

"Then confront the problem and resolve it. Don't let it get a foot in the door."

Tinker smiled wanly.

"Look, Joe," Scott said, "what I think you need happens to be what's just ahead of you—spring training. Six weeks in the Florida sunshine, writing about your favorite game. And with all the stars back from the war, it's going to be a particularly wonderful spring training. Christ, I wish I was going."

"It's going to be a hell of a time, no question. And it will be good to see those guys again. Reese. Reiser. Higbe. Hughie Casey. Lavagetto."

"Those are your Brooklyn Dodgers, Joe," Scott said, removing the cigar and smiling. "Two million readers are going to want to know how they look, how they came out of the war."

Tinker got to his feet. "Everything starts afresh in the spring, right, Scotty?"

"That's the way it's always been, Joe," Scott said, his contemplative gaze watching Tinker return to the large room beyond the glass walls.

5

A New York City patrol car deposited Detective Lieutenant Roger Selman in front of the Manley townhouse. Carrying his topcoat folded over his arm, the neatly dressed cop—dark suit, blue tie, sharp-brimmed gray fedora—mounted the brownstone stoop, his eyes "reading" the building, from the below-sidewalk-level service door to the front door to each shut and blind-covered window.

In his mid-thirties, Selman was a ten-year veteran of the NYPD, a man whose abilities had caught the attention of department brass. He was an honest cop, tough and sharp, and was expected to go far, though the fact that he was studying nights at CCNY for a law degree had people wondering if he might not be planning to go into private practice or perhaps into politics. His face was roundish, full-lipped, intelligent. A partner from his early years on the force had once given Selman this accolade: "If you were stepping back to crash in a door in some smelly tenement hallway, Roger Selman was the guy you wanted standing next to you."

Selman rang the bell and was admitted by a patrolman.

"Who's here?" the detective asked.

"Just me and the girl's father," the patrolman said.

"Has anything been disturbed?"

"Not since I got here, about ten minutes ago. I was phoning in from the corner and they told me to get over here."

"Where's the body?"

The patrolman jerked his thumb toward the living room.

"And the father?"

The patrolman stepped aside and pointed to the end of the hallway. Now Selman saw Warwick Manley sitting in a chair, head down, shoulders heaved forward, hat in lap.

Selman walked to the living room, took a long look at the sprawled body of Gloria Manley, not yet as a policeman but more as a spectator, curious, detached, then turned and went to her forlorn father.

"Mr. Manley?"

The grieving man's head rose and he fixed the detective with a pair of pain-bruised eyes that for several moments seemed lost and puzzled.

"I'm Detective Lieutenant Selman of the New York police."

Manley nodded vaguely.

"I'm sorry, sir," Selman said softly.

Manley's eyes squinted, and he said, "Would you kindly remove your hat, sir?"

Selman did so. He placed his hat and coat on a nearby chair.

"Is there a place where we can sit and talk?" Selman asked.

Manley got to his feet and Selman followed him to a small parlor on the side of the hallway opposite the living room. The windowless room contained several uncomfortable-looking high-backed wicker chairs, a small desk, and a large painting of woodland and foamy waterfall that Selman involuntarily remarked as being of the Catskill School.

"You found the body, sir?" Selman asked quietly when they were seated opposite each other.

"No one answered the bell. So I used my key."

"The door was locked?"

"Yes."

"You have a key to the house?"

"I used to live here. But everybody has a key to this place. She let people use it when she went away. She was very generous. And foolish. The kinds of people she knew . . . it wasn't a good idea. As you can see."

Manley's voice sounded disembodied. He was elsewhere; his voice was here. He was staring just over Selman's right shoulder, but there was no focus, just a flat, almost blinkless gaze.

"You were stopping by to see her?" Selman asked.

"We had a luncheon engagement. It was very strange. I felt removed, but she felt close. I know she did."

"Why did you feel removed?"

"Oh," Manley said mildly, lifting his hand for a moment, "you don't want to hear about that."

Yes I do, Selman thought. But later.

"You see," Manley said, "when she had some problem she would telephone me. As independent as they get, when there's some sand in the engine they call Papa. That's the way, isn't it?"

"What problem did she have?"

"I don't know. It could have been anything."

"Was it a man, do you think?"

"It could have been. Sometimes when she was changing them she would talk to me about it. Keeping me in her life, you see."

"Could it have been a financial problem?"

Manley looked at Selman now and smiled faintly, ironically.

"Money? No, Detective," he said. "She had more than enough of that."

"Ill health, perhaps?"

"I don't think so. She was a hardy little creature. Never sick a day in her life, even with the candle always going at both ends."

"What about her mother?"

"Her?" Manley grunted. "Long gone. Off to California to live with some bozo. Left us to go off and have her pleasures. She died eighteen months ago. I said to Gloria, 'Do you want to go to the funeral?' And she said, 'We'll send flowers.' And we did."

"Gloria lived here alone?"

"Officially," Manley said dryly. Then he looked sadly at Selman and said, "Is this really happening?"

Manley lapsed into a somber silence, like a man adrift on waves of bittersweet remembrance. Selman excused himself and left the room. It wouldn't be long before this place was going to be overrun with people, with more policemen, medical examiners, photographers, forensic experts, and all the paraphernalia with which a murder investigation is launched. He didn't know what they would find, but he did know what would be lost forever—that poised, pristine aftermath of violent crime, that undisturbed air that still contained in its molecules the victim's last breath. Selman wanted to absorb that silence, sense that frozen aura of horror and death before it was permanently shattered. Selman was no mystic, he knew he could not deduce evidence from atmosphere; what he wanted was a mood with which to begin this case.

He mounted the carpeted staircase to the second floor. There were four rooms here, the doors to three of them shut. Selman opened each of the doors and surveyed the rooms without entering. He was looking at what he imagined were guest bedrooms, each immaculate. The fourth door, which was only half open, was obviously Gloria Manley's bedroom. Selman paused for several moments; because its occupant was recently murdered, the room did not look natural, but rather like a stage set, everything too purposefully in place. With slow, self-conscious steps, he entered.

Two lights were burning, one in a bedside table lamp, the other in the bathroom. A silver fox jacket and a small, dark, velvet-covered purse lay in the midst of the king-sized bed, as though casually tossed there. The bed was undisturbed, its weighty-looking maroon outer cover, which seemed worthy of a royal sarcophagus, pouring yellow fringes to the carpet. A pair of high-heeled shoes lay on their sides in the middle of the room. The chair at the vanity table was pushed in. The room bespoke the maid more than it did the mistress. Selman reasoned that Gloria Manley could not have been here very long before going downstairs to meet her death. The bathroom likewise looked fresh from the maid's hand, each towel hanging in symmetry.

Selman went to the window, pushed aside the thick drapery with his hand, and then parted the slats of the blind with his fingers and looked out.

The view gave out on a fenced yard and the backs of the buildings on East Fifty-First Street, another row of townhouses. There was a fire escape outside. The window was locked.

He turned around, folded his arms, and studied the room, his mind working as his eyes moved attentively from place to place and object to object. She came in and closed the door behind her. She turned on the bedside lamp, then threw her purse and jacket onto the bed, then kicked off her shoes. She went into the bathroom, switched on the light but got no further. Because she heard a noise from downstairs. She went to the door and opened it partially, as a wary person might. She heard something, slipped out through the door into the corridor, went downstairs to investigate. A few moments later she was dead.

A thief? The place was not touched, not up here, not downstairs, nor had the jewelry on her body been removed. Selman's first guess was that she had been killed by somebody she knew. She gave keys to "everybody," according to her father. The odds were that there were a lot of "everybodys" in the life of a rich, beautiful young woman who lived alone in high style in an East Side townhouse.

Selman walked out into the corridor. Unless lights had been turned on and then off, it would have been pitch dark, making it nervy of her to have walked downstairs to investigate a noise. Unless she had been expecting someone, or heard a voice she recognized.

No, Selman thought, she turned on the light in the upstairs corridor; she would have had to. The switch was at the head of the stairs. He began descending, one slow step at a time. She said: *What are you doing here?* Or: *Oh, it's you.* Whoever it was withdrew to the living room and she followed. And he killed her. And turned out the light, using the downstairs switch, and left.

Pausing, thinking these things as he stood in the middle of the staircase, Selman's intent reverie was abruptly interrupted by the sound of men coming through the front door. They were here now, the scene-of-the-crime boys, with their satchels and powders and cameras and envelopes. Selman's solitary introspection was broken, his exclusive possession gone. The murder of Gloria Manley was now like something awakening, about to take on a life of its own.

Selman came down the rest of the stairs and went to Heathcote, the bald, cherub-faced man from the Medical Examiner's office.

"I want to know how she died and when," Selman said.

"I just got here," Heathcote said. His face wore a perennially pained expression. One of his shirt lapels stood out straight.

"Listen," Selman said to a uniformed officer, "her father's in that room over there. Stay with him. See if he needs anything. Mitchell," Selman said to a plainclothesman, "go and check the backyard. See what you can see. I also want to know if the door was locked or not." Another officer was sent to check the basement, with special attention to the service door.

Heathcote rose from kneeling over the body.

"You want science or an educated guess?" he asked.

"Go ahead," Selman said.

"I'd say she's been dead from eight to ten hours."

"How?"

"Broken neck."

"Could she have fallen down the stairs, crawled over here, and died?"

Heathcote shook his head. "No," he said. "The way that thing was snapped she was dead instantly."

"Did it take a lot of strength?"

"She was a slim person," Heathcote said as they gazed down upon the body of Gloria Manley. "An average man could have done it. Especially if he was angry. Those are diamond earrings she's wearing, and that ruby ring's the real thing. Does that tell you anything?"

"It might," Selman said absently.

The living room drapes had been pulled aside now, the blinds raised. What light there was from the dreary February afternoon, looking like it was being filtered through soiled gauze, entered the room. Selman, with his mordantly qualifying mind, couldn't help but feel there was something voyeuristic about *that* light falling into *this* room, touching *that* body. A glance through the window showed the expanding scene: several police cars, one of them double-parked; an ambulance just appearing; a *Daily News* radio car; a crowd of people beginning to grow, faces fixed upon the building with that adamant curiosity common at a police scene.

The uniformed officer sent to check the basement returned to report that the service entrance was bolted shut from the inside. A moment later Mitchell, the plainclothesman, reappeared.

"Lieutenant," he said to Selman, "there's another one. In a room at the back."

Selman followed him along the hallway,

through the kitchen and large pantry. They stopped at an open door. It was a small room, furnished sparsely but functionally with bed, chair, bureau, floor lamp. The floor was not carpeted, but there was a shag rug at the side of the bed. The body lay on its side near the rug.

"Was the door open?" Selman asked.

"Wide open," Mitchell said. "As you see it. The maid, huh?"

"Maid's room," Selman said. "Send Heathcote in."

Selman crouched over the body. She was slender, dark-haired, Hispanic-looking. Probably in her middle to late twenties. This one looked like she had put up a struggle for her life; her white nightgown was splattered with blood. There were bruises on her cheek and dried blood around her mouth, where she had evidently received a heavy blow. Her neck lay in the same sickeningly askew way as Gloria Manley's.

The chill in the room sent Selman to the window. Behind the drawn blinds he found the window half raised. He turned around and studied the room. The bedcovers were thrown back, and there was an indentation on the pillow. She heard something, he thought. She was awakened, got out of bed, and . . . And.

Selman looked around the room that was perhaps one quarter the size of Gloria Manley's. There was an unframed painting of a crucified Christ tacked to the wall, a pair of tall candles in brass holders on the bureau with a cheap plaster Virgin Mary between them. Also on the bureau were a missal and a paperback Spanish-English dictionary that looked well-thumbed.

"Standing from here," Heathcote said from the

doorway, "I would say refer back to what I told you about the other one."

"Looks like it, doesn't it?" Selman said.

With a sigh Heathcote got down and crouched over the body.

"Except for the smack in the mouth," he said. With one finger he raised the upper lip for a moment. "He knocked out a couple of teeth. Then took hold of her neck. It looks exactly the same."

"He could have blood on him."

"Given the force of that blow, I'd say it's a good possibility."

"Time?" Selman asked.

"Probably the same as the other one, even though the room is colder. Is that window open?"

"Yes."

Heathcote sighed again, this time as he stood. "I would like to finish inside first."

"Go ahead," Selman said. "We'll leave everything as is for you."

Selman and Mitchell left the maid's room, went through the kitchen, unlocked the back door, and went down a short staircase to the yard.

The concept of a backyard in the middle of Manhattan in the year 1946 seemed incongruous, given what backyards (along with front lawns) conjured in the imagination. This particular yard was little more than a patch of claimed soil, little more than a place for lawn chairs and hammocks. It was dirt-topped with tiny patches of grass scattered like green toupees here and there, surrounded by a wooden fence some six feet high. The view was confined to the backs of the buildings on East Fifty-First Street, with their windows and fire escapes. You had to crane your neck a bit to find the sky. The first ten or so feet from the house had been paved, creating a patio. The yard was absolutely empty.

"Send somebody around to those houses," Selman said, pointing toward East Fifty-First. "I want to know if anybody saw or heard anything last night. According to Heathcote's educated guess it would have been around three or four in the morning."

They stood beneath the open window of the maid's room. The ledge was about six feet above the ground.

"What do you think?" Selman asked.

"It would take some strength and agility," Mitchell said. "But hardly anything superhuman."

"She slept with it unlocked?" Selman murmured, speaking more to himself.

"Apparently. Unless she slept with it open."

"It was around thirty degrees overnight. I doubt if that window was open when she went to sleep."

Selman turned around, folding his arms, surveying the yard, underlip protruding for a moment.

"A guy who could climb into that bedroom," he said, "certainly wouldn't have any problem getting over that fence. Are all these yards shut off from the street?"

"No," Mitchell said. "A few of them have narrow alleyways that feed out."

"All right," Selman said, staring at the bare, winter-hard earth. "He hoists the window and climbs in. The noise disturbs the maid. She wakes up."

"He drops into the room and she jumps out of bed," Mitchell said, picking it up. "She screams, he hits her in the mouth, she screams again, and this time he cracks her neck."

"Pretty extreme for your common everyday burglar, don't you think?"

"Panic," Mitchell said, shrugging.

"In that case," Selman said, "he would have jumped right back out the window and taken off. Instead, he stayed in the house and calmly went about his business."

"Maybe he thought the place was empty. Nobody else home."

"How would he know that?" Selman asked.

"A guess."

"A pretty risky one, wouldn't you say, after the maid had screamed?"

"I don't know," Mitchell said. "But do you remember something the captain was talking about a few weeks ago? About guys coming home from the service. Some of them disturbed, mentally unhinged from too much combat. With all sorts of killing skills, in their hands and otherwise. We could have one of those guys here."

"Possibly," Selman said noncommittally. "So he goes on into the house. Miss Manley has heard something—the maid screaming—and comes downstairs to investigate."

"And walks right into our man."

"Who gives a repeat performance," Selman said. "And this time he does panic, or at least decides to get the hell out of there. Which is why the place wasn't ransacked."

"It could have happened just that way."

"Maybe."

"But you're not convinced."

"If I was convinced of anything at this stage," Selman said, turning around and studying the open window, "I wouldn't be much of a cop. Look, I want you to find out who her friends were, where she was last night, with whom, what time she got home, was she alone, etcetera. And see what you can find out about the maid."

"What about the father?"

"I don't think we're going to get a hell of a lot more out of him right now. I do want to talk to him again. Take him home in a car. But don't leave him alone. Make sure a friend or somebody comes over to be with him before you leave."

"And you?"

"I'll stick around here for a while, then go back to the station house."

"And check out the neck-snappers, huh?"

"If we have any," Selman said.

6

Yes, Tinker thought after his conversation with Scott, spring training was probably the tonic he needed to sweep out the mental cobwebs once and for all. He was, after all, primarily a baseball man, and this was when that wondrously long season stretched its limbs and then leaped to life again. After three years of tension and danger, of the most brutal uncertainties, the summer game with its artfully constructed schedule and soothing rhythms was probably just what he needed.

He understood the reasons for his lethargy. He had gone through combat that was hellish and terrifying, had killed men and watched friends die, had come home bemedaled, a hero. But coming home had not settled the ghosts. Combat experience had a dangerous and subtle afterlife. It could remain like an infection. He imagined that the only way to be truly rid of it was to face it cold-bloodedly, without sentiment or nostalgia. Avoid reunions. Cross the street to avoid wartime comrades. Resist the memories.

Tinker knew that he had brought the wartime perspective home with him, and he knew, too, that nothing he would experience for the rest of his life would equal it. So it was unfair and irrational to disparage sports as trivial engagements of little consequence. If allowed to go unchallenged, this brutal perspective could end up consuming him.

He sat down at his desk, rolled a sheet of paper into his typewriter, and began typing. From the top of the page to the bottom he punched out over and over: NOW IS THE TIME FOR ALL GOOD MEN TO GO TO SPRING TRAINING.

Later, he wrote a story about a minor player transaction between the Dodgers and Pirates that had come in over the ticker. When he was finished and read it through, he realized he barely remembered writing a word of it. The lead was fine, the story was good, the sentences flowed seamlessly one after the other—but from what level of consciousness it had emanated, he didn't know. While one part of him was still the functioning professional, another was still dead to the idea of writing sports.

Almost guiltily, he looked around at his colleagues, all sitting at their desks, all at the moment typing in unison, each concentrated and involved: paunchy Fred Mason, who covered the Yankees and who would soon be heading south with Tinker; stick-thin Jimmy Edgers, who covered boxing and horse racing and who always wore his gray fedora in the office; Tommy Curry, not yet thirty and with ambition deadly in its intensity, who covered pro football and college basketball, and who would soon be heading to Arizona to report on the Giants' spring training. The veteran Edgers had started in the business as an office boy before World War I and learned on the job; the other two had come out of college. Tinker had come here from high school, started as an office boy with a yen to write, been handed a dead-end

assignment to cover a track meet in Staten Island
and handled it so ably that he soon found himself
being given more assignments, and then more significant ones. The young man from the Capstone
section of Queens was on his way, his vivid style
and breezy irreverence a perfect fit for New York's
immensely popular tabloid, which was purchased
for two cents every day by one third of New York's
six million residents.

At four o'clock in the afternoon Tinker found
out how he had come to spend the night on the
floor of his apartment. He was sitting in a small
office one floor down from sports. Small and narrow, the office was part of the advertising department. It consisted of little more than a badly aged
wooden desk with broken drawers, a chair, and
walls of metal shelves filled with issues of the *Daily
News* dating back four months, there for the use
of people in the department who might want to
refer to some bit of past advertising. It was virtually an autonomously run office (the young man
assigned to it had little to do and was generally
elsewhere), and a place Tinker retreated to when
he wanted solitude.

Tinker didn't hear the woman enter the office;
when he looked up from his newspaper he saw
an irate face and then a hand flying laterally toward him, and he winced and shut his eyes as he
felt the flat impact against his cheek.

"What the hell was that for?" he demanded,
opening his eyes, more startled than angry.

"What was that for?" she said, then struck him
again. "*That*," she said, "is for not remembering."

He was about to ask what it was he hadn't remembered but refrained, afraid it might only earn
him another swat; and anyway something was be-

ginning to materialize from out of a hazy corner of memory.

"Rita," he said with a sad smile, "I apologize."

Exactly for what it was he was apologizing he still wasn't sure, though there was little doubt in his mind that he owed. This tall and beautiful brunette with the long, sensual legs hadn't come striding in here, obviously looking for him, without good reason.

"I should have left you there," she said.

"I'm glad you didn't," he said, wondering where "there" referred to. "You were very considerate."

He could see the anger beginning to abate in those dark brown eyes, a softening of the tension in that beautiful and intelligent face.

"You really don't remember, do you?" she asked, not belligerent now but curious.

"I can see the frame clearly but not the picture."

"One more smack might put it into focus."

"Go ahead," he said, closing his eyes, clenching his teeth, and lifting his jaw.

He felt that silky dark hair flood around his face, inhaled that alluring perfume that she dabbed behind her ears, and sat back with his eyes closed and allowed himself to be warmly and seductively kissed.

"You bastard," she breathed affectionately, withdrawing.

He opened his eyes. She was wearing a scarlet bolero jacket and a black skirt that was just a trifle snug around the hips and buttocks. And those legs. They were already legendary in the corridors of the *Daily News* building, and whoever thought about them would also hear the suggestive clacking of those high heels.

Rita Blasingame. Secretary in the executive suite. She was a year or two older than Tinker (which had her closing in on thirty), had married early and unwisely, and was currently separated from her husband. She was known in the building as The Great Untouchable, keeping herself aloof from her coworkers, receiving overtures from designing males with icy formality, leaving them feeling as though they had been nailed to the wall.

She had joined the paper in 1943, when Tinker had been an island-hopping Marine in the Pacific, and she was one of the first people he heard about when he returned to work, though at the same time being forewarned that she was not available.

He met her at the welcome home party thrown for him by the sports department, which the top executives and their staffs dropped in on. Tinker was asked to come in uniform, which he did, on his chest his Purple Heart, his Silver Star, his combat ribbons with battle stars. His initial conversation with her, after a cursory introduction, was brief. Alone together for a moment amid the banter and the toasts, she asked him how soon he would be going back to work.

"As soon as I can," he said. "I can't wait to get out of this uniform. And I'd like you to be there when I do."

And she was. That night, in her apartment on West Twelfth, just off Fifth. He saw her fairly regularly after that, though at her request discreetly, an injunction he adhered to, as much as he would have liked to have boasted of his conquest.

So after having been twice slapped and once kissed, Tinker remembered. They'd had dinner last night at one of those Village restaurants of good food and shabby ambiance and then, at his insistence, gone to a nearby bar, where he drank heavily while she, sipping from a single martini, watched in silent disapproval. Tinker's demons were loose; he had become captive to images of paralyzing fear, intense pain, graphic death. He saw things he had not realized had slipped into memory, and he felt the helplessness of knowing they would be there forever. As the haunting sea was to the old sailor, so were raw memories to the warrior.

And then Rita realized she had a drunken man on her hands and had to get him home. She helped him from the bar and when she had him on the sidewalk wrapped his arms around a streetlight while she stepped off the curb and hailed a cab. He stumbled several times before she managed to get him inside while the driver sat turned in his seat watching sullenly, wondering whether his passenger was going to leave a mess behind.

Getting Tinker up the several flights of stairs to his apartment was not easy. As with most drunks, his better thoughts were elsewhere. He was not obstreperous; indeed, he hardly said a word from the moment she got him out of the bar, but he was shambling and boneless as she guided him up step by interminable step. She knew that if she relaxed her grip on his arm for just a moment he was likely to go tumbling back down the stairs. But she guided him with extraordinary care and tolerance, remembering the times when as a child she had done the same for her father when he came home stunned with booze not from a saloon but from his lady friend, which everyone in the neighborhood knew about and which Rita sympathized with because her mother was a grim-faced virago with an emotional temperature set at freezing.

When she finally got him to his door she held him steady with one arm wrapped around his waist while she fished the key from his pocket and with it opened the door and then felt her strength give out. Tinker fell foolishly, first to his knees, like a supplicant, head bobbing over his chest, and then to the floor, graceless as an empty sack. He rolled over on his back. He was out cold now. Newspapermen, she thought sourly, gazing down at him. Her father had always warned her against involvement with actors and lawyers. Newspapermen probably seemed too unlikely for mention.

She switched on the light, then shut the door. She knelt over him, hauled him up from the waist, removed the jacket from his sagging shoulders, eased him gently back down, and then covered him with the jacket. That's it, you miserable bastard, she thought. You can sleep it off right there.

"How was I supposed to know what was eating you?" she asked. "You never said a word. You just started drinking and drinking."

"I don't like to talk about it," he said.

They were sitting in his apartment, sipping wine from the bottle he had bought on their way over from dinner. They both preferred her place, which was roomier and better furnished and benefited from the softer decors of the feminine touch. But her apartment was in the midst of being painted. So here they were, back at the scene of last night's soggy conclusion. Fortunately, the heat had been restored.

"How often does it happen?" she asked.

"Not often."

"What triggers it?"

"Nothing in particular. Well, something, I guess. It's not all that long ago. That's probably it. I think it has something to do with the chanciness of it all, guys ten feet on either side of you getting it and not you." He smiled wryly. "It takes away from the sanctity and high purpose of life."

"You feel guilty for having survived?"

"No, that's not it. It was the irrationality of it all. No reason for anything. The impartial scatter-gunning of fate. You just think about how close *you* came to getting it, and why you didn't. Anyway, I'll get over it. I'll grow older and wiser."

"So now I have to feel guilty for leaving you on the floor," she said.

"Nonsense," he said. "I deserved it. Getting me back here in that condition was positively heroic. Listen, I got a medal for doing exactly what you did. Most women would have left me there."

"Maternal instinct," she said.

"I guess going to spring training will help."

"Are you looking forward to it?"

"It'll clear my head. The official return to normalcy. Plenty of hot sunshine, some time at the beach, sipping exotic drinks in tropical nights. Spring training is really a six-week paid vacation."

"Will you miss me?" she asked with a slight curl of a smile.

"Of course. And I'll come back a better, more settled man."

"I hope you'll behave yourself down there," she said, sitting back in the apartment's one comfortable chair and crossing her legs.

He squinted one eye in frank appraisal.

"Those sculpted legs," he said, "convince me that there is a just God and a better world."

She raised one cynical eyebrow.

"Something on your mind, Mr. Tinker?" she asked coyly.

"Yes," he said, putting down his glass. "I want to see again just how far up those legs really go."

She smiled, as if at the antics of a child. Then she drew a deep breath and got to her feet and began to unbutton her blouse. Then she turned around and he rose and slipped the blouse from her shoulders. He unhooked her bra and let it drop to the floor. He leaned against her, kissing the nape of her neck, inhaling perfume and filling his hands with her firm, well-shaped breasts as she lifted her head and closed her eyes on a sharp intake of breath and arched her back.

He undid the buttons at the sides of her skirt and it dropped to the floor, unveiling her legs, which stood slightly apart, poised on her high heels.

"Black lace panties," he said.

"Do you approve?"

Still standing behind her, he unhooked her stockings and guided their sheer, almost airy essences down her legs. Then he inserted his thumbs inside the panties at either hip, pulled them away from her skin, and began peeling them off.

Completely nude now, still balanced on her high heels, she turned around and faced him.

"Mr. Tinker," she said, "you have the advantage of me."

Later, spent, exhausted, they were in each other's arms under the bedcovers. As she always did after sex, she was taking deep, soft breaths, as if to restore the cool natural gentility that had been swept passionately aside. Tinker cradled her against him, staring expressionlessly into the shadowed room, which was lighted only by the forty-watt bulb in the small kitchen.

Tinker's aimless reveries were interrupted by a sharp rapping at the door.

"Who the hell is that?" Rita asked.

Tinker looked at the windup clock on the bedside table. The hands read 11:05.

"I don't know," he said.

The knocking continued.

"You'd better find out," she said.

"Who is it?" he yelled.

"Joe, open up," a voice said with some urgency.

"My neighbor," Tinker said. "The NYU professor."

"Tell him to go away."

"What do you want?" Tinker called out.

"I have to talk to you."

"Is he the hysterical type?" she asked.

"Not usually."

Tinker threw back the bedcover and swung his feet to the linoleum-covered floor.

"For my next birthday," he said, bringing his tall, tautly muscled body to full height, "buy me a bathrobe."

He stepped into his trousers and raised them, leaving the belt ends hanging, and went to the door. When he opened it he was confronted by the highly animated face of Arthur Chiscomb.

"Do you have the radio on?" Chiscomb asked.

"I've got company," Tinker said pointedly.

Chiscomb tilted his head to one side and peered over Tinker's bare shoulder into the room. Rita had drawn the covers far up, and all he could see was a shapely form curled under them and a sprawl of black hair on the pillow.

"Oh," he said. "Sorry, Joe. Damned awkward. But I thought you'd want to know."

"Know what?"

"You heard about that society girl that was murdered uptown? Well, who do you think they've pulled in for questioning? I just heard it on the eleven o'clock news. That kid you were telling me about. Harvey Tippen."

7

The following morning Detective Lieutenant Selman was sitting behind the desk in his cubicle of an office on the second floor of his midtown station house. A uniformed officer appeared in the doorway and knocked on the wall.

"You've got a visitor, Lieutenant," he said.

"In a minute," Selman said abstractedly. His attention was focused on Gloria Manley's address book, which he had taken from a drawer in her night table yesterday afternoon. After dialing a few numbers he had been able to reconstruct the young heiress's final night on earth. The first step, he hoped, toward reconstructing her final moments.

Selman recognized quite a few of the names in the book, some because they were genuine celebrities, others because he made it his business to read the various Broadway columns, especially Ed Sullivan and Danton Walker in the *News*, Winchell in the *Mirror*, and Leonard Lyons and Earl Wilson in the *Post*. Selman's interest in this daily rendering of the night before was due solely to the fact that he worked the midtown beat, which encompassed Broadway, the theater district, the nightclubs, and Madison Square Garden. Over the past several years he had pulled enough celebrities out of drunken brawls to have become not unduly impressed with them. For one thing, he had seen too many of them fawning over known gangsters, a fascination Selman found repugnant.

"He didn't do it, Roger."

The voice came from the doorway, where Selman's visitor stood lounging against one wall, arms crossed.

"What the hell do you know about it?" Selman asked.

"I know the kid."

"Were you with him last night at about four A.M.?"

"No."

"So you want me to tell the D.A. that Joe Tinker of the *Daily News* knows the kid, ergo the kid is innocent."

"Have you charged him?" Tinker asked, walking into the tiny windowless office and sitting down on a wooden folding chair.

"No."

"Why are you holding him? That's what you're doing, according to the morning papers."

Selman closed the address book and leaned forward and folded his hands on the desk. His jacket was hanging on the back of his chair. He was wearing bright red suspenders; with his white shirt and blue tie they gave him a fleetingly patriotic look. A bench stood against one wall of the narrow office, its surface covered with unsteady-looking stacks of manila folders that, in their disorganization and irregularly thrusting sheets of paper, resembled a flourishing undergrowth. The wall behind the detective was an informal rogues' gallery of tacked-up wanted posters. The room was lighted day and night by a ceiling bulb that hung from a metal collar.

"Joe," Selman said, his voice sounding like it was on borrowed patience, "I've been up all night."

"Guys like you and me, Roger," Tinker said, "we're never off duty."

"This is not a sports page story."

"It's a front *and* back story. Harvey Tippen is the most exciting rookie the Dodgers, or anybody else for that matter, is bringing to camp this year."

"His debut might just be postponed for a while."

"I don't understand how he's tied in to this."

"He was having an affair with her. With Gloria Manley."

Tinker smiled incredulously. "Harvey? With *her*? He's just a bumpkin. You've got to be kidding."

"Oh, he's admitted it," Selman said. "She was probably just amusing herself. He seems to have been a change of pace for her, if you don't mind the baseball analogy. How well do you know him?"

"Well," Tinker said, "he's been hanging around New York over the winter and I've run into him here and there. He's subletting a place not far from me downtown."

"What do you think of him? Off the record. This is *all* off the record," Selman said pointedly.

Tinker shrugged. "A nice enough kid. A bit naive. Certainly not the sharpest tack in the box. Happy-go-lucky. If he's got one passion, it's to play for the Dodgers. It's the central focus of his life."

"Does he drink?"

"Not really. I'd describe Harvey as a chameleon personality. He tends to take on the coloration of his surroundings. If everybody else is drinking, so will he. If everybody else decides to jump in the East River, so will he. He's one of these guys who's flawless and graceful on a ball field. He's got every gift, including magnetism. He's a man with a milieu. In it, he's unique. Out of it, he's a face in the crowd. Jesus, Roger, I can't see him killing anybody. Seriously."

"Well, Joe," Selman said, unfolding his hands and drumming his fingertips on the desk for a moment, "he may be the second coming of Ty Cobb, but to me he has to be the face in the crowd."

"Can you tell me why?"

"Why don't you get it from Tony Marino? He's your paper's ace crime reporter. He's covering it for the *News*."

"Tony's a good boy," Tinker said, "but he's an intellectual. He theorizes too much. I'd rather get it from a cop. I always prefer the undecorated Christmas tree."

Did Tinker know El Morocco? Selman asked. By reputation, Tinker said. Well, Selman said, the East Side nightclub was where Gloria Manley had spent her final hours. She arrived at about one o'clock in the morning, accompanied by a group of friends, Harvey Tippen among them. They had been to several clubs previously and when they arrived at El Morocco they were in what the maitre d' described as a "spirited" state, particularly Miss Manley, who led her troupe into the place and who when she encountered the maitre d' executed a deep curtsy.

Seasoned veteran of nocturnal vivacity that he

was, the maitre d' sized up the group's too-resolute desire to enjoy themselves and placed them at a round table at a far wall. From the discreetly whispered reports he heard from the table's waiters as well as from his own observations, the maitre d' knew that the weather over that table was growing steadily foul. Miss Manley was becoming increasingly "snappish" (the word used by one of the waiters), with the husky young man her particular target. Some of the people at the table seemed to be enjoying the display, others appeared embarrassed.

Miss Manley's was "a controlled displeasure," the maitre d' said. She never raised her voice. Several times he drifted over and heard ridicule and sarcasm. What had provoked it he did not know. The young man, whom the maitre d' had seen in there with Miss Manley several times before, appeared bewildered and flustered by the verbal assaults, smiling awkwardly and looking to the others for support. Then suddenly she threw her drink at him, not the glass, just the contents, splashing the front of his suit. Startled, the young man pushed his chair back from the table and looked down at himself, astonished. Then he looked across the table at her, his face without expression. You couldn't guess what he might be feeling, the maitre d' said: anger, outrage, humiliation, indignation. It could have been anything. Everyone else seemed taken aback. Then she clapped her hand over her mouth and started to giggle, like a schoolgirl caught in a prank. Then she picked up a napkin and tossed it across the table into his lap and tried to mollify him. She said something consoling, though not quite an apology, the maitre d' didn't think.

"That was Harvey," Tinker said. "Who got rained on."

"Your boy," Selman said. "Playing out of his league, you might say."

"That kid has as much business in El Morocco as an owl."

"But there he was."

"Then what?"

"By now," Selman said, "it's around three o'clock in the morning. The party breaks up and they leave the club, ready to go home. But Miss Manley decides she wants a corned beef sandwich."

"You're kidding," Tinker said.

"Joe, to make jokes in the middle of a murder investigation would be in very poor taste."

"So is a corned beef sandwich at three o'clock in the morning, but go ahead."

"We're now going on the statement of Mrs. Juliana Overman."

"Who is she?"

"A friend of the late Miss Manley's. A chatterbox. She was among the party at El Morocco. She's a wealthy divorcée, about thirty or so. A prewar debutante, and very attractive. She inherited 'old' money, which doesn't mean it has wrinkles, only that people never question how you spend it."

"No jokes, I thought."

"That was a social observation," Selman said. "Her first husband, whom she married when she was eighteen, was trampled to death by a rhinoceros while on safari in Kenya. Stop smiling; there are such people in the world. She recently divorced her second husband. Anyway, Miss Manley knows of this all-night kosher deli on the

Lower East Side that makes the best corned beef sandwiches."

"She wanted to go all the way down there for heartburn?"

"Joe, these are the kind of people who fly to Boston for a cup of coffee. Do you want to hear this or not?"

"The mad adventures of the carriage trade," Tinker said, shaking his head. "Go ahead."

"So three of them get into a cab and begin heading downtown."

"Three?"

"Miss Manley, Mrs. Overman, and your boy."

"Harvey went along? After that scene?"

"Maybe he likes corned beef. I don't know. But he went. But after a few minutes Miss Manley decides she doesn't want a corned beef sandwich after all and wants to go home instead. So they turn around, go uptown to drop Mrs. Overman off at her place on Riverside, and then head back down to Miss Manley's."

"Harvey and Miss Manley."

"That's right. It's now three-thirty or so. According to Harvey, they had a little spat in the cab and when they arrived at her townhouse he decided he didn't want to go in. Now, this is his story. He saw her enter the house, then he paid off the cabbie and decided he would walk home. All the way to Tenth Street."

"And did he?"

"He claims to. He says he walked over to Madison and then downtown. He cut through Madison Square Park to Fifth and took that route home."

"It's crazy, but he could have. After a night like that a guy might want to . . ."

"Joe, there was a fire last night at Madison and

Thirty-Second. A gas explosion in a store. A three-alarmer. The fire gutted four retail stores and some offices upstairs. From about three-fifteen A.M. on the scene was a circus of fire engines, police cars, Con Edison boys, and probably even somebody from the *Daily News*. Harvey never noticed any of it."

"Look, he's a country bumpkin, he probably doesn't know the difference between Lexington and Madison, or Madison and Fifth."

"He said Madison. He was very clear on it."

Tinker sighed.

"But there's more," Selman said. "All right. It's possible he doesn't know the difference between Madison and Fifth; and at that hour, with enough booze in you, maybe you *can* walk through an emergency zone filled with lights and smoke and noise and not notice anything. He says he got home at whatever time it would have been; maybe four o'clock, maybe a little later. He says he went inside, got undressed, then put on a robe and went outside and put his suit in the trash barrel."

"He threw away his suit?" Tinker asked.

"So he says. You see, Miss Manley bought it for him. It seems she bought him quite a few gifts during the past month or so. He says that after the scene in the nightclub he made up his mind to end the relationship. By the time he got home he was so angry and so resolved to prove to himself that he was serious, he threw away the suit as well as some gold cuff links and a few ties she had bought him. As well as a few shirts."

"But you don't believe any of it."

"Oh, I believe he got rid of the clothing all right, since he's unable to produce it. I just think it may have been for another reason."

"Blood," Tinker said.

"The maid bled quite a bit."

"So you're saying that after the cab departed Harvey followed her into the house and killed her . . ."

"Don't forget the maid."

". . . and the maid, then went back downtown to his apartment and disposed of the suit and shirt, which may or may not have had bloodstains on them."

"I'm telling you how the thinking around here is beginning to stack up," Selman said. "There is nothing definite yet. I've still got a lot of people to talk to. But for an early suspect, Harvey's a pretty good one. In the parlance of some of your Broadway buddies, he's going off as the favorite."

"It still sounds very circumstantial to me."

"Most murderers are convicted on circumstantial evidence, the chief witness being unable to speak."

"I still don't think what you have is enough."

"Do you know what a good prosecutor—particularly one with political ambitions—could do with it? Anyway, there's more. Harvey can't account for his whereabouts from the time he got out of the cab until about ten-thirty A.M., when he walked into a cafeteria on Fourteenth to have breakfast."

"I thought you said he got home at around four," Tinker said.

"No, Joe; *Harvey* says he got home at around four. But a neighbor who came home at about nine o'clock in the morning, who didn't have his front-door key, tried to rouse Harvey to let him in. No answer. No Harvey."

"He might have slept through it," Tinker said.

Selman leaned back in his chair, folding his arms, smiling indulgently.

"You're a good defense lawyer, Joe," he said, "but you've got a poor client. When we mentioned that to Harvey he said that he heard the guy ringing but was too tired to get out of bed to answer."

"So?"

"One of my men spoke to the neighbor last night. It seems that Harvey lives on the first floor, his bedroom window level with the top of the stoop. Instead of ringing, the guy leaned over and with his cane—this is an old guy with a World War I injury—tapped on Harvey's window. The bedroom window. No answer."

Tinker shook a cigarette from his pack of Old Golds, put it in the corner of his mouth but did not light it.

"The sad thing," Selman said, "is I don't think this kid realizes yet how serious this is for him."

"Which probably means he's innocent."

"With that story?"

"Geez, but it is strange," Tinker conceded.

"Looking at it objectively," Selman said, "very strange. Right from the moment he gives up the cab at that hour and decides to walk home. It was a pretty cold night, Joe. He says he was on Madison, but we know he wasn't. He says he was in bed at nine in the morning, but he wasn't. He disposes of an expensive suit because he says he was mad at his girlfriend. Since most of his story is bullshit, where the hell *was* he between three-thirty and ten-thirty A.M.?

"*If* he did it," Selman said, "then he came out of the Manley house one scared kid. He probably moped around for the rest of the night wondering what the hell to do. I've been on a few cases, and in my experience murderers, unpremeditated especially, generally don't go straight home. They wander around trying to come up with a story. Maybe that's what he did. Then he realized he had blood on his suit and shirt and knew he had to get rid of them. So he went home, God knows when, changed clothes, and went out again with a parcel under his arm and got rid of it. Into the river probably."

"Pure speculation."

"Put it in the mouth of a good prosecutor and it'll come out sounding like the gospel. And remember something else, Joe. This is no tenement murder case. This involves a young, wealthy, beautiful café society girl. This is front page all the way. The public is interested. The D.A. is going to want a conviction."

"Guilty or not," Tinker said morosely.

"Don't give me that fish-eyed look. My job is to gather the facts. Once that's done it's out of my hands."

"Where is he being held?"

"He's still here, for the moment."

"Can I talk to him?"

"I'd rather you didn't."

"Come on, Roger, for Christ's sake. I know the kid. He must be scared to death. It'll do him good to see a friendly face."

Selman thought for a moment.

"It'll have to be off the record," he said.

"This is not my story," Tinker said.

"The poor sap doesn't even have a lawyer yet."

"What about his family?"

"From what I hear," Selman said, "they're kind of confused. I don't think they're going to be much help."

"I would imagine the Dodgers would get him somebody. This kid is as valuable to them as Ebbets Field."

"They're waiting for the owner to get back to town."

"That's right," Tinker said. "Bollinger is in Chicago on some baseball business. He's not due back for a few days."

"He's a mean son of a bitch, isn't he?"

"As a rule, yes. But this is his prize prospect. He's going to have to do something."

"All right, Joe," Selman said, rising. "Fifteen minutes and that's all. And if he says anything interesting, I wouldn't mind hearing about it."

"I thought it was to be off the record," Tinker said with a look of exaggerated innocence.

"Move it," Selman said.

8

It seemed esthetically wrong as well as an insult to the laws of nature. It was like damming a river or bottling the wind. You did not take a youngster who had been designed to fly across the bright green grass of America's outfields and lock him behind bars in a windowless concrete-walled cell, eight feet by ten feet. That was what Tinker thought as he approached the cell and saw Harvey Tippen sitting inside. And he thought this, too: *You poor dumb son of a bitch. They're going to pin it on you, guilty or not.*

Harvey was sitting on the edge of his cot, leaning forward with his hands clasped. His face was studiously blank. He was wearing a white shirt and khaki trousers. Tinker thought Harvey's black curly hair was worn just a bit long, to a length that callow schoolboys associated with concert violinists. No doubt Miss Manley had found it pleasing.

The short corridor that divided the eight cells was quiet except for the music from the radio on the table at the guard's station that seemed to be drifting after Tinker. Harvey's eyes moved sharply into their corners when he saw Tinker, who was walking with self-conscious quietness, even though the other cells were empty. Tinker was approaching Harvey's cell as he might a sickbed, with qualms and uneasiness. But when he saw Harvey's sudden smile of recognition and delight, Tinker's doubts quickly melted.

"Joe," Harvey said, getting to his feet. "Boy, is it nice to see you." He shoved his large hand through the bars in greeting, but Tinker did not accept it.

"It's best we don't," he said, jerking a thumb toward the head of the corridor where the guard was sitting. Tinker had left his topcoat there and submitted to a cursory frisking, even though he had been brought down by Selman.

"How they treating you, Harvey?"

"I'm locked up, Joe," Harvey said, wrapping his fingers around the bars. "That's how they're treating me. And I haven't done anything. I swear. What the hell am I doing in here?"

"They're just holding you for questioning. They haven't charged you with anything."

"That cop keeps asking me a lot of suspicious questions," Harvey said.

"That's his job, Harvey. He's going to be questioning a lot of people. Don't worry; they'll get it squared away."

"He thinks I did it."

"Don't be so sure. Never try and guess what a cop's thinking."

"Well," Harvey said sullenly, "I'm the only one that's locked up, far as I can tell."

He was a good-looking boy all right, Tinker thought, with ruggedly handsome features and a strong-looking jaw that a heavyweight contender might envy. But his eyes were most telling; round and dark, they were bright with naiveté, with an appealing guilelessness. Just the plaything for some frivolous little rich girl who had grown up from playing with toys to playing with real people, and probably with the same sense of insouciance. Harvey was a center fielder who was built like a catcher—an ideal catcher. An inch or two over six feet, he was two hundred pounds of wondrously trimmed muscle. Shirtless, he looked as though he had been quarried. What enabled a boy of his size to run with such breathtaking speed was one of those inexplicable mysteries of nature that elevated athletes to their special plane.

"If he doesn't think I did it," Harvey said, "then why am I here?"

"I didn't say that he didn't think you did it. All I'm saying is that I don't think he's made up his mind. And anyway, Harvey, you haven't made it easy for him."

"What do you mean?"

"He's found some inconsistencies in your story," Tinker said with what he thought was delicate understatement.

"Like what?"

"Oh, some odd things. Like, for instance, why did you decide to walk home on a cold night instead of keeping the cab?"

"I felt like walking. I wanted to think."

"They seem to feel you can't account for the time you got out of the cab until around ten-thirty in the morning."

Harvey stared blandly at Tinker, eyes unreadable.

"And then," Tinker went on, "this business of throwing away your suit and your shirt."

"Well, man, I explained that. I was so sick of her that I wanted no part of that stuff anymore. She'd bought those things for me, you see, because she said she wanted me to look like a gentleman," Harvey said, enunciating the last word with some disdain. "I went along with it for a while because I figured what the hell."

"She buy you a lot of things?"

"Well, the suit, some shirts, cuff links, a pair of shoes. She bought me a fancy hat once but I wouldn't wear it. Had to draw the line somewhere. And when we went out she always paid. I mean, she'd give me the money up ahead, so as to make it look right."

"You were like a fuckin' gigolo."

"So I was told. I never knew what that was, except they mostly gigolo older women."

"So you threw the suit and shirt away," Tinker said.

"That's right," Harvey said, suddenly animated. "You see, I'd made up my mind. After what happened in that nightclub I was mad as hell. I said to myself that I wasn't going to take that crap anymore. And just to make it stick, when I got home the first thing I did was take that suit and shirt outside and put them in the garbage barrel, and the goddamned cuff links too. What the hell do I need cuff links for? I'm going down to spring training soon."

"What else you throw away?"

"That's all."

"Did you keep anything she bought you?"

"A couple shirts." Harvey shrugged. "I figured what the hell."

"They're probably useless without the cuff links."

Harvey frowned. "Really?" he said.

"Why was she picking on you in the club?"

"She did that every so often. When there were

other people around, never when we were alone. Like she was showing off or something, like she wanted to prove she could get away with it. I'd ask her not to do it again and she'd say okay, she wouldn't. But then she would. Like I was some kind of joke or something. Then she threw a drink at me. For no reason. I hadn't said anything."

"You got angry."

"Well," Harvey said sullenly, "I didn't like it. Then all of a sudden she clammed up and it was over. She was like that. Sweet as pie one minute, a goddamned bumblebee the next. But I told myself right then and there that I'd had enough of it. That I wasn't going to see her again, her or her weird friends. I was planning to go back home for a while before heading south. Jesus, I don't know what my old man must be thinking just now."

"He must be worried as hell."

"Not worried—mad. He was drooling over the fact that I was getting a chance to play for the Dodgers. That's all he's ever been dreaming about, ever since I was a kid. And now this. Christ, Joe, he'll break me in two. I'll tell you this as no joke —with the mood he must be in right now, I'm safer in here than anyplace else." Harvey forced a foolish little laugh.

"I'm sure he's very concerned," Tinker said soberly.

"No, Joe. He's mad. He wanted me home weeks ago. Good God. I wonder if the fuckin' house is still standing. He's six-foot-four and two hundred fifty pounds. An ox. And he's got a temper like that mountain."

"Which mountain?"

"The one that blows up."

"Etna."

"That's the one."

"What'd you do that night, from the start?"

"Well, Gloria said let's have dinner at Shor's. She'd meet me there at eight o'clock. Well, I got there but she didn't show. So I sat around talking to people on and off and then she called at about ten, or maybe it was earlier, and said to come over to the house. She said some friends were there and we'd have a couple snorts and then go out. We hit a few places and then ended up in El Morocco. That's what happened."

"Then you agreed to go downtown with her to get a sandwich."

"That's right. I figured it would give me the chance to tell her I was kissing her off. That other woman came along."

"Juliana Overman."

"That's right. Another good-time Annie. She's all right, I guess. Hell of a body. Then we no sooner start than Gloria says she wants to go home."

"Why?"

"I don't know. She'd quieted down quite a bit. She knew I was sore."

"Was she drunk?"

Harvey made a face. "Not really. She could hold it. She'd told me that she'd been drinking since she was twelve. No, I wouldn't say she was drunk. She said she just wanted to get home, that's all."

"Did she want you to stay the night?"

"I'd told her that after we got the sandwich I was going home. They were going to drop me off on the way back. I told you, I'd made up my mind that it was all over. I'd taken enough crap."

"After you dropped Mrs. Overman off, did Gloria ask you to stay?"

"No, because that was when I told her I was kissing her off, that it was over."

"In the cab?"

"Right."

"What did she say?"

"She didn't like it at all," Harvey said. "She always liked to be the one to break it off, you see. She gave me some lip, but by that time I didn't give a damn. Then we reached her house and got out of the cab."

"And she walked into the house and you discharged the cab and walked home."

"That's it, Joe. That's what happened. The next thing I know that cop is at my door and zippo, here I am. I don't know what the hell's going on."

"Look," Tinker said, "just hold on. Don't get discouraged. When Bollinger gets back he's sure to hire a lawyer and get you out of here."

"You think he'd do that for me?"

"I'm sure he will."

"He's a tough son of a bitch. He's not gonna like this. Can't Mr. Rickey do something?"

"Rickey's only the GM; Bollinger owns the team."

"Bollinger," Harvey murmured, as if to himself. "He wouldn't like it one bit, would he?"

9

After leaving Harvey, Tinker returned to Selman's office.

"So?" the detective said when Tinker walked in, looking up from the papers on his desk.

"This room looks like an attic," Tinker said, looking around at the small, cramped office.

"Claims he's innocent, right? Sometimes I think there must be some sort of purifying agent distilling itself over the front door of this station house, because the moment a guy walks through it he becomes innocent."

"Or cynical," Tinker said, taking a seat.

"No, Joe," Selman corrected, "skeptical. There's a difference. Sometimes it's the first line of a cop's defense. Anyway, you know why you'd never make a good cop?"

"Tell me."

"Because you have to be ready to run in your own brother if you have to."

"Are you telling me I'm sentimental?"

"I don't want to make it sound negative," Selman said with a mischievous smile. "Hell, sentimentality in a newspaperman is probably a good thing. So Harvey didn't tell you anything you think I should know?"

Tinker shook his head.

"Well," Selman said, "maybe the next customer will be more helpful. We've just brought a guy in for questioning. It may be something and it may not. He's from your neck of the woods, as a matter of fact."

"Where?"

"Sunnyside," Selman said. The neighborhood, built up in the 1920s with neat semidetached red brick homes, was just a few minutes away from Manhattan by subway. "His name is Norman Buxton. He's a chef, works the midnight-to-eight shift in an all-night place on Second Avenue in the Fifties. He's about thirty-five years old, married, with two kids."

"Rotarian or Kiwanian?"

"He's in the interrogation room now. I'll ask him."

"Who is this guy? Aside from being the pillar of Sunnyside."

"He was Maria Espardo's boyfriend." To Tinker's puzzled look, Selman said, "Maria Espardo. Gloria Manley's maid. Also murdered. This guy was seeing her. Discreetly, of course. We got a tip on him from a neighborhood source."

"You're going to talk to him now? Let me sit in."

"That's irregular, Joe."

"I'll keep my mouth shut. Eyes shut. I won't even listen."

"All right," Selman said. "But whatever you hear, you never heard."

Tinker followed him along a corridor with institutional gray walls interrupted by frosted glass doors with brass knobs. Uniformed cops were coming and going, some in visored caps and blue coats, others in shirt-sleeves. Tinker eyed the hol-

stered guns on the hips of the latter. He supposed
you never became blasé about guns.

The interrogation room was down a flight of
stairs, below street level. Tinker wondered if the
location was tactically chosen, to make a person
feel more removed, more isolated. The room was
large, without windows, sparsely furnished with
a card table and several gray metal folding chairs.
Unlike the interrogation rooms Tinker had seen in
the movies, this one was not sinisterly lighted,
with detectives standing behind blinding white
lights; a bulb of abundant wattage hung in the
middle of the ceiling.

When Tinker and Selman entered they found
Norman Buxton sitting in a chair, one hand resting
in his lap, the other on the table. He was wearing
a sports jacket over a tieless white shirt open at
the throat. He was a soft-looking man, sort of
pillowy between the neck and waist. His roundish
face was a bit too full, his reddish hair thin on top.
His eyes were filled with concern.

A uniformed cop was standing near the door,
and sitting on a chair across the table from Buxton
was a police stenographer, a thin, nicely tailored
mid-fifties woman with silver-rimmed glasses, a
receding chin, and no wedding ring. She remained
a totally autonomous, voice-activated presence
during the questioning.

Selman dismissed the officer, indicated a corner
for Tinker to stand in—it was a position behind
Buxton—and then pulled one of the chairs toward
Buxton and put one foot up on it, rested his arm
across his knee, and leaned forward.

"We appreciate your coming in, Mr. Buxton,"
he said.

"I want to help," Buxton said, "but I really don't

know anything." There was a soft, eager-to-please sincerity in his voice.

"Well, sometimes we don't actually know how much we know," Selman said with a pleasant smile. "How did you meet Maria Espardo?"

"She came into the restaurant occasionally, at the odd hour. I mean odd for a young woman coming in alone. Like midnight or one o'clock in the morning. I'd spot her from the back and if things were slow I'd come out of the kitchen and have a cup of coffee with her. She seemed alone in the world."

"And you were just being friendly."

"That's right. She hardly spoke any English, you see. Well, I'm a high school graduate and I speak very good English, if I may say so, and I tried to teach her a few words."

"That was thoughtful of you."

"Well, I don't think she had any friends and she had no family here. She was from Spain, you know. She came here by herself. That took some courage."

"It certainly did," Selman said.

"So it became a little game between us, me trying to teach her a few words from my vocabulary and also trying to figure out what she was saying to me. We'd laugh a lot about it. She was a great kid. She finally conveyed to me that she was working for a rich lady over on Fiftieth and that the lady went out often and stayed out late. She—Maria—would sometimes get lonely and walk over to the restaurant and have a snack."

"When did you start having an affair with her?"

A pained expression filled Buxton's face. He slid his hand back off the table and dropped it into his lap with the other. He passed an uneasy glance at the stenographer, whose eyes never rose from the page she was working on.

"I'm a married man, Lieutenant," Buxton whispered.

"This is confidential," Selman said. "You can tell us."

After stirring uneasily in his chair for a moment, Buxton said, "About two months ago. Around Christmas. I think she was kind of blue. People get that way during the holidays. The lady she worked for went away over Christmas. I thought rich people always took their maids with them, but I guess not. So," Buxton said, shrugging helplessly, "the place was empty."

"You went to the house?" Selman asked with some interest.

"I shouldn't have done that?" Buxton asked with alarm.

"It's all right with me. I'm just surprised."

"Where else were we to go?" Buxton was whispering again, sidling his eyes from Selman to the stenographer and back again. "I'm a married man."

"Happily?"

"Happily what?"

"Married."

"You may not think so, but I am. Does my wife have to know about any of this?"

"What would she do if she did?"

"I don't know. You can never tell with them, can you?"

"Is she a hysterical woman? Violent?"

"No, no," Buxton said. "She'd probably cry."

"How often did you go into the Manley house?"

"During the holidays mostly, when the woman

was away. We'd go straight to Maria's room; I never saw any other part of the house."

"Did you want to? Weren't you curious?"

"No, sir."

"How about other occasions?"

"Since the holidays, maybe three or four times. I don't think she was allowed to bring anybody in. Anyway, she didn't want to get caught. She conveyed that to me."

"What about the other night? Were you there then?"

"Which night?"

"When the murders were committed."

"I was home. It was my night off. Why?"

"Nobody is accusing you of anything, Mr. Buxton. You came in of your own free will and you can walk out at any time. Since one of the victims was a young lady of whom you were very fond, we just assumed you'd want to help."

"I do," Buxton said emphatically. "That's why I'm here."

"Did you see Maria that night?"

"Well, sometimes on my night off," Buxton said reluctantly, "I'd come into town. You know how it is, I'm used to the hours. My wife hits the hay the same time, whether I'm there or not. So I went over to the restaurant for a cup of coffee."

"And to see if Maria was there."

"She knew I'd sometimes drop in on my night off," Buxton said. "I had conveyed that to her."

"What time did she come in?"

Buxton eyed Selman resentfully and said, "If you know she came in, you must know the time."

"We just want to see if you do. It's a memory test."

"Around ten-thirty."

"And?"

"She was very upset."

"About what?"

"I don't know. I'd never seen her like that."

"Like what? Describe it."

"Scared. I'd say she was scared of something."

"Did she tell you what she was scared of?"

"No," Buxton said. "Remember, she didn't speak much English. But I don't think she wanted to tell me."

"Then what?"

"We walked back to the house. Then we went inside. I figured maybe if we . . ." Buxton's voice trailed off as he gave the stenographer a quick, furtive glance.

"You went into the house?"

"Only for a few minutes," Buxton said quickly, raising his finger. "She suddenly started shaking and all. She said she was going to see the priest. The 'padre,' she said. She was able to convey that to me. All of a sudden it became a big obsession. She gave me a hug and asked me to go. So I left. That's the last I saw of her."

"And did she go?"

"I'm sure she did."

"But you didn't wait around?"

"She was pretty plain about the fact that I ought to leave. I'd bet a new hat that she left a few minutes later. She was shaking like a leaf."

"Do you know what church she attended?" Selman asked.

"There's a Catholic church a couple of blocks away. I know she used to go there for Sunday Mass. She'd get some time off on Sunday afternoon and sometimes we'd get together. Walk around Tudor City. Sit on a bench. Have a little lunch. All very innocent. You know what I mean."

"You never went to church with her?"

"I'm not a very religious man, Lieutenant," Buxton said, sounding self-conscious about it. "I mean, I'm God-fearing and everything, but just not a churchgoer. Anyway, I'm a Methodist."

Buxton was dismissed a few minutes later, with the usual injunctions: don't leave town without notifying us; don't talk to anyone about this (he was only too eager to reassure Selman about that one); and if you think of anything else, contact us. Then he left in a hurry, as though afraid he might be summoned back.

"So?" Selman asked as he and Tinker walked down the front steps of the station house.

"He admits to being in the house that night."

"At around eleven. I want the guy who was there five hours later."

"This guy's alibi has got rubber legs," Tinker said. "He claims he was home in bed with his wife. What kind of alibi is a sleeping wife?"

"What's his motive?"

"The maid was going to blow the whistle on the affair, threaten his marriage. Look, he admits he was there. How do we know he left when he says he did? He could have stayed there, sacked out with her, then had a falling-out later, did her in, and was about to leave when Gloria walked in. He'd have no choice but to silence her, too."

"I suppose it's possible," Selman said noncommittally as they walked through the early afternoon crowds on Lexington. Whenever Tinker glanced at him he saw that Selman's eyes were continually watching faces, picking them up and dropping them with quick, penetrating glances.

The cop looked like he was searching not for the guilty but the guiltiest.

After heading south for a few blocks they turned at East Forty-Eighth and arrived at the Catholic church identified by Buxton as the place where Maria Espardo had gone to worship.

They walked up a dozen very long, low steps toward a pair of large, formidable front doors that looked designed to withstand a siege. Tinker, deferring to Selman, followed him inside. The contrast between the muted church aura and the hum and beat of the perpetual city outside was sudden and soothing. Several lonely-looking people were scattered through the pews.

A priest was standing at the chancel rail, staring at the high altar as if considering a job of renovation. He was a large, brawny man whose long black cassock made him appear even bigger. When he turned around, Tinker saw a good old Irish face, keen blue eyes and ruddy cheeks roadmapped with broken capillaries, under a full head of thick, wavy white hair. On appearance he was the kind of man who made you wonder about his choice of vocation.

Tinker took an aisle seat while Selman spoke to the priest. He had not been in a church since before the war, though he had attended a few rudimentary services under hot Pacific skies before and after campaigns, with death a raw presence. He had no thoughts one way or another about religion, though he was conscious of how serene he felt at the moment, how at ease; but he was also aware that there was a subtlety to this sense of relating, an element of old subversion. The emanations of understanding were almost oppressive. Tinker began wishing he had waited outside.

After about ten minutes of quiet conversation Selman and the priest shook hands. Tinker followed the detective back along the carpeted aisle, through the doors and down those long, low narrow steps that seemed indigenous to churches and government buildings. The two men walked to the curb and leaned against the fender of a car.

"Zero," Selman said. "He didn't see her."

"Was he here that night?"

"It so happens, yes. Until after midnight. And he did not talk to a distressed young woman with a poor command of English. So says Father John Michael Martin O'Shea."

"Was there anyone else here she might have spoken to?"

"He says no."

"Did you tell him what it was about?" Tinker asked.

"Yes. He'd read about the murders, but he didn't know one of the victims worshiped here. I showed him Maria's picture and he said yes, he recognized her, had seen her in here frequently, but that she absolutely did not come in that night."

"Then what do you make of it?"

"She could have changed her mind. Simple as that. Maybe whatever was frightening her wasn't as serious as Buxton thought."

"Or he could have made it up."

"It would be a strange thing to make up. I don't know," Selman said, then looked at Tinker. "I just don't know, Joe."

"Maybe you ought to talk to Buxton again."

"He'd tell us the same thing. But I'm not ruling him out, Joe. Not by any means."

"Damn," Tinker said. "I thought for sure we'd

get some answers here. Is there another Catholic church in the area?"

"About ten blocks away. But this was her church, this is where she came every Sunday. I tell you, Joe, this one is shaping up as a real nut-cracker. You know what Father O'Shea said? When we shook hands and I was ready to leave he looked me in the eye and said, 'It's just the beginning for you, isn't it?' "

"That's when they sound most profound," Tinker said. "When they can't help you. It's their training."

10

It was unusual for a sportswriter to envy anyone else on the paper. Not only was writing sports the attainment of a goal that had usually been nurtured since early in life, but it was also the job looked upon most enviously and wistfully by the hired hands in other departments. The job seemed adorned with perquisites: travel, attendance at games, association with celebrities who could be at once heroes and idols, and columns and stories that were read as avidly as any in the paper. Because he covered the Brooklyn Dodgers, a team the *Daily News*'s brash and outspoken style seemed to represent, Tinker's stories were devoured by millions of people every day, leading one editorial page writer to lament to him one day, "If I had your readership . . ." "You'd have to be more careful," Tinker said.

Nevertheless, Tinker believed he would have readily swapped jobs with the paper's police reporter, Tony Marino. Where Tinker saw himself as a man doomed to cover bunts and double plays, he saw Tony sitting in on courtroom dramas and exploring the more intriguing depths of human nature. Since returning home from the war, Tinker found himself, reluctantly, regarding sports as artificially structured theater, with the same representation of reality as a motion picture screen. Real life did not follow a schedule, nor was it precisely and unambiguously recorded on statistical sheets.

"This is one of the few murders that would have held its own during the war," Tony said to Tinker.

"What do you mean?" Tinker asked.

They were sitting at Tinker's desk in the sports department, where Tony occasionally dropped in to see if he could pick up a tip on a horse. Tinker was amused by this sporting inclination in the otherwise sober-minded intellectual. Tony was a second-generation Italian and the first of a large family to graduate college (CCNY, in 1934), a distinction that filled his family with pride.

"I mean as far as headline noise is concerned," Tony said. "Study history's memorable murders and you'll see my point. This one has all the classic ingredients. A young, beautiful woman. Always an attention-getter. And wealthy. That spices a case. An apparent dissipated lifestyle. That adds dimensions of characterization. Suddenly a glamorous and pseudodecadent life becomes an open book. The rabble develop this morbid thirst for information: What's going on with the rich? What are they doing? Why are they killing each other?"

"Each other?" Tinker asked. "You think it was somebody who knew her? One of her friends?"

The husky, broad-shouldered, softening-in-the-middle Tony sat back in the chair alongside Tinker's desk. A retreating hairline was ennobling his forehead, rendering him increasingly professorial in appearance.

"Possibly," Tony said, "when you stop to realize how liberal she was in handing out her key."

"I don't think Harvey did it."

"That's your heart talking, not your head."

"I spoke to him."

"You did?" Tony said with some interest. "Well, I'm not surprised, seeing you're friends with Selman. What do you do, get him tickets or autographed baseballs?"

"I knew him before the war, when he was a plain flatfoot. He had a beat around Ebbets Field and we got to know each other. I brought him into the Dodger clubhouse once and introduced him around. Roger's a good guy."

"Well, he hasn't let me or anybody else see Tippen."

"Harvey's just a plain, simple kid. I'm telling you, Tony, he's no murderer."

"Well, if he's not," Tony said, "then I hope they catch who *is* real soon, because they won't want to let a case like this go unsolved. A case like this is fed to the public like Elizabethan tragedy, and believe me, it's got to have an ending that satisfies that public."

"Meaning what?"

"The accused has to be credible, that's all. And from what I hear, they've got enough circumstantial on Tippen to make it stick, if they have to."

"His story isn't the most convincing I've ever heard," Tinker conceded.

"It's got built-in termites."

"But don't you think, if he was guilty, he'd have done better? Isn't a preposterous alibi sometimes an indication of innocence?"

Tony laughed. "No," he said. "This idea of murderers being sly and crafty and cunning and gifted with a sense of self-preservation is a lot of crap. If they were so clever, they wouldn't have murdered in the first place. And alibis? Some of them are corny enough to have been grown in Iowa.

We had a guy up in the Bronx a few months ago. Shot a grocer in a stickup. He had no intention of doing so, he claimed. But while he was holding the gun on the guy, he sneezed, inadvertently pulling the trigger."

"What the hell kind of alibi is that?" Tinker asked.

"That's what he came up with. But as far as Tippen is concerned, let me ask you frankly: Do you think he's telling the whole truth and nothing but?"

The nagging thought had been in the back of Tinker's mind ever since his conversation with Harvey. He had tried to ignore it, but it had remained, like a sharp glint of light in darkness.

"No," Tinker said. "I had the feeling he might be keeping the lid on something. But that wouldn't make any sense."

"Unless it was incriminating," Tony said quietly, lowering his head for a moment and raising his eyebrows slightly.

"What do you know about this Manley girl?"

"Well, as you know, extremely wealthy. Inherited six or seven million from a grandparent and would have gotten another large parcel someday from her father, not to mention some more millions from the will of another grandparent when she hit her twenty-first birthday."

"Which she missed by a few months. So who stands to inherit?"

"I'm not sure yet," Tony said. "She's only got one other relative, a cousin named Norah Gregg who lives over on Park."

"Wealthy?"

"Not nearly in Gloria's class."

"It's worth looking into," Tinker said. "Tell me more about Gloria."

"Party girl. Loved nightclubs. Picked up and discarded lovers rather frequently. Went out with all sorts of characters, reputable and otherwise, including actors, socialites, charming ne'er-do-wells, and, apparently, baseball players."

"How the hell did she ever meet him?"

"Believe it or not," Tony said, "at a baseball game in Montreal last year. She and some of her friends went up there for a party and just for a lark went to a game. She saw Tippen, thought he was 'cute,' and sent him a note asking him to join them after the game. Which he did. She told him that if he was ever in New York to look her up. He may be a whizzer on a ball field, Joe, but basically he's still a rube from some small town in Connecticut and when he got into her crowd he was dazzled. Famous people, bright lights—you know the drill. Gloria Manley was very headstrong and fun-loving and a lavish spender. Your boy fell into a bucket that had champagne at the top and a cesspool at the bottom."

"That poor stupid kid," Tinker said, shaking his head.

"You're not going to find much sympathy for him," Tony said. "He's going to be seen as a jealous or thwarted lover, which lends itself to crude jokes and ridicule. He's going to look confused and out of his element, and that's not going to soften any hearts. I can tell you one thing: John Q. Public returns the quickest verdicts. In a case like this, just being suspected equates with guilt. Having that electric chair up in Sing Sing makes every honest citizen feel lethal, and it's a feeling they enjoy exercising from time to time."

"Scary," Tinker muttered.

"You bet it is."

"So what are you going to do now? How do you follow this story?"

"I'll see what the police come up with. I'll talk to some of her friends. This job isn't really as exciting as you think, Joe. In fact, most of the time it's quite prosaic. While I'm slogging through the unfriendly climes of March, you're going to be down in Florida getting paid to watch big leaguers play baseball. Anyway, the reason I came in: Are you sure you don't have any inside information from the sporting ovals of America?"

After Tony had left, Tinker stared moodily at the small calendar tucked into one of the leather corners of his desk blotter. His departure for spring training was now less than ten days away. Normally a time of anticipation, of hearing the wisecracks and receiving the backslaps of the envious. But, Christ, Tinker thought, how could he just pack up and go away with Harvey under suspicion of murder? And anyway, part of the excitement of this particular spring training was the thought of watching Harvey Tippen hit and run and throw and crash his way into the Dodger lineup. But now that wasn't going to happen. Baseball's brightest young talent was sitting in a cage in midtown Manhattan.

Tinker was called into Scott's office, where the editor complimented him on the Harvey Tippen story Tinker had banged out that afternoon.

"Nicely done indeed," Scott said. "I liked the way you described them trimming the grass in Florida, getting it ready for a kid who might never get there."

"I'd like to do some followups," Tinker said. He

was standing over the boss's desk, arms folded. His tie knot was dropped, his top shirt button undone.

"What kind of followups?"

"Talk to his family, boyhood friends, maybe some of his Montreal teammates."

"Is that really necessary?"

"There's a lot of interest in this," Tinker said. "He's not just a great prospect, but with a local team."

"Yes, but it's more a front-of-the-paper story. As you say, he's just a prospect, not a star. It's not as if his loss is going to put a hole in the team, since he's not even on the team. The core of this story is—did this kid kill that girl, not what a jolt it would be to the Dodgers if he goes to the clink."

"But, Scotty, how often do we get something like this on our side of the paper?" Tinker leaned forward, flattening his hands on the desk. His tie hung straight down. "It gives us the chance to really see the human side of an athlete, in a tragic dimension. Most of what we write about these guys is game-related and superficial. Here we suddenly have an opportunity to do something meaningful. If this kid is guilty, it's a genuine sports tragedy. You know how romantic this whole business is. Hell, it's the *press* that's made it romantic. Harvey Tippen might become one of the great What Ifs of sports legend."

Despite his skeptical look, Scott said, "I suppose that's legitimate enough. I saw you talking to Tony Marino out there. It's his story, isn't it?"

"Only in its banal life-or-death aspect," Tinker said, straightening up. "He's got the song, we've got the ballad."

"You have such a line of shit, Tinker."

"I sat at your feet, Scotty."

"You could sell suspenders in a nudist colony. All right. But bear in mind that the team is very upset and embarrassed by this, so go easy. Avoid the sordid; that's not your department. Write a few stories along the lines you described. Stay in your element and don't try to be Sherlock Holmes."

"I'm just a humble sportswriter, Scotty," Tinker said blandly. "Just trying to do his job."

"Joe, why is it," Scott said, sitting back and clasping his hands together behind his head, "that when you're being lazy and cynical I don't worry, but when you turn serious and dedicated I start to become uneasy?"

Turning to leave, Tinker paused, feigned great seriousness for a moment, then said, "I don't know, Scotty. It sounds to me like one of us is all mixed up."

11

You always have to feel you're making progress, Selman told himself, even if it was not evident. You were making progress if you were gathering information, and he certainly was doing that. The question of what was relevant and what was significant would gradually answer itself, if everything was studied acutely enough. Every major crime had its own unique code and signals wherein lay its flaw and solution. Break the code and read the signals, Selman told himself; what had been committed by one man could always be solved by another.

The first bit of information had come from Detective Mitchell, who had accompanied Warwick Manley home on the day of the murders. Mitchell said it hadn't been necessary for him to detain himself until the grieving father had summoned companionship: the companionship was already there.

"A fruitcake," Mitchell said. "The guy is living with a fruitcake."

"Fruitcake?" Selman asked.

"A fairy. They're both fairies. Can you imagine? He was married, had this beautiful daughter, and he's a fairy."

"You're sure?"

"Lieutenant," Mitchell said, mildly emphatic, "I'm sure. The guy walks around like he doesn't have a bone in his body."

"Who is he?"

"His name is Albert Jones. He's about twenty-five. He's an unemployed architect, from Buffalo. Very effeminate. They were home together the night of the murders. I established that."

"Discreetly, I hope," Selman said.

"Of course. Frankly," Mitchell said, "I think either one of the women could have taken him."

So that, Selman thought, was why Manley had felt "removed" from his daughter. Also, Selman had the feeling that the daughter had not been embarrassed or offended by the father's predilections, which probably distressed the father even further. Manley had impressed him as being a self-flagellating sinner (if sinning was what the old man was doing), and to have his own daughter cast an indifferent or even sardonically amused eye upon the source of his anguish could not have been pleasant.

Selman was sitting at the desk in his small windowless cubicle. Half a container of cold coffee stood at his elbow. He was sifting through reports and documents and statements and scribbled notes, feeling very much like a man standing outside a locked house trying to figure out some way of getting inside. And he would find the way if he persisted.

The reports from the coroner's office established the time of death at between 3:30 and 4:00 A.M. for both Gloria Manley and the maid, Maria Espardo, who seemed little more than an adjunct to the case, like a crossfire victim. What was the ancient culture, Selman found himself thinking, that slaughtered a household servant belonging to a deceased ruler in order that the ruler might be attended in the hereafter? That almost seemed to have been the fate of poor Maria Espardo, who from what little was known of her had had a luckless life. According to information received from Immigration, she had arrived in the United States from Spain in 1940, at the age of eighteen. The only one of Gloria Manley's friends who seemed to know anything about Maria was Juliana Overman. The others had barely known of her existence, which didn't surprise Selman. He supposed that to these people a maid or any other servant was little more than part of the furniture, though Selman reproached himself for making these judgments; it could only impair his objectivity.

Nevertheless, he did not feel comfortable investigating these people. Though he prided himself in being insightful about human nature, he found those of wealth and privilege a bit more difficult to understand. Their values and their styles of living, so radically dissimilar from his own, seemed to throw smoke screens over their motives and to distort their personalities as he perceived them. People who regarded physicians and attorneys as part of the serving class certainly did not defer to policemen, and so there were layers and attitudes and postures to penetrate before one's instincts could begin working.

According to Mrs. Overman, Maria had had a difficult time in Spain during the Civil War, with her parents and most of her family having been civilian casualties. Despite having been in residence in the United States for six years, she spoke little English. She had been in Gloria's employ for several months, her previous position having been with a wealthy Spanish woman, an aristocrat who had left Spain in 1936. Upon the death of this woman, Maria was hired by Gloria, who found her "quiet and efficient," according to Mrs. Overman. Little else was known of Maria. Her funeral expenses were being seen to by Warwick Manley. And so, Selman thought, went the story of Maria Espardo.

Selman wished he knew who had died first, maid or mistress. If the killer had gained entrance to the house through the window, then doubtless Maria had been first. If he had come in through the front door, either with Gloria or by using one of those keys she had so generously handed out, then Gloria had been first, followed by Maria, who had either witnessed it or been alerted by the noise.

For the moment Selman chose to believe Gloria had been killed first, in all likelihood by someone she knew. In his mind Selman had just about ruled out a burglar, for no burglar, no matter how unnerved by committing a pair of murders, no matter how anxious to get off of the premises, would have left that jewelry on the body. He would have taken at least that.

Whoever had done it could have entered with Gloria, or been waiting inside, or let himself in soon after her arrival. After killing her, he probably decided it would be more prudent to leave through the rear of the house, and in so doing encountered Maria, killed her, and left through the bedroom window. Very possible, Selman thought, except that it would have been easier to exit through the back door rather than opening a window and dropping out. Unless he didn't know there was a back door, or was just befuddled and wanted the quickest way out. Which brought Selman to his only suspect so far.

He still had an open mind about Harvey. Harvey had a motive—Gloria had insulted and humiliated him. He had opportunity—he was right there. And means? Well, you couldn't help noticing that this kid had a pair of hands on him like steam irons. And that story he told—was anyone supposed to believe it? The problem was, Selman just couldn't see him wringing necks. But determining Harvey's guilt was not going to be Selman's job; the D.A.'s office would make that judgment, and if Selman didn't give them anything better than what he already had, he had a pretty good idea about what they would do.

Selman stared at the names listed on the piece of paper before him. They were the people who had been at El Morocco with Gloria during the hours before she was murdered. He had spoken to each of them and would again. In addition to Juliana Overman and Harvey Tippen, there were five others, and Selman was meticulously impressing each on his mind, focusing on their images, as if trying to get them to involuntarily yield something to him.

They were a mixed bag, all right. An actor, a Broadway producer, a "man about town," a lawyer, and a young lady who was Gloria's cousin. Only the cousin showed any genuine grief over Gloria's death. The actor had been sullen about it, the producer a bit too solemn, the man about town coolly detached, and the lawyer, well, law-yerly.

He had obtained their names, as well as a brief rundown on each, from Mrs. Overman, who was more than eager to help, though not, Selman suspected, because she had been Gloria's best friend (self-described) but because she was one of those people who were animated by being part of something like this; one of those privileged people that Selman tried so hard not to be biased about, who behaved as though a couple of gruesome murders had been committed simply to entertain them. Nevertheless, the chattery Mrs. Overman had said some helpful things.

Selman stared dispassionately at the list, written in a column on a sheet of white lined paper:

> Frank Serrano
> Brandon Pfund
> Bobby Pilleter
> Vernon Slate
> Norah Gregg

Strangers to him the day before yesterday, they had now become integral to his every thought, and then when this was over, strangers once more.

Serrano was the actor. Up from Philadelphia, he was twenty-five years old. Muscular. Intense. With the kind of vanity that could wear out a mirror. That, anyway, was the professional facade, and Selman wondered what lay beneath it. He knew that insecurity and fragile egos were endemic to the profession. It was one of those vocations—athletics was another—where time worked insidiously against you. A profession

where you could be rejected because your face
wasn't "right." But there was a toughness about
this guy that a mannered exterior didn't quite
cover, and Selman had asked the Philadelphia police to run a check on him. As far as his career
was concerned, Serrano, who shared an apartment
with two other actors in a tenement just north of
Rockefeller Center, had a handful of modest cred-
its, taking minor roles in a few Broadway plays.
He admitted to having had a brief affair with Gloria
and apparently had been dumped for Harvey
Tippen.

Brandon Pfund was the producer. "They call me
'Brandy,' " he told Selman. Selman didn't want to
call him anything. Homosexuals made him uncomfortable, though he wouldn't have guessed it about
Pfund if Mrs. Overman hadn't told him. Pfund
was a sturdy-looking man who spoke in deep,
cultured tones. He lived in a nicely appointed
apartment in the Sixties, off Madison. He had pro-
duced several moderately successful shows on
Broadway before the war, but nothing lately. Gloria had told him she would back the play he was
planning to produce in the fall. Her death, he told
Selman, was "a great personal loss and an artistic
tragedy for the American theater."

The only one of the group that Selman had felt
comfortable with was Bobby Pilleter. Selman knew
a con man when he met one, no matter how elegant the trappings. Pilleter lived quite nicely in a
large apartment in the East Forties, off Lexington.
He was thirty-five years old, tall and ruggedly
handsome, soft-spoken, with an easy, free-flowing
charm. But there was a wary glint in his eye—
Selman recognized it—that was alert to the po-

liceman's reaction to every word. *This guy*, Selman thought, *has had conversations with the law before*. Pilleter described himself as "a sportsman," a characterization he pronounced, Selman thought, rather derisively. *Probably lives off of women*, the cop told himself. Pilleter said he had known Gloria only casually, had in fact been to her house that evening for the first time in months when they gathered to have some drinks before going out. How had he come to know her? Selman asked. Everybody knew Gloria, Pilleter said with a taunting smile, as if to say, Go have fun, copper.

Vernon Slate was the lawyer. He represented both Warwick Manley and Gloria. His office was in the Chanin Building on Forty-Second, where Selman spoke to him, his apartment a few blocks south, on Thirty-Eighth. An unctuous-looking character, he was in his middle forties, his pencil mustache and shiny black hair giving him a villainously handsome aspect. Divorced, he led a quiet life, he said, except when summoned out for an evening by Gloria. Summoned? Selman asked. She was an extremely wealthy client, Slate explained with a helpless shrug.

From Norah Gregg Selman got very little. Gloria's cousin, aged twenty-two, single, short, and rather mousy (of the group, Selman noted, she was the only one who was not in any way physically attractive), she lived alone in a small but expensive apartment on Park Avenue in the Sixties. Norah was still red-eyed from grieving. She and Gloria had not been particularly close, but her cousin was kind, she said, a happy, fun-loving girl. She didn't have an enemy in the world, Norah said, and Selman didn't know if the remark was naive or the product of a mind befuddled by grief.

Selman gathered together his various sheets of paper and placed them in a manila envelope, which he then slipped into one of the desk's gnarled and splintery drawers. He shut his eyes for a moment, placing thumb and forefinger into their corners. It had been a long day, filled with questions and speculative theories. He was afraid this case was going to have a lot of the latter, with the city's wide array of dailies leading the way.

He reckoned he'd pick up a bag of Chinese on the way uptown to his apartment on Seventy-First and Broadway. He'd eat and sit and listen to the radio for a while, then try to get to bed early, if the theories circulating through his head would allow it.

The telephone on his desk rang and Selman stared at it dubiously for a moment, then picked up the lone-spined black receiver and brought it to his ear.

"Hello?"

"Lieutenant Selman? Is that you?"

"This is Selman."

"This is Juliana Overman."

"I recognized your voice."

"I just received a call from a newspaperman who wants to come over and interview me."

"So?"

"I was just wondering if it was all right."

"You're free to talk to whomever you wish, Mrs. Overman," Selman said.

"He's from the *Daily News*. I don't think I've ever read it in my life."

"Is it Tony Marino?"

"No. It's a Mr. Tinker."

Selman smiled and shook his head.

"Do you know him?" Mrs. Overman asked.

"Yes," Selman said. "A most able man."

12

Tinker decided he would start at the beginning, and so he was sitting amid the black-and-white zebra decor of El Morocco, having a drink. Though he had been to the Copa, the Stork, the Latin Quarter, Billy Rose's Diamond Horseshoe, and many of the other glittering harbors of nocturnal New York, this was his first visit to the club at 154 East 54th Street. He felt a bit uncomfortable sitting in this high-toned atmosphere; he was more accustomed to sipping his booze at Shor's or Lindy's or Jack Dempsey's or at one of those soul-of-the-earth bars on Third Avenue that gained character from the monstrous pillars and rackety trains of the el that seemed to wall off the avenue.

The place was quietly elegant, without the icy snobbery of the Stork, where Tinker, on his infrequent visits, was always made to feel conscious of his off-the-rack Robert Hall suit. The voices here were more subdued than in his familiar haunts, less competitive, with none of the loud, sometimes uncivil cross-currents of raucous argument. Laughter in this place did not seem to erupt from the belly. These people were not discussing Rocky Graziano or Rapid Robert Feller. The men looked like they were still filled with Groton and Andover starch, the flawlessly coiffed women suggested slightly stale ex-debutantes, their smiles chiseled into faces of such fixity of expression as to make one wonder if those heads were removable appurtenances that were put into silk-lined hatboxes at bedtime.

Of course, it was early to be in El Morocco. The place was known as one of café society's favorite after-theater stops. It then became an aquarium tank that drew some very ornate schools of swimmers, their buzz attended by the piranha columnists on the prowl for "items" and anecdotes with which to edify the toiling millions already abed. No doubt the place was livelier at those hours, Tinker reasoned, when the socialites were known to fatten a lip or bloody a nose, things that just didn't seem to happen at the Stork.

One of those fish had definitely been out of water the other night. Tinker couldn't begin to imagine Harvey Tippen in this place. A stein of beer among the long-stemmed crystal. A baked bean in the caviar. DiMaggio could handle these places; he always had, even as a youngster, because you could never be quite sure what was behind that poker face. Joe had grown from princeling to monarch, as close to royalty as you got in democratic America. When Joe walked into a nightclub, his companions, whoever they were, were with him, not the other way around. Harvey Tippen? He was Gloria Manley's amiable teddy bear, carried here and there to be set up for display.

Tinker tried to be objective. What would he have done if a beautiful young heiress had beckoned him out of the rabble and bought him expensive clothing and swallowed the tabs and bedded him in her townhouse? Not having been asked, he couldn't be sure, nor would he pretend to know. He hoped he would have been able to rely on his integrity and self-respect, but it was only the un-tempted man who could pride himself on pos-sessing those qualities. Of one thing he was certain: she would never have thrown a drink at Joe Tinker. If she had, he would—

Have what?

Broken her neck?

Tinker found a waiter who had been serving the Manley table that night.

"Why do you want to know about it?" the waiter asked.

"My name is Rodney Flicker," Tinker said. "I work for Winchell." He felt his suit being ap-praised, to his disadvantage. "Walter would like to know what happened."

The waiter barely shrugged; very Gallic, Tinker thought. "She just suddenly got nasty and started insulting him."

"For no reason?"

"Not that I could see. She was temperamental, you know. Sometimes she was very nice and sometimes she wasn't."

"Was she drunk?"

"I don't think so," the waiter said.

"What were the others doing while this was going on?"

"They seemed amused."

"Did Tippen say anything?"

"I don't think so. He seemed confused."

"He didn't threaten her or anything like that?"

"Not that I know of."

"Did you see her throw the drink at him?"

"Oh yes," the waiter said laconically. "You pretend not to, of course. If you ask me, she brought the whole thing on herself. She was asking for it."

"Then you think he did it?" Tinker asked.

"Didn't he?" the waiter asked, raising one supercilious eyebrow.

About ten minutes later, as he was preparing to leave, Tinker heard the waiter whisper in his ear, "He was in the party that night." It was done quickly and discreetly; Tinker had barely looked up when the waiter was on his way, but it was apparent whom he had been referring to, for a man had just slipped into a booth across from Tinker. The place was still quiet enough that you noticed people as individuals rather than as types or as parts of groups. The man, wearing a white dinner jacket, was thickly built, with wavy brown hair that looked combed with fussy care and a large, round, intelligently sensitive face that had put on just about all the weight it ought to; the fat looked recent, it hadn't begun to sag or crease.

Tinker flagged the waiter.

"Who is he?" Tinker whispered.

"Mr. Pfund," the waiter whispered back, then went on.

Tinker left a generous tip on the table and walked across to the booth. Pfund had just sipped from a cup of coffee and was replacing the cup on the saucer. He looked up at Tinker, frowning for a moment, as if asking himself whether he knew this man and, if not, whether he should.

"Mr. Pfund," Tinker said, "may I join you for a moment?"

Pfund gestured to the seat opposite.

"I won't take but a moment of your time," Tinker said, sliding in and seating himself. "My name is Flicker, Rod Flicker. I work for Winchell."

"I know Walter," Pfund said. His voice was deep, mellow, almost self-consciously refined. It was a highly trained instrument and Pfund, a theatrical man, employed it effectively. He looked to be in his late thirties, although the fleshy face probably added a few years. He wore a red carnation on the lapel of his dinner jacket. Whatever cologne he was wearing gave off a sweet smell, like gumdrops.

"As you know," Tinker said, "Walter has taken a deep interest in the Manley murder."

"No," Pfund said, "I did not know that." The fattening of his cheeks seemed to have narrowed his eyes slightly, making him look shrewder than perhaps he was.

"So I'm just going around town asking a few questions here and there," Tinker said. "And just by luck you happened to walk in."

"I'm a fairly regular visitor to El Morocco."

"And you were here with Miss Manley and her friends that night."

"You mean the night of the tragedy. Yes, I was part of the group."

"Not an entirely happy group, I gather."

Pfund thought about it for a moment, then said, "You gather correctly. There was a bit of tension."

"What was your relationship with Miss Manley?"

"Just a friend. I recently optioned a new play and she was considering backing the production. Gloria was an avid devotee of the theater. We're all going to miss her."

"So her death was quite a blow to you."

Pfund sipped some coffee.

"I don't like to personalize such a tragedy," he said, putting the cup back down, "but yes, it is a blow, without question. This play was going to be my first truly important piece of work since before the war. It's a first-rate script."

"Did you do any theatrical work during the war?" Tinker asked.

"No," Pfund said, staring him straight in the eye. "I spent my war in the infantry. In North Africa and Italy. I was wounded twice during the Sicilian campaign. I had a hellish, miserable war and I was anxious to return to my life's work. As you know, Mr.—"

Tinker had to think for a moment. "Flicker," he said.

"Producing plays seems like a very glamorous occupation to the outside world, but the realities are something else. Creating culture and enter- tainment is a hard-nosed business."

"Had Miss Manley irrevocably committed her backing?"

"No, not irrevocably. I wouldn't say that. She had the right to change her mind." Pfund added quietly, "They often do." He looked at Tinker with an ironic smile. "And who do you think is usually the last to hear about it?"

"Do you think she was a dilettante?"

"It wouldn't have surprised me. Her good friend certainly is."

Tinker looked inquiringly at Pfund.

"Mrs. Overman," Pfund said with, Tinker thought, just a note of mockery. "Mrs. Juliana Overman."

"I'm going up to see her in a few minutes," Tinker said.

"Give her my regards. If you want."

Tinker didn't think he would.

He had some time to spare before heading uptown to keep his appointment with Juliana Overman, so after leaving El Morocco Tinker walked a
few blocks downtown to Fiftieth Street. Scene of
the crime. Or the exterior, anyway. Yesterday's
Mirror had carried a photo of the curious standing
outside the Manley house, some of them pointing
up at the windows. Tinker didn't doubt that the
house had become this week's tourist attraction in
New York. Nor could he be critical of that, since
his own stories were contributing to the morbid
interest.

When he got to the street with its small trees
and genteel townhouses he turned the corner,
bending his head in momentary deference to a
gust of late-February wind blowing in off the East
River.

There were lights in every dwelling on the north
side of the street except one. There were no yellow
windows or open blinds at the Manley house,
where there was a look of winter shrouds and dark
abandonment. This house, where once the chan-
deliers burned warm and golden over Gloria Manley's roaring parties, was now nothing but cold
rooms and empty staircases. A patrol car was sta-
tioned outside, a uniformed cop sitting at the
wheel smoking a cigarette.

Tinker kept going. At the corner he waved at a
cab pausing for a red light and got in and sat back
as they raced uptown on Park, that most Episco-
palian-looking of thoroughfares. He stared moodily out from the backseat darkness at the opulent
buildings on either side. Elegant by day, Park Av-

enue at night exuded an aura of privacy and re-
striction.

At Seventy-Second Street the cab made a left
and went crosstown in a westerly direction. Running easily in light traffic, they entered the park
at Fifth and Seventy-Second and drove through to
Central Park West and kept going. When there
was no traffic and the lights were with you, Tinker
thought, it made you realize how small and con-
vergent this city really was.

13

She was my closest friend. My dearest friend. The difference in our ages and the fact that we'd only known each other for a few years meant nothing. But she was in many ways much more mature than I. Sometimes I'd introduce her as my older sister, just for a laugh, but also to underline how much I respected her. I met her right here, right in this apartment. Someone brought her to my party and the moment she walked through the door I said to myself, 'That girl is going to be my friend.' She absolutely lit up a room. She was one of these gorgeous young creatures who know exactly the impression they are making, who can size up a roomful of people and not make eye contact with any of them. Oh, the public Gloria could be haughty. Be sure of that. But then we'd laugh about it later. It was just an act, you see. She should have been born to royalty. I told her that. She had all the airs, but at the same time a genuine compassion and humanity. She would have made a wonderful princess. This is going to be a grayer, sadder world without Gloria. What happened to her is a scandal. Don't you think so, Mr. . . . ?"

Juliana Overman was indeed a chatterbox, as Selman had described her. She hadn't stopped talking from the moment Tinker walked through the door of her penthouse apartment on Riverside in the Seventies. She seemed delighted to have the ear of a newspaperman, though her visitor carefully avoided mentioning that he worked out of the sports department and that he was more interested in Harvey Tippen than he was in Gloria Manley.

He asked for bourbon and got a triple scotch on the rocks as she kept right on talking as she poured the drink and handed it to him where he sat in a deep maroon-colored leather chair that looked like it had come from the lounge of a venerable English club. Then she paced back and forth across the thick brown carpeting as she continued to chatter, and Tinker had the impression of a woman trying to purge herself of thoughts before they hardened into painful memories.

"Tinker," he said.

"Yes," she said, and went on. "She called me that afternoon and said let's get together tonight. When I asked her what she had planned she said she wanted to remake New York in her image. Gloria sometimes talked like that. A childlike romantic, that's how I saw her. A woman trying to grow up in a hurry to get away from what must have been a wretched childhood. But you can't really leave those things behind, can you, Mr. . . ."

"Tinker."

"That mother of hers. A textbook of inept parenting. Selfish. Vain. Neglectful. A queen bitch. And her father. Well-meaning, but I guess you know about *him*."

"Yes, ma'am," Tinker said, sipping, watching Juliana over the rim of the glass.

"When I think back about how fast Gloria

lived—the men, the drinking, the parties—it sometimes seems that she knew she was going to die young and wanted to be sure she got it all in. There was a *recklessness* about it all. I've broken my share of the commandments. I suppose we all have. But most of us come up for air occasionally."

Tinker had expected Juliana Overman to be attractive and he wasn't disappointed. She was tall, with very blonde hair swept up from the back of a long white neck and piled neatly on the top of her head. She had bright blue eyes and a fun-lover's quick smile. Tinker could see the ghosts of a thousand such smiles etched ever so faintly at the corners of her mouth. She was wearing a pair of navy blue slacks that were snug over a shapely rump, and a white knitted sweater just a bit too bulky to show off what chest she might have. Six of her fingers wore rings that Tinker knew didn't come from Woolworth's. She was barefoot, her toenails painted crimson.

The apartment had a hearty masculine ambiance, with beamed ceilings, a lot of leather, wood paneling, a large stone fireplace. It looked more like a wealthy hunting lodge in the Adirondacks than a penthouse on Riverside. The huge windows that fronted onto the terrace gave a sweeping view of the Hudson (like any river, sinister at night) and across to New Jersey. A black leather banquette ran along one set of windows. One wall was decorated with framed and autographed photos of Juliana at various nightclub tables with recognizable faces ranging from actors, comedians, and singers to mayors and governors; photos of Juliana in full riding habit astride a horse; Juliana posing in front of mountains, lakes, on the verandas of resort hotels, on yachts, and even one perched on the wing of a small two-seater. The vast living room seemed to be completed by the grand piano that stood in one corner.

"I understand," Tinker said, "that you all gathered at Miss Manley's earlier in the evening, before going out for the night."

"That was Gloria's idea," Juliana said, still pacing around the room, bare feet sinking into the rug. She paused at the window for a moment and studied the night over New Jersey. "Makes you grateful for high-rising architecture, doesn't it?" she said absently. Then she turned around and folded her arms. "She had the soul of a social director," she said. "Can you imagine—a twenty-year-old planning for the rest of us? We allowed her to do it. She loved doing it. And hell, she was good at it. She called me first. Gloria always called me first."

"At what time?"

"Around seven. I took a cab over. We sat around for a while trying to plan the evening. Gloria started calling people. It was a peculiar roundup, if you ask me. There was her lawyer, Vernon Slate; that dreary little cousin, Norah; Frank Serrano, the actor; Brandy Pfund, the sometimes well-known director; and Bobby Pilleter."

"Who is . . . ?"

Juliana smiled, as if amused by some idle caprice.

"Who is Bobby?" she asked. "I guess he's what is known as 'a man about town.' "

"That covers a lot of sins," Tinker said.

"So does Bobby," she said, tucking tongue in cheek for a moment. "But who is he? Oh, one of those tall, dashing creatures who was baptized in a font of pure charm."

"In other words, one of those enigmas who lives well on no visible means of support."

"My dear," Juliana said archly, moving away from the window and finally sitting down, sinking languorously into a sofa opposite Tinker, "if you attended the right parties you would see that Bobby's means of support are quite visible."

"Was Gloria one of them?"

"You'd best ask him that."

"Okay," Tinker said. "By what time had you all gathered?"

"I would say around nine. That was when Gloria remembered the baseball player."

"Harvey."

"Sweet Harvey," she said with what Tinker took as mild, airy dismissal.

"What do you mean, 'remembered' him?"

"She'd made a dinner date with him. Eight o'clock at Toots Shor's. That's where the sporting crowd gathers, so she thought it would be appropriate. But she forgot all about it. Gloria did that now and then. Part of her wayward charm. One afternoon she walked up to me at The Colony and said, 'Oh, Juliana, how nice to bump into you.' And I said to her, 'Gloria, darling, we have a luncheon date.' That was Gloria."

"What about Harvey?"

"She was getting tired of him, you see. I knew it wouldn't last. It couldn't. He was a nice boy, but was always the odd penny. When she remembered him she was kind of irritated about it because she knew she'd have to call him. And she wasn't in the mood for him."

"But she did the right thing," Tinker said.

Juliana nodded. "She called him at Shor's and told him to come over. Which he did."

"Did she explain to him?"

"My dear, if Gloria had to explain or apologize for everything she did she would never have had time for the next breach of ethics. So Harvey showed up and off we went. The first stop was Billy Rose's, where we listened to some delightful tunes of yesterday; then to the Taft lounge, where Gloria wanted to hear some piano player; and then finally to El Morocco."

"What was her attitude toward Harvey during the evening?"

"Boredom. Indifference. And then irritability. It wasn't anything the poor dear had done or said. It was just that she was tired of him. A more alert man would have known it and gone away. But he hung on like a puppy, laughing at all the jokes—laughing last, I might add. Harvey never knew it was a joke until everyone else laughed. It was like we'd picked up a refugee who didn't know the language."

The telephone rang and Juliana excused herself as she reached out and lifted up the receiver. She said hello, then smiled and closed her eyes lightly for a moment, as though listening to some extremely pleasant flattery. Then she said, "I'm really sorry, my sweet, but I can't. I have the press here at the moment. I've been trying to re-create that awful evening. . . . Yes, I know it is. But I'm just trying to help. . . . Yes, in a day or two. Call me." Then she said goodbye and hung up.

"Have I gotten in the way of something?" Tinker asked.

"Nothing that won't keep," she said. "Anyway, I enjoy talking to the press. I always have. They're the only ones who really listen."

"I'm listening, all right," Tinker said. "What happened at El Morocco?"

Juliana sighed. "It wasn't very pleasant," she said. "She began insulting Harvey. Right out of the blue. Called him a clod, a parasite, leech. Things like that. She told everyone that she'd bought him the clothes he was wearing."

"What did he say?"

"He tried to laugh it off. Then he started saying things like, 'Come on, Gloria.' Then she threw the drink at him. Bobby reproached her for that."

"No one else said anything?"

"They wouldn't have dared. She's Slate's wealthiest client. He wouldn't open his mouth. And Brandy Pfund, well, he was still hoping Gloria was going to back his new show."

"And was she?"

"No," Juliana said unequivocally. "I'm afraid she'd led him up the garden path on that one. Oh, she might have meant it in the beginning. But that was Gloria at her mercurial best. Make a promise and then let it wither. But Brandy was still hoping, as was young Mr. Serrano, who was supposed to be in it, and who had gone far beyond the call of duty to get the part."

"What do you mean?"

Juliana laughed, stretching her arms up and out for a moment.

"Oh dear, but it's a naughty world, Mr. Tinker. Do you really want to know about it? I really shouldn't tell."

"Mrs. Overman, you're dying to tell."

"It's not for the newspapers," she said, raising one cautionary finger.

"You have my word."

"Gloria thought it was hilariously funny. That

girl had the most decadent sense of humor," Juliana added, as if having a brief, nostalgic trip into the past. "You haven't met Frank Serrano?"

"No."

"That young man considered himself one of the world's great lovers. Always had some little ingénue on his arm. A man among men, our Frank. So Gloria decided she'd take him down a peg. She thought it would be a great joke if . . . well, you know."

Tinker didn't know, but wanted to, and so smiled conspiratorially.

Juliana rose, poured herself half a tumbler of scotch, and resumed her seat.

"All right," she said, taking a sip. "I daresay half the Broadway theater knows about it anyway. You've heard of the casting couch? Well, there's the usual one and the pink one. Mr. Pfund uses the pink one."

Tinker got it.

"If you're casting a play," Juliana went on, "and there's a role that can be played with equal élan by any number of sturdy young men . . ."

"You get the one who's anxious and pliable."

"It's an ugly thing, but common enough in the theater. I suppose it's an agonizing decision for a young actor to have to make, but then their careers are so chancy and so tenuous anyway. So they compromise. They barter their pride and self-respect for advancement, for opportunity. Predators like Brandy Pfund—and he's not the only one, believe me—take full advantage."

A twice-wounded infantryman a fairy? Life, Tinker told himself, was surely a learning process.

"Frank Serrano," Tinker said, "was willing to do anything to advance his career."

"He loathed it," Juliana said. "He confided in Gloria one night, drunkenly, with tears in his eyes. She pretended to be aghast, of course, but she had put him up to it in the first place, telling him to go and see Brandy, that there might be something for him, and then telling Brandy that she wanted Frank in the play and that Frank would do anything to be in it. So Gloria made the match, so to speak, and then wheedled all the lurid details from Frank, which she couldn't wait to tell me all about. God, Mr. Tinker, the *things* they do to each other."

"So Serrano got the part?"

"Punning, Mr. Tinker? Yes, he did. He told Gloria he was showering six times a day because of it. And then Gloria, with her delightful sense of the infuriating, told Brandy she'd changed her mind about bankrolling the play, which devastated him. And heaven only knows what it's done to the equanimity of young Mr. Serrano."

"Does he know the whole thing was a sordid practical joke?" Tinker asked.

"I don't know."

"What was he like that night?"

"Sullen. But what was there for him to say? The poor boy was beginning to realize that he'd been buggered for naught. Gloria didn't help with her wisecracks. At one point she asked Harvey if he'd like to be in the theater. She said it was already filled with ballplayers. Isn't that awful? God, I'm going to miss her."

Jesus, Tinker thought, it was no wonder that Gloria Manley was dead; it was only a wonder that she'd been able to live as long as she had.

"Those wisecracks brought out the storm clouds," Juliana said, "but no thunder or lightning. When seven million dollars is talking, you bend the knee."

"Is that what she was worth?"

"Give or take a farthing," Juliana said, tipping another swallow of scotch through her lips. "But she was very generous with it. You never wanted if you were a friend of Gloria's."

"So Pilleter was the one who calmed her down," Tinker said.

"Bobby has this commanding way, when he wants to use it. He just told Gloria that that was enough. Quietly but effectively."

"Had they ever had a romance?"

"Why are you asking so many questions?" she asked with a quizzical smile. "Oh, all right, you're a newspaperman. You people want to know everything. And then you go and use five percent of what you were told."

"And usually half of that we make up," Tinker said, responding with a wink and his rogue's smile.

"Well, I suspect that Gloria and Bobby had a bit of intimacy late last summer. I know that they went to Saratoga together in August. But it didn't last long."

"Was it serious?"

"On his part, no doubt. Mr. Tinker, any man who gets hold of a beautiful young woman who's worth millions is serious. But they parted amicably. Bobby is too much a man of the world to do otherwise. Like you."

"Like me?" Tinker asked, caught off guard.

"You look like a man of the world. Are you?"

"I've been out in it."

"What's your first name?"

"Joe."

"That was my second husband's name," she said. "This was his apartment. It's a bit masculine," she said, looking around at the heavy furniture and the beamed ceilings, "but I like it. I got it as part of the settlement, though he gave it voluntarily. He's gone off to Paris to live. He couldn't wait for the war to end, so he could get to Paris."

Tinker supposed that was as good a reason as any to want the war over with.

"It's hell to live with a man who loves Paris," she said. "That's one city a woman can't compete with. It's so feminine."

"Your second husband?" Tinker asked innocently, hoping to induce the story of the first one, which Selman had alluded to briefly.

"Yes. I've been married twice. My first husband was killed."

"I'm sorry."

"Ivan Overman. He was Social Register. We were on safari in Kenya. On our honeymoon, actually. He was hit by a rhinoceros."

She made it sound like a traffic accident, Tinker thought.

"Terrible way to die," he said, unable to think of anything else.

"I don't think he knew that," Juliana said, biting at the tip of her pinky for a moment. "He was drunk. He shouldn't have been out there with a rifle in that condition."

"Did you see it?"

"No, I was in camp. Apparently the thing came out of nowhere and just ran right over him before anyone could do anything."

"You were awfully young to be a widow."

"Listen, Joe," she said, "better a young widow than an old one. Trust me on that one."

"Anyway," Tinker said, "getting back to the other night . . ."

"Have you ever been on safari?"

Yeah, he thought, for three years with the United States Marines.

"If you shoot things in Africa," she said, "it's a safari. If you shoot them in this country, it's hunting."

Tinker imagined she had regaled many a dinner party with that one.

"After you left El Morocco that night," he said, "Miss Manley had this sudden urge to go down to the Lower East Side for a sandwich. What was that all about?"

"It was all about nothing, as it turned out. We were all standing on the sidewalk when she suddenly announced she wanted a corned beef sandwich and that the only one that would do came from this place she knew down there. A twenty-four-hour place. Naturally I was asked to accompany her. I don't think she wanted to be alone with that baseball player."

"No one else wanted to go?"

"Would you have wanted to go to a kosher delicatessen at three o'clock in the morning?"

"So the others all went home."

"I imagine. The night was pretty well used up."

"After what had happened in the club," Tinker said, "I'm surprised Harvey went with her."

"In a way, it tells you why she wanted to be rid of him. She would have respected him more if he had told her to stick her corned beef sandwich up her ass and gone home."

"So what happened?"

Juliana shrugged, then took a long swallow of scotch.

"We started out for the delicatessen but then the flighty little beast changed her mind. Decided she didn't want one of those revolting sandwiches and wanted to go home instead. So they came up here, dropped me off, and that was the last time I ever saw her."

"Did they talk much in the cab, Harvey and Gloria?"

"No. I think by that point she was tired and he was confused. Frankly, I was a bit thinned out myself by then and wasn't paying much attention. But I don't think they said very much."

"Do you think he was expecting to spend the night with her?"

"I have no idea, Joseph. Gloria didn't like to sleep alone. It wasn't just physical bliss; she just didn't like to be alone. Something back in her wretched childhood, I suppose. She was a sad person, Joe. The whole thing is a sad story. And that poor maid. Look how she got caught up in it. Poor wretched little thing. Timid as a mouse. You know how these refugees are, especially when they don't have the language. I guess we don't really think of Spaniards as refugees, but they did have their little war. She dropped a tray of drinks that night, breaking some very fine glassware, right in front of everybody. My God, you never saw a person so mortified. She was in a frightful way, poor girl, near tears. I felt so sorry for her that I helped her clean it up. 'She'll do it, Juliana,' Gloria said. I think Gloria was appalled that I was helping the maid. Everyone else just sat back and watched. I don't normally assist the help in cleaning up—I'm sure you understand *that*—but my heart broke for her. Servant or no servant, you don't want to see them trembling like that. And what did I really do? Just picked up a few pieces of glass and put them on the tray. Gloria could be such a snob. Later, when we were leaving, she, the maid—what was her name?"

"Maria."

"Was it? She came over to me and whispered to me in Spanish to thank me. I have a smattering of the language, you know; we'd exchanged a few words from time to time. I suppose it made me feel democratic. But she was so intense, you'd think nobody had done her a favor in years."

"It was very kind of you," Tinker said.

"All I said to her was not to worry, that everything would be fine. Actually, that was about the extent of my Spanish. Would you like that glass filled?"

Without waiting for him to answer, she rose, crossed the room, took his glass, and poured him three fingers of straight scotch. After handing it to him she resumed her seat, drawing up her knees and embracing them with her arms. Her painted toenails looked like an irregular crimson necklace strung along the edge of the sofa.

"I'm glad you dropped by tonight," she said. "I'm not in the mood to go out or to see any of the regulars."

"You're in mourning for your friend."

"Yes, I am," she said pensively. "I wonder who killed her."

"You don't think Harvey did it?"

"I don't know. I suppose he could have. Who knows what went on in that cab after I got out. She could have said something that incited him. Or he could have been saving up his anger. He

wasn't my type, but he seems a nice boy. Frankly,
I find it hard to believe that he could have done
it."

"They're going to try and pin it on him."

"Well," she said, "I guess I feel sorry for him."
Then she smiled coyly at him. It was apparent to
Tinker that her mind had taken a quantum leap.
"I bet you'd be fun on a safari," she said.

It occurred to Tinker that arousing this kind of
interest from women had not happened to him
before the war. He'd done all right, of course, but
it was mostly at the rumble seat level. Before the
war a woman like Rita Blasingame would have
remained an unfulfilled fantasy. But now it was
different, and whatever accounted for it—experience, maturity, self-confidence—had left him al-
luringly scented.

Juliana Overman was not a woman for indirec-
tion, nor a woman who could imagine a man being
embarrassed or reluctant. There was a candor in
her desire that Tinker found appealing. But when
he heard just what it was she had in mind he
decided to reserve judgment. He realized that with
a woman like this, desire was an extension of play-
fulness. But there was no question about going
along; he was no less the adventurer than she.

When she told him she wanted to make love
next to a crackling fire, he thought it a splendid
idea. Tinker had never made love before a roaring
fire and it seemed the soul of romantic rapture.
Putting desire into action, Juliana had removed her
slacks and was padding softly about in her pink
underpants. She was a trifle heavy in the thighs
and bigger in the can than had first appeared, and
that dark shadow at her pubic area told him she
wasn't really a blonde. Removing that bulky

sweater, she revealed a pair of full, womanly breasts.

He began undressing right there in the chair, peeling off his jacket and dropping it on the floor, then unbuttoning his collar and undoing his tie, at the same time trying to kick off his shoes. His face wore a slightly inane smile, as if he had been following this routine in this spot for a lifetime and had yet to tire of it. But then his smile faded.

"What are you doing?" he asked.

She was crouched before the fireplace—to start a blaze, he thought. But what she was doing was lifting out some logs and tinder and, holding the wood to her chest, heading for the terrace. She pushed aside the glass sliding door and went outside. When she returned, unencumbered, she was smiling brightly.

"Oh," she said, reaching up and unpinning her hair and letting it fall below her shoulders, "it's a brilliant night for it. Cold but no wind. And the stars are right there. Alfresco sex! There's nothing like it, Joe."

She went around turning out the lights, and soon Tinker could feel the cold air permeating the darkened room. Wearing only his shirt now, he was passing in and out of the terrace door, carrying logs and tinder and newspapers and placing them in a circle on the terrace that was formed by a low wall of bricks. Black smudges on the concrete floor told him this wasn't the first time she had indulged herself out here, but whether ever before in February he didn't know.

Wearing a dark brown sable coat and nothing else, she carried out an armful of cushions and arranged them neatly alongside the bricks.

"You can hear the traffic," she said, "and see

New Jersey and the lights on the river. It's going to be beautiful, Joe. Lovemaking should never be mundane. Have you ever done it in an airplane, Joe?"

Tinker never had. Nor, he was forced to admit as she went through a litany of variegated experiences, had he ever done it in a tent in Kenya, nor in London's Hyde Park at midnight, nor in a motorboat in Bar Harbor, nor on straw in the stables at Belmont Park. He didn't say it, but a blow job in the schoolyard of Junior High School 73 in Capstone was as exotic as it had ever been for him. Until now.

Once they got the fire going it helped considerably, as did the body heat they soon began generating. Juliana, with her elevated thighs embracing the sides of his body and her fingers locked at the back of his neck, was eye-closed and ardent, panting toward ecstasy and murmuring compliments about his prowess. Tinker, who had called for a bathrobe for some added protection from the elements, kept pounding away upon the cushions, feeling the fire's soft crackling warmth, wondering whether some of his impaling stiffness could be attributed to the thirty-five-degree temperature. He wasn't sure if he was really enjoying this and resolved to get it over with as quickly as possible. There was nothing wrong with screwing on a penthouse terrace, but there were surely better times for it than a February evening.

He kept at it until she began to buffet and then to moan. She threw her head wildly from side to side, the long blonde hair flailing in his face. A moment later he let himself go with a thrust and a spasm that left her invoking the name of the deity over and over.

"What do we do now?" he asked a few moments later. "Roast some hot dogs?"

They were sitting cross-legged on the cushions, she clutching her sable coat around her, staring dreamily into the waning fire. Joe Tinker, ace sportswriter and bemedaled war hero, was wearing a pink silk bathrobe with a floral design on the back.

"I always wanted to do this on a cold night," she said quietly.

The sinking fire was throwing less and less heat.

"You were divine," she said. "You will come back, won't you?"

"Sure," he said.

"Thank you for not laughing at me," she said idly, continuing to stare into the fire with fixed eyes. "You're a sensitive man, Joe. That's so rare."

She shifted her eyes to him. Certain people he knew were able to do that with ease, to shift their eyes without moving their heads. He never felt comfortable doing it. She did it now and gave him a slow, sad smile.

14

Tinker supposed one must be grateful for reality and its dogged intrusions, no matter how sobering and chastising its lessons. It was the sole repository and dispenser of social gravity.

When the fire had burned down they dressed and then stood holding each other at the edge of the terrace and stared off into the cold night. Beyond the running Hudson currents there were lights on the Jersey side, and further north along the shoreline a large electric sign that advertised a product called SPRY, and beyond that the Palisades in their rugged gloom and the graceful cables of the George Washington Bridge with their countless electric lights. Closer to hand was the swish of traffic on the Henry Hudson Parkway, the darkness of Riverside Park, and the warm yellow lights scattered through the surrounding buildings. Tinker was taking deep draughts of these twin wonders, the majestic creations of nature and the inspired works of man.

After talking of millions of dollars, of African safaris, and after making love on the terrace of a penthouse, here he was now, riding the subway home, sitting on the hard wicker-covered seat with his arms folded and his legs crossed, oscillating with the train's motion, half-shut eyes staring moodily at the empty seats opposite.

Reality didn't come just with the long descent in the self-service elevator or when the doorman in the visored cap and braided coat ignored him, it also came, and most emphatically, when he hit the sidewalk outside of the building and found he didn't have enough money for a taxi. So he walked east on a quiet windswept Seventy-Second Street, heading for the Broadway IRT, feeling not larger but smaller for having just come from a penthouse.

He realized now how easy it had been for Harvey to have fallen in and been caught. That style of life, that casual ease, that almost insouciant unawareness that there even was another way of living, could be very seductive. To a bumpkin like Harvey a well-heeled idleness could seem like hectic sophistication, while a pointless existence, if it wore the right clothes and traveled at the right speed, could seem fascinating. One couldn't really fault Harvey for succumbing. After all, this was a kid who wasn't that far removed from malted milk dates at the local ice cream parlor.

Tinker wondered how many steps he himself was from the edge of the abyss into which Harvey had fallen, and what it would take to push him over. The idea of his vulnerability amused him. Juliana wanted to see him again, and it hadn't been said casually. He had agreed, but kept it vague. He couldn't afford to take her to the places she preferred going. So she, if she wanted his company, would have to advance him the money before the evening started. She was no doubt a more mature and prudent woman than Gloria had been and wouldn't try to make a bagatelle of him. Joe Tinker, kept man. Gigolo. Newport in the summer, Palm Beach in the winter. Or was it the other way around? It wasn't easy sorting these things out when you were riding in the subway.

But he had seen how it could happen, how a man could be turned into a plaything. And then he saw how worse could happen. At Forty-Second Street a man boarded the train carrying a copy of the *News*'s pink edition, which had hit the streets several hours ago. When the man sat down opposite and spread the paper out in his hands, Tinker saw the headline: D.A. PREPARED TO CHARGE TIPPEN.

He left the subway at Fourteenth Street and began walking north on Sixth Avenue, heading home. It was after 1:00 A.M. now and the streets were nearly deserted. At Fifteenth Street he crossed to the west side of the avenue. The row of stores here and the office building above were dark. He paused for a moment to light a cigarette, bending his head toward the match held in his cupped hands. The streets were at that moment so quiet he could hear the clicks made in the signal boxes as the traffic lights changed. As he flipped the match aside he turned his head for a moment and in that moment saw reflected in the window of a furniture store a flash of light and at the same time heard the blunt nasty roar of a handgun and then the large plate-glass window shattering and collapsing in a ringing cascade of glass.

He began running—he realized later that he had made the decision without thinking, that some of the old combat instincts that had helped bring him through one campaign after the other in the Pacific were still sufficiently honed to impel him to do the right thing. He could have dropped to the sidewalk, but there was no cover, not a parked car, nothing. So he had run. He had about seventy-five feet to go to the corner, running with his right shoulder raised and his hand covering the side of his head, waiting for the second shot. But there wasn't any.

He wheeled around the corner and pressed himself against the brick wall, panting. He forced the breath to stay in his lungs for several moments while he listened, expecting to hear footsteps running across the street toward this corner. If the guy did come and made a tight turn around the corner, Tinker might have time to tackle him; if the guy made a wide swing around—gun in hand—there wouldn't be enough time for a prayer.

Then he began running again, staying close to the wall. He ducked behind the fender of the first parked car he came to and glared through the darkness toward Sixth Avenue. He had never seen an empty street corner look so sinister, so lethal. *He's not coming*, Tinker thought. *He'd be crazy to.* Nevertheless, he waited for about five minutes, feeling the old familiar frozen fear he had experienced for nearly three years and which he had thought he was through with forever.

Finally he expelled a deep breath and stood up tentatively, still wary, his eyes fixed on that corner. He took several backward steps, still mistrustful, then turned and hurried to his building, taking frequent backward glances.

Upstairs, he picked up the telephone and reached Selman at home. The detective's cranky hello indicated interrupted sleep.

"It's Tinker. Somebody just pegged a shot at me."

"Where?"

"On Sixth Avenue, between Fifteenth and Sixteenth. I was on my way home."

"You okay?"

"He missed. He took out a store window instead."

"You get a look at him?"

"No."

"It seems you may have involved yourself in something, Joe. Whatever it is you're doing, you'd better back off."

"Is that your best advice?" Tinker asked facetiously.

"It's the only advice," Selman said.

Tinker was at his desk early the next morning, earlier, in fact, than anyone else. That gunshot had resounded through his dreams and he had risen early, had some toast and coffee, and then decided to walk to work. Before heading uptown he went around the corner to have a look. The glass had been swept away and the furniture store's window was boarded up, a large, irregularly lettered BUSINESS AS USUAL sign nailed to it. It would have been business as usual even if he had taken that slug in the head, Tinker told himself. That was the cold side of life.

He walked along Sixteenth to Fifth and then north on the sidewalks of that thriving canyon. He had decided to keep mum about last night's target practice and had asked Selman to do the same. Scott would throw a fit if he heard about it, probably insist his ace writer leave for Florida immediately, or at least insist that Tinker stop writing about Harvey.

Harvey. In the midst of his own excitement Tinker had momentarily forgotten about his favorite young ballplayer. Christ, Tinker thought, if the kid had heavy legs and a slightly slower bat I probably wouldn't be involving myself in any of this. It was all a paean to talent. It made Tinker, in that respect, the purest and most dedicated of sportswriters. As far as he knew, no other baseball journalist, going all the way back to the 1840s and Henry Chadwick, the father of the genre, had ever put his life on the line (literally now) for the greater glory of the game.

At Twenty-Third Street he entered Madison Square Park, reversing now the route that Harvey claimed to have taken home on the night of the murders. A few snowflakes scattered themselves over the park as he paced along the concrete paths, past the pipe-iron railings and empty benches. He followed Madison north to Forty-Second, then went east, shouldering his way through the crowds hurrying out of Grand Central. Passing the newsstands, he saw that every morning paper had Harvey Tippen on its front page. Tinker silently cursed him. Guilty or innocent, Harvey had no business getting himself into a mess like this. The kid was one of nature's jokes: every physical attribute possible, but not a finger's worth of common sense.

"Well, Joe," Scott said, coming through the door, topcoat over his arm, "bright and early, eh?"

"Early, for sure," Tinker said.

Scott paused at Tinker's desk.

"Did you see that little wisp of a snowfall? I'll bet that got you to thinking about Florida."

"It sure did," Tinker said.

"You're still on the Tippen story, right? Well, if you're going to do it right you're going to have to go up to his hometown and talk to his family, his neighbors, friends, maybe his old high school coach. That sort of thing. And then wrap it up. You'll be leaving in a week."

"Yes," Tinker said. "I was thinking of that."

"You've seen the papers; it looks like the D.A. is on the verge of charging him. I imagine that would dry the story up for a while. Either way, it gets it out of our bailiwick."

"I still have this feeling he didn't do it," Tinker said, hoping that perhaps Scott would clap him on the shoulder and tell him to go out and prove it.

"Maybe, maybe not. But that doesn't concern us."

"Jesus, Scotty, this kid is a hell of a ballplayer."

"That doesn't make him innocent," Scott said, going on to his office.

Tinker tried a few leads for a story on Harvey Tippen the ballplayer, but all he could think of was Harvey Tippen the prisoner sitting in that cramped cell with spring training looming just days away. He wanted to write that no ballplayer who had a clear chance of realizing his life's dream of making the Brooklyn Dodgers would commit murder a few days before the opening of his opportunity. He wanted to write that ballplayers weren't real people to begin with, that they lived only when the sun was bright and the air warm, that the greater part of their lives was spent in the imaginations of other people, and that when the season ended they became empty uniforms and were packed away in crates. He wanted to write that ballplayers were not murderers, but he knew that none of it would ever leave Scott's desk, and so he sat there with his elbows on the desk, face in hands, staring at the blank sheet of paper in his typewriter.

Just before noon Tinker was called into Scott's office.

"I've just had a call," the sports editor said. "The Dodgers have called a two o'clock press conference at the Hotel New Yorker."

"By the Dodgers you mean . . ."

"Yeah, Bollinger, the big cheese himself. He's finally back in town and he's deigned to talk to the press. He's going to address the Tippen business. Get down there and cover it."

"What do you think he's going to say?"

"I can tell you what he's saying off the record: This is a goddamned disgrace, a black eye for the team, and the kid ought to fry. But for the edification of the public, and Dodger fans in particular, he's going to say a man is innocent until proven guilty . . ."

"That old saw," Tinker said dryly.

". . . that Harvey has the team's full support, and let the legal process take its course."

"What about 'let the chips fall where they may'?"

"He'll probably say that too. Toddle along, Joe."

The New Yorker, at Eighth Avenue and Thirty-Fourth Street, was known as "the baseball hotel." It was a favorite port of call for teams in town to play the Yankees, Giants, or Dodgers, with about half of the big league clubs stopping there. The others preferred the Commodore and the Roosevelt in the Grand Central area, which was convenient for Tinker if he had to see somebody, those hotels being virtually across the street from the *News*.

Tinker walked into the New Yorker's lobby at ten minutes to two. There was always a good deal of smartness and spirit in the lobby of a first-class hotel, with well-dressed people purposefully criss-crossing the marble floor, uniformed bellhops in crisp animation, revolving doors making what seemed perpetual revolutions. When the season started and the teams began coming through, a giant banner hung from the mezzanine ceiling, welcoming whatever club was in residence.

Tinker bumped into Larrimore Henry, who covered the Dodgers for the *World-Telegram*. With his three-piece dark suit and neatly parted gray hair, the tall, erudite Henry looked more like a State Department attaché than a reporter of squeeze plays and groundouts.

"Where is it, do you know?" Tinker asked.

"Just follow me, Joseph," Henry said, adding airily, "as you always do."

They began mounting the stairs to the mezzanine.

"Did you know this hotel had forty-three floors?" Henry asked.

"I only knew it was tall."

"It's only a remotely relevant fact, but you never know when it might come in handy. When you're covering a press conference in a place it's good to have a sense of the place's minutiae."

"That word sounds positively obscene."

"Minutiae? I never thought about it."

"I bet they'd never let you say it on the radio. Why is Bollinger having this thing here and not at 215 Montague Street?"

"He obviously thinks the team office is inappropriate. Or, given the character of this situation, maybe he prefers it not be stained. Anyway, you know Bollinger; he'd rather be in Manhattan than Brooklyn. He thinks it suits him better."

"Bollinger only thinks he thinks," Tinker said.

"Watch your catcalls, sonny," Henry said, "we're here."

The room at the end of the mezzanine corridor had a neatly lettered sign on the door that read BROOKLYN DODGER PRESS CONFERENCE. When they walked in Tinker and Henry were greeted by front office executive Horace Glickman, a Columbia University Phi Beta Kappa who was conversant with all of history's heavy thinkers from Aristotle to John McGraw, but whose greatest skills lay in flattering and cajoling the press corps.

"It hasn't started yet," Horace said. "But soon."

"You serving anything?" Tinker asked.

"Persiflage and cheese dip," Horace said. "Look, it's going to be brief. You know how he is."

"Not if we ask a thousand questions," Henry said.

"I guarantee you won't get a thousand answers. He's in a lousy mood."

"Is that news?" Henry asked.

Tinker moved through the crowd of about twenty reporters and photographers, patting a few shoulders by way of greeting. He was surprised to see Tony Marino there.

"Listen, ginzo," Tinker said to his colleague, "do I come to police headquarters and poach on you?"

"As a matter of fact, yes," Tony said. "According to Lieutenant Selman."

"I'll buy you a drink downstairs when this is over. I want to talk to you."

Outside of a few straight-backed wooden chairs

against the wall and a desk and swivel chair in the center, there was no furniture in the room. Andrew Bollinger was standing behind the desk, cigar in mouth, churlish expression on his face. He was wearing a cheap brown suit that belied his wealth but bespoke his origins. This thin, sour-faced, fifty-year-old baseball executive had come up from poverty in Cairo, Illinois, made his packet in Northwest lumber, and bought a controlling interest in the Dodgers in the 1930s, when the team was near bankruptcy. It was said of him that he was the only baseball executive who didn't know the difference between a double bourbon and a double play, but he'd been shrewd enough to hire first Larry MacPhail and then Branch Rickey to run his investment.

Sitting in the swivel chair was Mrs. Edena Bollinger, who was the paradigm of a successful man's second wife. A good twenty years younger than her husband, she had the cuddly blonde looks of an aging starlet and the good legs of a Rockette. Extra helpings of rouge and lipstick enhanced the pleasant vacuity of her face, while she had the gorgeous smile of one who had unexpectedly triumphed over adversity. She had been working as a waitress at the Bear Mountain Inn, where the Dodgers took spring training during the travel-restricted war years, and where Bollinger had met her. In rapid order Bollinger took her as his mistress, punched out a writer who wanted to know what was going on, shed his first wife of twenty-five years, and married Edena and moved into a lavish apartment on Sixty-First Street between Fifth and Madison.

Bollinger ran his hand over his thin gray hair, puffed several times on his cigar, eyed the assemblage with undisguised hostility, and asked if everyone was there.

"Everyone, Mr. Bollinger," Horace Glickman said from his position at the door.

"All right," Bollinger said. He spoke with a rasp. Here was, Tinker thought, the epitome of the self-made millionaire, the man with little patience or empathy for the suckers he'd left behind. Tinker glanced at Edena; she was smiling sweetly, legs crossed, a silver fox wrap sitting on her shoulders, a diamond brooch resting upon her well-filled cashmere sweater.

"I was out of town on business when this thing happened," Bollinger said. "Naturally I was shocked. You all know the details of the tragedy, so I don't have to go into that. I don't know Harvey Tippen personally, but the boy is a member of the Brooklyn baseball organization. We have hundreds of players in our organization and we're proud of them all. Along with baseball skills, we try to impress upon them a standard of moral behavior as well as just plain common sense. If a man gets into trouble it's a reflection upon himself and not upon the organization. Now, Harvey's gotten himself into a mess of trouble and we feel for him and his family. The truth of the accusations that have been made against him have not yet been established, and until they are we see Harvey as innocent. That's the American judicial system, is it not, that a man is innocent until proven guilty. We intend to stand behind Harvey and support him in every way we can, within reason. If he's guilty, then we wash our hands of him and assure you he'll never again play in the Dodger organization."

No, you jackass, Tinker thought; he'll be playing

for the Sing Sing Dodgers, unless and until they
sit his ass in the electric chair.

"But we're going to do whatever we can to
help," Bollinger went on. "I've instructed one of
our lawyers, Mr. Milton Miller, to represent
Harvey in this matter. And I'd like to add one
other thing, a word to our many millions of loyal
Dodger fans. I want to assure them that the Brooklyn organization is not going to let this incident in
any way, shape, or form distract us from what is
our principal goal in 1946—winning the National
League pennant and bringing Brooklyn its first
world championship. The war is over, all of our
players are back sound and healthy and ready to
bring the highest brand of major league ball to our
fans. So," Bollinger said, "this is going to be the
only official statement the club is going to make
on this matter. I'll take a few questions and then
we're going to leave the whole thing in the hands
of the law."

Tinker had the first question, the only one he
wanted answered.

"Mr. Bollinger," he said, "regarding Milton
Miller: does his legal experience extend to criminal
law?"

"I don't know," Bollinger answered with a note
of irritation. "You'll have to ask him."

"What kind of legal work has he done for you?"
Larrimore Henry asked.

"Real estate. I assure you he's a very able man."

"Why not hire an experienced criminal lawyer?"
someone asked.

"We're doing the best we can for Harvey," Bollinger said. "Remember, we're not obligated to do
anything." He was biting down hard on his cigar
now, his eyes beginning to squint as they moved

from face to face, as if daring someone to put a question.

Tinker stared at Edena. Nothing, it seemed, could disturb that apparently impermeable equanimity, not the plight of Harvey Tippen, not the flow of sometimes trenchant questions, not her husband's increasing impatience. When the photographers came close and began aiming their flashbulbs she smiled and decorously patted the side of her head, providing a delightful contrast to her scowling husband. When one writer, probably playfully, asked her what she thought of the situation, Bollinger answered irascibly for her: "She hasn't studied the issues."

"What issues?" he was asked.

"Guilt or innocence," Bollinger said, his voice raising. "The biggest issue of all."

After several more questions, Horace Glickman, with an acute sense of his boss's rapidly draining patience, entered the group, clapped his hands, and announced that the press conference was over. Edena Bollinger rose from her chair, smiling at the photographers.

"Mr. Bollinger," one of them said, "can we have one of you and your wife standing away from the desk?"

"Stick it up your ass," Bollinger said.

"The theme of that press conference," Tinker said to Tony Marino as they headed for the hotel bar, "was we're standing behind you but we won't be sending flowers to the funeral."

"He's a real bastard, isn't he?" Tony said.

"A crude sketch in a cheap frame."

"He impresses me as the kind of man who believes that accusation equals guilt. It's a primitive

ethic and probably one of the qualities that's made
him a success. The self-made man often is given
to thinking the worst of everyone; it makes it easier
for him to trample them down on his way to the
top."

"But in this case he's trampling on what is potentially a very valuable piece of merchandise."

"Doesn't bother him," Tony said. "Curiously,
these guys are often moral puritans. He's probably
offended by what Harvey was doing."

"But he himself," Tinker said as they entered
the lounge area of the bar, "was playing around
with that adorable little trinket and ended a long
marriage for her."

"Joe, when a man writes his own moral code he
tends to exclude the author."

They sat down at a small table that had a blue-
and-white-checked cloth and a basket of peanuts
in the middle. A waiter took their orders and soon
placed mixed drinks before them.

"A real estate lawyer?" Tinker asked after taking
a sip. "Did you get that?"

"It may all be academic. I can tell you, unoffi-
cially, of course, what the strategy is. I've been
talking to a few people in the department. This is
not for the paper, Joe, but they're advising Harvey
to make a statement."

"Who's advising Harvey?"

"The police. They're telling him that there's a
strong case against him because of all the discrep-
ancies in his story, that it doesn't look good, and
that the best course open to him would be a signed
confession, which would lead to a charge of sec-
ond-degree manslaughter. He'd get five to seven
and could be out in three. That's what they're
feeding him. They're even writing the script for

him, which he then dictates back to them and
signs. They want him to say that he followed her
into the house, she provoked him—continued to
provoke him, actually, since everybody saw what
she did at the nightclub—and he lost his head.
That episode at El Morocco could work to his advantage. The judge could be extremely sympathetic, if Gloria is painted vividly enough as a
snotty rich kid."

"That's very nice," Tinker said, "except the guy
may be innocent."

"He's at the front of the line, Joe. They don't
have anybody else. And there are just enough
shades of gray in his story to make him a credible
suspect."

"But why should he sign a statement like that,
if he's innocent?"

"I'll tell you why—because our system is more
immediately geared to handle the guilty, not the
innocent. Once you're brought in, the presump-
tion is no longer with you, especially in a case like
this. Without having been there, I can tell you
what Harvey's been through. He's been sitting for
days either in his cell or in an interrogation room,
without benefit of legal counsel. He's been asked
to tell his story over and over, and each time
they've punched more holes in it, showing him
how vulnerable to attack it is and telling him what
a bloodthirsty prosecutor would do to it. He keeps
telling them he's innocent and they keep telling
him he can't prove it, but that they *can* prove he's
guilty. He's a simple kid and gradually they're
convincing him that they're his friends and are
trying to do him a favor. They'll talk a little baseball
with him from time to time, ask him how big
Gloria's tits were, then remind him what a jam

he's in and occasionally refer to that chair 'they' have got up in Sing Sing. 'They' becomes a very important word, Joe. These guys are very smooth, very skillful; gradually they peel Harvey and themselves away from the rest of the world. 'They' are trying to get him. 'They' want to fry him. 'We' are the only ones who can help you."

"What about Bollinger's lawyer? Can't he stop this?"

Tony shrugged. "He can, but will he? When he sees what the D.A.'s got he might very well advise Harvey to go along. You heard Bollinger. That wasn't exactly a fight-to-the-death declaration of support. And I'll tell you something else, Joe: Harvey can sign a statement and be given all the assurances in the world; but they're hardly a contract. He can still walk into court and find himself facing murder one."

"Jesus Christ," Tinker murmured. "You going to drink that?" he asked, pointing to Tony's untouched drink. His own glass was by now empty. Tony shook his head, then watched Tinker appropriate the glass.

"They just want to get this off the front pages," Tinker said.

"That's right. They get a confession, then there's an arraignment before a judge, a trial date is set, the headlines go elsewhere, and it's forgotten."

"And you know what the worst thing is?"

"The cops close the books on it."

"The investigation goes into the record books like yesterday's ball game," Tinker said, "and the guy who really did it goes to sleep with a smile on his face. I can't believe Roger Selman is part of this."

"He probably isn't. He's the investigating officer, but I understand that the interrogation—the one we've been talking about—is being done by others."

"I don't think Roger believes the kid did it."

"It wouldn't be easy, or in some ways advisable, for him to continue an investigation into a case the department considers closed."

"Roger's a good cop. I can't believe he's buying all this bullshit. How are you going to handle the story?"

"Not the way you'd want me to, Joe. I don't know for sure whether Harvey's guilty or not. If some dignified assistant commissioner stands up and tells us that the kid has signed a confession, what do you want me to do—not print it?"

"You can say that he was subjected to unreasonable pressures and subtle coercion."

"How do I know it's true?"

"You do know it's true," Tinker said.

"I know what a friendly source told me. I can't print that as a fact."

"You know, Tony," Tinker said with a wry smile, "look at the structure of this thing. One of the reasons the department is anxious to cut a few corners and accelerate this case is because of the weight of those big black headlines—which *we* write, and by 'we' I mean the universe of journalism, with our almost panic-stricken priorities, our almost immoral need to overstate. We help to put Harvey in the kettle and then we're outraged because the cops light the fire."

"Complicity, huh?" Tony said with an understanding smile. "Well, it's a working relationship the press has with the public. We tell them what's interesting about them and that motivates them to make us make it even more interesting. You think the front page is any different from a movie marquee? The public wants to know what's playing today."

"If I was working your street . . ." Tinker said.

"You'd be fired in a week," Tony said.

At six o'clock that evening Tinker was sitting in a bar just off Columbus Circle with Roger Selman. The detective, who looked drawn and tired, had ordered a soft drink. Tinker was holding a shot glass filled with bourbon between his fingers.

"I didn't want to talk to you in the station house," Tinker said.

"That doesn't mean I'm going to tell you anything here I wouldn't tell you there."

"I want your candor, Roger."

"It's off your desk now, Joe. They're charging him."

"Has he made a statement?"

Selman nodded.

"He's being badgered into a manslaughter charge, isn't he?" Tinker asked.

"You writing this?"

"No. For my information only."

"The interrogation is out of my hands," Selman said.

"Do you believe he did it?"

"I haven't made up my mind."

"But if he signs a statement, then it's over."

"I should think so."

"And you'd let it drop?"

"Look, Joe, a newspaperman has a story, he runs with it and nothing else. Correct? Well, that's not the way it works with a cop. Since the other night I've got two more homicides—not page one homicides, but real people nonetheless. Not to mention holdups, assaults, and all the other peccadilloes of midtown Manhattan."

"But you can't let an innocent kid go to hell because he happens to be in the middle of a crowded agenda."

"You don't know that he's innocent," Selman said with some resentment. "Joe, this is not a show trial in the Soviet Union. We don't beat confessions out of people and then put them on trial for the greater glory of the NYPD."

"It sounds pretty close," Tinker said, emptying his glass with a single swallow.

"I didn't say I liked it. But you people have put us under a lot of pressure. 'Diamond Hero, Diamond Girl.' 'The Town House Murders.' 'Gloria's Last Hours.' Where's *your* responsibility in all this?"

"The press can afford to make mistakes, the police can't."

"You poison the air, we breathe it," Selman said in a surly tone. "And if you want to be coldly objective: why did Harvey lie about what he did after leaving her? It *is* a lie, you know, his story of a long walk home. And getting rid of his clothing—possibly blood-splattered clothing. If he is innocent he's certainly not helping his cause."

"You must have other suspects," Tinker said. "The more I find out about Gloria, the less loveable she becomes."

"Joe," Selman said wearily, "I'm sure we know everything that you do, and more. We checked out the people she was with at El Morocco. They all went home after they left the club."

"Were they seen?"

"At that hour of the morning, no. But we've no reason to suspect them of anything. There's nothing to place them in the house at the time of the murder."

"They all had keys."

"They openly admitted that, all of them."

"That theater guy had a motive," Tinker said.

"Pfund? We know that. She withdrew her backing for his play. That happens all the time in the theater. He's an experienced theatrical man; these people live in cathedrals of disappointment."

"One too many, perhaps?"

"You're grasping, Joe."

"How about break-ins in the area? Any pattern?"

A tired smile crossed Selman's face. "No, Joe," he said indulgently.

"It could've been an honest burglary that went wrong."

"You can theorize all you want, but where was Harvey for seven hours and why'd he get rid of the suit and shirt? Look, Joe, no matter what you think, the boys genuinely believe he did it. Sure, they want to wrap it up, but they're not trying to railroad him."

"But you have some doubts."

"I admit I'm not a hundred percent convinced."

"You heard about the press conference."

"I would say that was not very helpful."

"Jesus Christ," Tinker said, "I felt like decking him. Pompous, sanctimonious, hypocritical son of a bitch."

"Different from you only by sweep and degree," Selman said.

"What the hell does that mean?"

"Bollinger is trying to protect the good name of baseball. You guys do that, don't you? If a player gets drunk, if he beats his wife, if he gets in a brawl, you don't print it, do you? At all costs, protect the team."

"Yes, we do that," Tinker said. "That's the way the relationship works. Baseball's pure and unstained image must be preserved. But in this case it's a man's life we're talking about. And to hear that talk coming from a goddamned hypocrite like Bollinger. Him and that silly simpering bauble of a wife of his. She looks like something you'd find hanging on a lecher's Christmas tree."

"When are you going to Florida, Joe?" Selman asked with a cordial smile.

"I may not go."

"No? I would have thought you'd be looking to the tropical sunshine, leaving this whole sordid mess behind. Especially with people taking potshots at you."

"What the hell could that have been about?" Tinker asked.

"It could have been a nut, a would-be robber, an irate husband, a literary critic."

"Or," Tinker said, tapping the table with his finger, "because I'm starting to get close to something."

Selman smiled tiredly. "Go to Florida, Joe," he said.

15

Tinker had been told by one of the actor's room-mates that he could find Frank Serrano at a rehearsal hall at Eighth Avenue and Fifty-Fifth Street. The entrance was between an empty store and a hole in the wall that sold grilled hamburgers and hot dogs. Tinker jogged up a tall staircase whose yielding steps gave out creaking noises under every impact. Beyond a double glass door at the head of the stairs was a large anteroom that was bare except for a desk and chair that looked as though they had been unattended for years. An enormous bulletin board hung on the peeling yellow wall, covered with a potpourri of tacked-on leaflets, notices, and index cards. A telephone booth stood in one corner, its walls scrawled with numbers. The glamour and glitter of the theater were not evident in this place.

There were two widely separated, hideously painted green doors. On one was taped a piece of typing paper on which were printed the words THE YELLOW CATERPILLAR COMPANY. Tinker opened the door and entered the large room. About a dozen casually dressed people were scattered around, most of them holding limber-covered scripts. On the apron of a small stage a white-haired man in a black turtleneck was sitting and talking to several people in front of him. A few others were in earnest conversation around a card table. Against one wall were several dozen wooden folding chairs, most of them shut. The room was windowless, the light coming from tracks of fluorescent bulbs overhead. A piano was in the corner. To one side actors' blocking marks had been chalked on the floor.

The only one not casually dressed was a young man in a three-piece blue pinstriped suit who was standing with his arm around an attractive young blonde. When he saw Tinker he whispered something to her, withdrew his arm, and walked toward the visitor with an outstretched hand.

"Mr. Tinker, I presume," he said.

Tinker didn't know if this was supposed to be parodic or not.

"Yes," he said, shaking hands.

"My roommate telephoned and told me you might be up. I'm Frank Serrano."

The stride had been confident, the handshake firm. An inch or two over six feet, Serrano, in his middle twenties, was a man of extraordinary good looks, with thick wavy black hair that glistened, dark eyes, and a sculpted smile that broke out like a neon light and with just as much sincerity. He spoke in a warm baritone that sounded pretentious in so young a man.

"It wouldn't do to talk in here," Serrano said. "The other room is available."

They left the cast and director of *The Yellow Caterpillar* and went into the adjoining studio. Serrano turned on a single track of overhead light, pitching the studio's further reaches into shadow. This capacious room was a twin of the other, with folding chairs, a couple of card tables, a piano, and a small stage.

"I hope I'm not pulling you away from anything," Tinker said after the light had gone on and the door was shut behind them.

"Not at all," Serrano said, slapping his hands together and rubbing them for a moment. "They're mounting a new play in there and I have a few friends in the cast and I just stopped by for some shop talk. The theater thrives on that. We have an underground network of information to rival any Fifth Column's." Serrano smiled—he seemed to turn it on and off like some secret weapon—and chuckled self-indulgently. Actors, Tinker thought. They were always on stage, but it was a perilous place to be without a script.

Serrano pulled a pair of chairs away from the wall, slammed down the seats, and placed them about five feet apart in the middle of the room, directly under the light. The two men sat down facing each other. In the large, nearly empty setting, under the narrow fall of light, they looked conspiratorial.

"You say you're doing a story about Gloria for the *News*?" Serrano asked.

"The New York City angle," Tinker said. "How treacherous the carefree life can be, how fickle. How the stars can suddenly turn to hailstones and the melodies fall into a dirge." Jesus, Tinker thought, there'll be roses growing here tomorrow.

"I know what you mean," Serrano said, nodding his head, that honey-dipped baritone turning solemn for a moment. "This city can break your heart in a hurry."

Or your neck, Tinker thought.

"Gloria's death," Serrano said, "was, among other things, a great tragedy for the Broadway theater. For so young a woman she had a mature appreciation and sense of responsibility toward the performing arts. I realize that that might be looking at her death narrowly, but I would like to stress her finer qualities, since the newspapers have been going off in other directions. I mean no disrespect."

"No, no," Tinker said, "you're quite right. Perhaps we can do something to redress the balance. From what you're saying, I take it she didn't just buy orchestra seats, that her patronage went deeper."

"Quite. Her generosity toward the theater was both personal and impersonal. By that I mean she sometimes helped individual artists personally as well as being prepared to provide backing for a show. Where, I ask you, is the theater without such people? You know what we call them in the profession."

"Angels," Tinker said.

Serrano nodded and smiled, as if giving Tinker an A. "Not an ill-chosen word, Mr. Tinker."

"But am I correct in assuming that she had offered to back Mr. Pfund's new play and then abruptly withdrew that support?"

Serrano's dark eyebrows came together for a moment, as though he had come across an unexpected phrase in his script.

"There was some talk of that," he said. "I don't know if a final decision had been made."

"I understand you were to be part of the production."

"That's right. It could have been a breakthrough

role for me. Something I could really sink my teeth into."

"I guess part of one's theatrical art is mastering the pangs of disappointment."

"Disappointment is built right into the heart and soul of the theater," Serrano said. "I'm afraid it wouldn't be much of a profession without it, sad to say."

"How long had you known Gloria?"

"Several months. We met down in the Village. I was attending a workshop that Mr. Pfund was running on Bank Street and one evening she came by and sat in. We struck up an acquaintance and the next thing I knew she was inviting me to parties, both at her place and as an escort to others."

"Pretty heady stuff, I imagine."

"I met a lot of people, made some contacts. It was helpful."

"Were you romantically involved with her?"

Serrano paused. He smiled slyly for a moment. His ego can't resist it, Tinker thought.

"For a while," Serrano said, making an effort to sound casual.

"She was kind of flighty about those things, wasn't she?"

"What do you mean?"

"She changed partners a lot."

"We're all young, healthy, virile people, Mr. Tinker."

"Were you in love with her?"

"Heavens, no. Gloria had a lot of friends and so did I. You seem to have some bourgeois notions."

"Sheltered life," Tinker said, flashing an ingenuous smile. "How well do you know Harvey Tippen?"

Serrano grunted, disparagingly, Tinker thought.

"What is there to know?" Serrano said. "He was just a face in the crowd. Gloria was temporarily infatuated. Mr. Pfund described him as an automobile without an engine. Ultimately he became an irritant, to Gloria, to all of us."

"She did a job on him that night, didn't she?"

"No more than he deserved. The fellow couldn't take a hint."

"That's no reason to humiliate him."

"I think it was the only way to get through to him."

"What did you do after the party broke up at El Morocco?"

"I walked home. I live just a few blocks away."

"Were you upset with Gloria? For withdrawing her backing, I mean. After all, it cost you a good role."

"I was distressed, of course. But in an impersonal way. It was her money, after all, to do with as she pleased. It was a business decision."

"Do you think she ever seriously intended to back the play?"

"What do you mean?"

"Well," Tinker said, rubbing his face, then leaning forward on the chair, "I heard she had something of a capricious nature. A weird sense of humor."

Serrano wet his lips, gazing steadily at Tinker.

"In what regard?" he asked warily. "What kind of angle are you pursuing in this story?"

"Well," Tinker said, "I was speaking to Juliana Overman."

The curiosity that had been in Serrano's face slowly changed to an expression of hardened neutrality.

"I wouldn't put much store in what she says," he said.

"She was very close to Gloria."

"So?"

"Apparently they had no secrets between them. None."

Tinker could see from Serrano's taut, expressionless face and unblinking eyes that the mine field was at hand.

"What did she tell you?" Serrano asked. "She's not the most reliable of people. Drinks like a fish. I heard that's why the second husband walked out on her. She's been carrying a grudge against mankind ever since. Believe me, you've been wasting your time if you've been talking to Juliana Overman."

"Are you saying she makes up stories?"

"What stories?" Serrano asked. "What has she been telling you?" A certain insistence was building in his voice, ruffling the measured hues and tones of that resonant baritone. It was apparent to Tinker that this fellow lacked the temperament needed to sustain high indignation.

"Stories that Gloria told her," Tinker said.

Serrano frowned, then wiped his lips quickly with his tongue, staring severely at Tinker, sitting stone still, though not, Tinker sensed, without some exertion.

"Those bitches gossiped about everybody," Serrano said. Signs of perspiration had appeared on his upper lip. "What did she say about me?"

"Gossip is never flattering, Mr. Serrano," Tinker said quietly.

"Which is why people will always listen." Serrano began nodding his head vigorously. He smiled; the smile wasn't as bright as earlier, was too broad, like mirth without sound. "I know what you're talking about," he said, almost as if in accusation. "Those two bitches were snickering about it, weren't they? You talk about an incestuous world, Tinker, you're talking about the theater. It's a fucking collection of dreamers and phonies and perverts. Let me tell you, I wanted no part of that. I'm a serious artist."

Serrano got to his feet and began pacing back and forth in front of the small stage, all of it in darkness except for the forward part of the apron.

"You might ask yourself what a serious artist is doing selling his soul to the devil," Serrano said. "Well, who hasn't done it, Tinker?" And then, as if in formal recitation: "Let him who is without shame come forward, and we'll call him a hypocrite. You never know when you're going to get an opportunity, do you?" Serrano said, pacing in a tight line back and forth in front of Tinker, expelling his words in an angry rush, jabbing his finger at Tinker for a moment as he said, "You know, they say that nothing is for sure in the theater, that there are a million surprises. Well, I can tell you one thing that's for sure—you get older. You can't imagine how fast you do that when you're an actor. Listen, Tinker, I'm not just some good-looking kid who decided he wanted to be a star. I went to drama school. I studied. I've worked goddamned hard."

Serrano wheeled and jumped up onto the low stage and now Tinker, still sitting, had to raise his eyes to watch him.

"Here's where I want to be," Serrano said loudly, stamping one shoe on the boards. "I've

made plenty of sacrifices, and so I've made one
more. But don't get the wrong idea, Tinker. I'm a
tough kid," Serrano said, jabbing his thumb pug-
naciously toward himself. "I come from a family
of hard-assed Philadelphia wops. I'm the first son
of a bitch in my family who doesn't have callouses
on my hands. And you know what? I'm proud of
that."

"Gloria talked you into it, didn't she?" Tinker
asked.

"She said it would get me a leading role on
Broadway," Serrano said. "You don't know what
that means to an actor, do you, Tinker? You don't
know what that *sounds* like inside his head. You
tell yourself you'll do whatever it takes to get the
job. It happens all the time in this business, Tinker.
More than people think. You'd be surprised at
how many goddamned fairies there are in the theater. Agents, producers, directors, performers. I did
what I did to get ahead in the world. Gloria said
that Pfund had a dozen guys he could cast in the
role. She said why the hell should I be sitting in
the audience on opening night instead of being up
on the stage? She said all I had to do was compromise myself a little and I'd get the job and
nobody would ever be any the wiser. And do you
know why Pfund wanted me? Because that fucking miserable son of a bitch knew I was a man, a
real goddamned man. Make sure you get that
right."

"And then you started wondering if she ever
really intended to back the play," Tinker said, "or
whether she was just having some fun at somebody's expense. She and Juliana were capable of
cooking that up, weren't they?"

Serrano did not answer.

Tinker stood up slowly. "You must've been good and goddamned mad," he said.

Serrano made an odd, unpleasant movement with the corner of his mouth. He spoke in a voice deadly in its calmness.

"When I heard that somebody had wrung her neck," he said, "I felt like celebrating."

16

I want to ask you a question," Tinker said.

"I hope it's not a proposal of marriage," Rita said.

"Since you're officially still married, no. Anyway, I'm planning to wait until I'm old and gray for that."

"That's your side of it. All right, what's your question?"

They were sitting on the floor of her apartment eating dinner out of an array of white cardboard containers brought in from a Chinese restaurant on Sixth Avenue.

"I want an honest answer," Tinker said. "Have you bedded down with anybody else since we've been going together?"

Rita arched an elegant eyebrow.

Tinker had come to accept the fact that, since his evening with Juliana Overman, his conscience had been bothering him. As far as he could tell, the sensation was unprecedented in his life, particularly in this context. He had always been one to accept gifts and opportunities—lawful and moral, of course—as part of life's unpredictable mélange. To accept some and reject others on grounds of scruple would have made things too complicated. He had formed the vague philosophy that prudent decision making was too inhibiting an onus for a young man. Conscience, Tinker decided, would determine when a man was no longer young. He was wondering now whether the day had come.

"Simply on the grounds of principle," Rita said, "a question like that should never be answered."

"Oh."

"But I would like to know why it was asked."

Tinker pondered as he gulped down food he liked but could not always properly pronounce. He had no ready answer.

"I don't think that was an idle question," Rita said. "A good journalist, like a good lawyer, never asks a question unless there's a point to it."

Sitting cross-legged on the lushly carpeted floor, Tinker continued to eat, his lower jaw moving rhythmically up and down. He stared inquiringly at her. She was sitting with her back to the sofa, over which hung a large reproduction of Brueghel's *Hunters in the Snow*. She was wearing a pair of white slacks, and now she drew her knees up and rested her chin on them, an expression of subtle intrigue in her eyes.

"Are you doing a story on the sexual mores of executive secretaries," she asked, "or are you perhaps seeking predispensation to do anything you want to in Florida?"

He continued spooning and forking his food up from the containers, jaws rotating.

"I may not go to Florida," he said. "I may ask Scotty to let me stay here until the Tippen case is resolved."

"According to the papers it's all but been resolved."

"Not to my satisfaction," he said.

"Well, then to the satisfaction of all the ladies at my beauty parlor."

"What are they saying about it? I'm serious. I want to know what people think."

"They think he did it but they feel sorry for him. They hope he gets off lightly. Murdering the spoiled and petulant rich, it seems, is an acceptable blood sport for the lowly."

"You think he's guilty?"

"I have no opinion one way or the other. But everyone seems to be forgetting that whoever killed Gloria also went on and did the same to her maid."

Finishing eating, Tinker put his utensils into a soggy container and wiped his mouth with the back of his hand.

"Harvey wouldn't have done that. He might have done it to Gloria; she certainly provoked him. But not the maid."

"It's not a sports story, Joe. They'll never let you stay here and cover it."

"There are still people I've got to talk to."

"You don't have much time."

"Tomorrow I'm going over to Capstone, get hold of a car, and drive up to Connecticut to see Harvey's family. It's legitimate; Scott wants the story."

"Let's get back to your question."

"I'm sorry I asked it," he said, gathering together the containers, the utensils, and the napkins and placing them on a tray.

"I know. Nevertheless I'm intrigued. You can't ask a woman a question like that and then change the subject."

"Not even to murder?"

"Some things transcend murder."

"Well, hell, you said you weren't going to answer."

"I want to know why it was asked."

There were two ways to deal with an aroused conscience: tell the truth or contrive a lie. The truth was laudable, but it also had the tendency to widen the scope of a problem. And while a neatly packaged lie could not put out a fire, it could certainly be a lid with which to hide the smoke.

"I was thinking," he said, "if I was so human as to err while I was in Florida whether I should feel guilty."

"That's not why you asked that question," she said after studying him with a long gaze that disconcerted him with its shrewdness. "Have you been seeing someone? You're certainly free to."

"If I was—*if*—wouldn't you be pleased that I felt guilty about it?"

"That is just about the most tawdry plea for nobility I've ever heard. Who have you been seeing, Joe?"

"I haven't been *seeing* anyone."

"Then who did you *see*?"

Jesus, he thought, how did I get into this?

"You said I was free to do as I pleased," he said.

"But I didn't say I was obligated to like it."

"Hell," he said, "I feel just like Harvey; you *think* I'm guilty, ergo I am guilty."

She smiled wryly.

"Why don't we sleep on it, Joe? You in your apartment, and me in mine."

As he walked home along a nearly deserted Fourteenth Street, Tinker felt the uncomfortable self-reproach of a man who had just allowed his pocket to be picked. Why the hell had he brought that subject up? Was it because he had actually been tempted by Juliana's high-toned glamour, by the rarefied airs of her highly perched world? Was he nursing some secret desire to be the next Harvey Tippen?

But then something else moved into his mind. Maybe he had become overly sensitive since having been shot at, but as he walked home Tinker began having the feeling that he was being followed. As he turned at Sixth Avenue and began heading north, he looked back and saw a man about half a block behind, walking in a way that Tinker in his suspicions thought was furtive. If the guy was a tail, then he wasn't very good at it, slowing perceptibly each time Tinker turned to have a look at him. The guy was wearing an overcoat with the collar up, a fedora with the brim pulled forward, and had his hands in his overcoat pocket. Since having been shot at, Tinker told himself, he no longer had the luxury of being entirely trusting.

Though the night was cold and the hour late, there were people on the avenue, on both sides of the street. If this guy was planning to take another shot at him, Tinker thought, it would be when they had turned the corner and were on what was at that time of night usually a deserted Sixteenth Street.

When he got to the corner Tinker spun around it and began running. He kept going until he reached the grocery store—closed now—in the middle of the block. There, he crouched down behind the large wooden crate that was used to hold the early-morning milk deliveries. Resting his fingertips lightly on the splintered sides of the box, he peered around, his gaze riding along the street.

He felt a pang of fear when he saw the man come around the corner—at a rather accelerated pace—take a few steps, and then stop and survey the empty street. *Son of a bitch*, Tinker thought. *He is following me*. And though he did not think it he felt it: *He's got a gun and he's going to try it again*.

A few cars were parked on either side of the street and Tinker guessed that behind one of these would seem the logical hiding place, ahead of the milk box. The man began walking slowly forward, on the same side of the street as Tinker, who slid back into the store's doorway, looking behind him for a moment: if he were discovered, his one hope would be to plunge through the glass door, get inside the store, and take his chances there. Or he could start shouting. Make a racket. Get some lights on in the buildings around him, get people at the windows. But the son of a bitch was probably too close for that now. The shouting would be a giveaway; it only took a few seconds for a gun to be drawn, aimed, and fired.

As he crouched in the doorway, an acrid odor began offending Tinker's nose and he realized that someone had stopped by here earlier and urinated against the door. Some honest New Yorker who couldn't wait to get home. Tinker cursed, feeling some ultimate indignity as his anger rapidly built. Here he was, hiding in a doorway on a cold night, about to be murdered, his shoes resting in somebody else's piss. Goddammit, he thought. Enough. He'd had three years of this crap and . . .

He shot out of the doorway as if off a line of scrimmage, wheeled, and with sudden unbridled fury went charging along the sidewalk directly toward his tormentor, who, about fifty feet away, stopped, froze for a moment as he appraised the shouting, cursing Tinker coming at him, and spun around and began running, which only galvanized Tinker further, filling him with a manic energy.

"You son of a bitch!" Tinker roared, infuriated by some perverse sense of triumph.

The man bolted across Sixth Avenue, made an abrupt right turn, and continued along on the far side of the street, flying past the darkened stores, startling several pedestrians. Tinker, still yelling, ran diagonally across the avenue, causing a car to swerve around him. He saw the man's hat fly off as if snatched by wires, saw him run across Fifteenth, leap onto the sidewalk, and keep going, arms pumping, overcoat whipping.

Continuing his pursuit, Tinker watched the man rush toward the green lamps over the subway kiosk and then fairly leap into the entrance, silhouetted against the stairway lights for a moment. Tinker followed, galloping down the steps, passing a woman still pressed against the wall in fright from the previous apparition. Taking the final half dozen steps at a single leap, he hit the concrete with an emphatic impact that made the soles of his feet feel momentarily afire. He saw his man crawling on all fours under the turnstile, then getting up and running for the platform.

"Hey!" Tinker roared and went on, taking the turnstile like a hurdles jumper, vaguely aware of a protesting shout from the change booth.

Several people standing idly on the platform came to attention as pursued and pursuer stormed past. At the end of the platform the man stopped, threw a wild, panicked look back, and then jumped off and ran into the tunnel.

Unrelentingly, Tinker followed, though not as recklessly—sitting himself on the platform's edge and sliding himself down, trying to recall what he had heard about a third rail and sudden death. Running awkwardly between the rails, he headed into the tunnel darkness, hearing the other's footsteps echoing ahead. Stumbling over one of the track bed ties, he felt himself hurling forward through the darkness, landing flat on his chest. Putting his hands in the icy water that was trickling between the rails, he pushed himself erect and continued running, closing in on his man now, whom he caught a glimpse of in the lurid illumination cast by a red signal light on the wall. The man was running awkwardly, brokenly, as if all his bones were straining to go in opposite directions.

The rumbling noise seemed to begin a great distance away, but it grew rapidly in volume like a billowing charge of thunder. A few moments later twin beams of white from the headlights of the downtown F train came ominously into view, splitting the darkness. Clearly outlined, the man stopped, spun about wildly, stretched out his arms, and froze like a piece of black sculpture.

Get out of the way, you asshole, Tinker thought, and then stepped carefully aside and pressed himself against the side of the concrete wall, stiffening his arms against his sides. He took a deep breath and held it as the train thundered by with a rush of cold wind. He looked up as the lighted cars rolled past, exchanging glances with several startled faces, and, once he realized that nothing was going to hit him, smiling foolishly at whoever noticed him.

He waited as car after car went by in metallically clattering procession, then found himself looking after the train as it headed toward the Fourteenth Street station.

He moved away from the wall like a man who had been reprieved from a firing squad, momentarily astonished by the sudden silence. He could hear the water trickling between the tracks. Then he heard gasping. He stepped gingerly over the rails and found his man still flush against the wall on the other side, too petrified to move. In the faint glare of a yellow signal light, Tinker, his fear suddenly replaced by his previous anger, went up to the gasping, quivering figure and seized him roughly by the lapels.

"Who the hell are you?" Tinker demanded.

For several moments the man fought to catch his breath. Then he stammered, "That train. My God."

"You'll be under the next one if you don't talk," Tinker said, tightening his grip.

"Please. Get me out of here."

Tinker pulled him away from the wall, gave him a shove, and began following him through the tunnel.

They emerged at the Twenty-Third Street station, where Tinker had to help his stumbling, gasping companion up to the platform, which was empty. In a state of near collapse, the man staggered to a bench and caved in on it. Tinker stood over him, waiting.

The man was about thirty-five, red-haired, with a bland, earnest face that was smudged with soot.

One overcoat sleeve was torn open. He looked plaintively up at Tinker.

"I'm sorry," he said. "It was foolish. But I wanted to know."

"Know what?" Tinker asked irascibly.

"Who you were. What was going on."

"What the hell are you talking about?"

"When you left the apartment I followed. It was foolish. But I have a right . . ."

"Who the hell are you?"

"Frederick Blasingame."

In a sudden fit of anger and frustration Tinker leaned forward, took him by the lapels, and half lifted him from the bench.

"You're her husband?"

Blasingame nodded, the corners of his eyes squeezing in for a moment. Tinker dropped him back down.

"Her husband?" he said, incredulously.

Blasingame nodded again. Tinker sat down beside him.

"We could have been killed in there," Tinker said absently.

"We almost were."

"What do you want?"

"I just wanted to know."

"Why don't you ask her?"

"She won't talk to me," Blasingame said.

"Where do you live?"

"Jersey City."

"It figures," Tinker said.

"What?"

"Nothing. Did you follow me the other night?"

"I haven't been in New York for a month."

"Are you sure?"

"I'm sure," Blasingame said, expelling a deep breath.

"Christ," Tinker said, wondering whether he might owe the man an apology. Instead, he said, "I don't like being followed."

"I know," Blasingame said sullenly. "But I saw you go into the house with her and I didn't know what to do. So I waited. When you came out . . ."

"You decided to follow me."

"I'm sorry," Blasingame said. "Believe me."

"You all right now?"

Blasingame nodded, then sighed.

Tinker left him there. Wearily, with aches and pains in his back and legs, he climbed the steps and emerged on Twenty-Third Street, feeling along with his fatigue a sense of disorientation. The cold, windless February night felt bracing. The sky was clear, with a few stars glistening icily over the skyscrapers.

There was an all-night cafeteria on Park Avenue South and Twenty-Second and he headed for it, in dire need of a cup of coffee and a bit of society. He supposed as a friend he ought to call Rita and tell her that her estranged husband was keeping tabs on her, but he was in no mood to play the good friend. And anyway, after tonight's experience he doubted if Blasingame would have the nerve to follow anybody for a while.

The cafeteria was a favorite coffee stop for cabbies, and when he reached it Tinker saw half a dozen Yellow Cabs parked outside. When he entered he found the garishly lit place virtually empty except for two tables of cabbies who were drinking coffee, smoking cigarettes, and engaging in the muted small talk of men who work through the night. Early editions of the *News* were lying about.

"You look great, Joey," a voice said.

Tinker squinted in the light and saw Maurie the Educated Cabbie, so self-proclaimed because he had spent a couple of early manhood years at CCNY. Maurie was wearing the flat cloth cap emblematic of New York City cab drivers, a shabby unbuttoned overcoat, and a sweater under it. Gray curly hair spun out from under the cap. The sight of Tinker had provoked a warm, friendly grin.

"You been digging tunnels?" Maurie asked as Tinker sat down at a table across from him and his cronies.

"Why?" Tinker asked.

"Look at yourself."

Tinker looked. His gray raincoat was black, his hands were black. He picked up a tray left on the table and in its imperfect reflection saw a face smudged with soot.

"You doing an Al Jolson imitation?" Maurie asked. Then he turned to his colleagues and announced that this was Joe Tinker, best sportswriter on the *News*, probably the best in New York.

A few moments later Tinker was surrounded by half a dozen idling cabbies, being plied with questions about the Dodgers and the Giants and the prospects for the coming season. His appreciative audience, which swelled as more cabbies came in, bought him a cup of coffee and several pieces of Danish, all the while asking questions and raptly absorbing his "inside" information. They wanted to know if Mel Ott would play another year for the Giants, if the Dodgers had enough pitching, if the Cardinals or the Cubs would be Brooklyn's biggest threat, if DiMaggio would be back from the wars in fine form. They quoted back to him some of his recent stories on Harvey Tippen, and he told them he was convinced the kid would be proven innocent before long. He answered everything politely and anecdotally, enjoying his temporary status as unquestioned expert, even as he began to wonder if this night would ever end.

It went on until two o'clock in the morning, when the men began drifting back to work, each leaving with a handshake and compliments and envious words about his upcoming departure for Florida. When they were gone he was alone with Maurie.

"The boys really appreciated that," Maurie said. "These are your people, Joe. You're a bigger celebrity to them than Clark Gable. Now go home and take a bath."

"I'm too tired to move," Tinker said.

"Come on," Maurie said, slapping a large hand on Tinker's shoulder. "I'll run you home. On the house."

"Maurie the Educated Cabbie," Tinker said with a tired smile.

"I read a book once," the cabbie said.

"It must have been the right one."

They went outside and got into Maurie's cab, Tinker sliding into the front seat next to the cabbie. As they cruised the few blocks over to Sixteenth, Tinker sighed and closed his eyes for a moment.

"Trouble tonight?" Maurie asked.

"You won't believe this," Tinker said, "but I was chasing somebody through the subway tunnel from Fourteenth to Twenty-Third."

"Oh, I believe it," Maurie said with a glance at

Tinker's soot-covered raincoat. "Who were you chasing?"

"My girlfriend's husband."

Maurie pondered it for a moment, then said, "It should be the other way around, shouldn't it?"

17

Although Tinker could be sentimental about his old neighborhood, he seldom got out there to visit anymore. Living in Manhattan, with its convenient proximities, had contracted his concepts of time and distance. Capstone was a two-fare neighborhood and the trip by subway and trolley car took forty minutes, an unreasonable amount of traveling time for a man who was never more than a ten-minute subway ride from wherever he wanted to go. (Ebbets Field and the Polo Grounds were tedious trips, but that was business.) Helping put Capstone in recession in his thoughts were the facts that his parents were dead, there were strangers living in his childhood home, and most of his close friends had scattered after the war.

Bypassed by the subway and surrounded on three sides by cemeteries, its growth had been precluded, and Capstone was one of the most provincial neighborhoods in Queens. As recently as Tinker's childhood in the 1920s Capstone had been the site of working dairy farms. The area's most distinguishing features were the pair of two-hundred-foot-high gas tanks that dominated the surrounding two-story clapboard and brick houses.

It was ten o'clock in the morning when Tinker

got off the trolley at Grant Avenue and Seventy-First Street. The sun was bright, the temperature a moderate fifty degrees, and he had a pretty good idea where he would find Harry Knackers, one of the few outposts of continuity left from Tinker's boyhood.

Tinker walked along Seventy-First Street and then turned through the open gate and into the schoolyard of Junior High School 73, which he had attended with more fidelity than enthusiasm from kindergarten through ninth grade and which remained for him a four-story half-block-long repository of pleasant memories.

On the books of the Board of Education the school was formally known as William Cowper Junior High. Tinker remembered that when he was in seventh grade his English teacher had deputized a committee of three (Tinker was one) to find out just who this Cowper person had been. After some investigation they returned with the information that Cowper had been an eighteenth-century English poet and hymnologist who had died in an insane asylum. This latter fact invoked great hilarity in the class: their school was named for a loony. It wasn't until he was almost out of high school that Tinker encountered some of Cowper's poetry and realized that if this was lunacy, then sanity was ill-named and a fraud. He didn't know whether to be impressed or depressed: impressed because when the school was built in the early 1930s some member of New York's educational system had been bright enough to name it for an outstanding poet, depressed because an English teacher had had to send out a research squad to see who Cowper had been.

And then, sure enough, there was Harry Knack-

ers, sitting on the cold ground against the handball
court. A relic of the old days, not yet thirty but
already permanently tethered, chronically jobless
but parent-supported and -tolerated, one of those
scraps that time in its passage leaves unswept.
Harry had always hung around the schoolyard,
pleasant and aimless, standing with his hands in
his pockets and smiling, and here he was yet, like
a man waiting for ghosts, confident that his per-
severance would draw them. He had drawn one
this morning.

As Tinker approached him, Harry got to his feet
and swung one arm far out to the side, waiting to
clap a heartily fraternal handshake into Tinker's
hand. The greeting made, Harry slipped his hands
back into the pockets of his peacoat. He was bald-
ing now and added weight had made him moon-
faced, but his friendly eyes had none of the mor-
bidity of the perennial lurker and his smile was
genuine.

"Joseph Tinker," Harry said. "Capstone's greatest writer."

"How are they hangin', Harry?"

"What brings you to town?"

"You," Tinker said. "I need a car. You got one?"

"You know me, Joe. I got four of them right
now."

Capstone's most anchored resident had always
had a passion for automobiles. Though he never
went anyplace beyond driving his mother shop-
ping, Harry always had a fleet of cars which he
bought and sold in transactions that never ex-
ceeded fifty dollars. Before the war he would buy
a heap for five dollars and on weekends come
barreling into the schoolyard with it, scattering the
crapshooters and the hangers-on and the softball

players as he careened around the large, concrete-surfaced yard, bouncing off the wooden fence on one side and the tall wire one on the other, picking up small, knickered passengers who jumped on and off the running boards.

"How long you need it for?" Harry asked as they walked to his house.

"A few days," Tinker said. "You got one that can get me to Connecticut and back?"

"Connecticut?" Harry whistled. "I think so. I got a Plymouth that should do it. The clutch is a bit tricky, but— You got to baby it."

"You still drive around the schoolyard, Harry?"

"Not since 1943. They banned me. I had a Dodge and the brakes failed. I went right through the fence and landed in the school's Victory garden. I killed a million radishes. But we won the war anyway, hah? Hey, I hear you won all sorts of medals out there."

"That's right, Harry," Tinker said. "I'm a killer."

"Well, anyway, they don't let me drive around the schoolyard anymore. I tell you, Joe, things are changing."

Even Harry Knackers knew.

Harry Knackers's 1937 Plymouth did not seem enthusiastic about making this trip, its engine uttering frequent peevish noises that Tinker pretended not to hear. But it plodded along, taking him out of Queens, across the Fifty-Ninth Street Bridge, then up through Manhattan and the Bronx toward Connecticut, a place as alien to most of New York's asphalt-bred residents as Idaho. Tinker's knowledge of this neighboring state was pretty much limited to what landscape he glimpsed from the window of the train that sped between New York and Boston. Connecticut was, in other words, a place that stretched out somewhere between Ebbets Field and Braves Field.

Harvey Tippen came from a small town in the northwestern part of the state. To get there Tinker drove through what he assumed must be very attractive scenery in the summer, but in late February it looked sullen and ill-used, much of it under patches of old snow, the trees looking as though they had been frozen into grotesque postures by winter. He stopped for gas and directions at a Socony station, received a small tin replica of the company's Flying Red Horse symbol as a premium for his purchase, and went on, feeling like a traveler from afar as he stared at small towns, scattered houses, and cold farms whose acreage was measured off by small stone walls, a two-lane blacktop unspooling ahead of him.

When he was pointed to the road to the Tippen house he was told he would need no further directions, that all he had to do was "keep going until you see the pile of shit on your left." Tinker had learned never to ask strangers to explain their arcana, and so he kept driving, assuming that after that description the Tippen house would prove to be self-revelatory.

After going several miles on a stretch of road that had been bruised and pitted by the rigors of New England winters, Tinker saw what had to be the Tippen house. The man who had described it to him had been a paragon of Yankee concision. While none of the homes along this stretch of country road could have been described as manorial, they had at least presented appearances of pride and warmth; the Tippen residence, however, looked like a place where the debris of an explosion had come down.

A broad, hand-painted wooden sign was nailed to a pair of thick posts that had been hammered into the front lawn. "Tippen's Things," the sign proclaimed in three-foot-high black painted letters, and Tinker reasoned that "things" was the best possible word to describe a pile of crap that you wouldn't call junk and couldn't call antiques. The front lawn and as far around to the back of the house as Tinker could see were covered with "Things": it was a turmoil of blackened stoves, wooden iceboxes, bedsprings, automobile tires, agricultural implements, bird cages, bathtubs, steamer trunks, and other detritus that accompanied the human adventure.

Tinker supposed that once upon a time the two-story house with the gabled roof and red brick chimney had been presentable. A stand of trees bordered the backyard. There was a white picket fence in front, but in front only, with no sides, as if someone had forgotten to finish the job; nor did it have a gate, simply an opening to walk through. A heavily wooded area was across the road, while the nearest house was about a hundred yards away.

Harry Knackers's faithful but feeble Plymouth seemed to blend into this setting as Tinker pulled into the driveway and parked behind a pickup truck that had four dented fenders. He got out and walked toward the front door, which opened and revealed an enormous man who fairly filled the entrance. The man wore a blue-and-red-checked flannel shirt that Tinker could see was bulging at the biceps, a pair of paint-stained khaki pants, and combat boots. He was a good six inches over six feet and must have weighed close to three hundred pounds. His large head was covered with thick black hair that bunched at his shirt collar. He had a scraggly black mustache that drooped at the corners like a Western gunfighter's. His mouth and jaw bespoke pugnacity, while his eyes seemed to be telling you you were guilty unless you could prove otherwise.

"Mr. Tippen," Tinker said as he walked across the dead grass, finding an aisle through the pile of shit.

"Do you want to buy something?" Tippen asked in a voice that suggested this was the only possible justification for anyone's existence.

"No, sir," Tinker said, stopping now, smiling amiably at Tippen. There were two steps up to the front door, so the man looked even bigger. "I'm Joe Tinker, with the *Daily News*." Tinker waited. "The *New York Daily News*," he added with quiet emphasis. This was usually enough to crack any ice. Not this time.

"So?"

"I'm a friend of Harvey's." Again Tinker waited. He was wondering if he might have to specify just which Harvey he was referring to.

"So?"

"I'm doing a story on him. The paper is very sympathetic to him. I'm very sympathetic to him."

"You are, are you?"

"Could we talk about him a little bit?"

"What good is that going to do? That stupid kid is in a shithole of trouble and nothing's going to get him out of it."

"You can never tell," Tinker said. "Public opinion is important. We have two million readers."

"That ain't worth a bucket of skim piss in a court of law."

"Can't hurt," Tinker said.

With fingers as long and as thick as frankfurters, Tippen rubbed the side of his face for a moment.

"That stupid kid's gone and thrown it all away, hasn't he?" Tippen said in a voice torn between anger and remorse. "If I'd known what he was going to do, I'd've held him upside down in a barrel of water for five minutes. That would cure anything, wouldn't it? Do you know how hard I worked with him? Right from the start. These eyes," Tippen said, tapping the bridge of his nose, "know talent. When he was six months old I started rolling a ball across the floor to him. When he was three years old my wife stitched together a uniform for him that had 'Dodgers' written in front. When he was five years old I took him to Ebbets Field and was able to introduce him to Babe Herman. 'Babe,' I said, 'here's the kid who one day is gonna come in here and break all of your records.' Babe Herman shook the kid's hand and said, 'I don't doubt that at all.' "

"That's a great story," Tinker said.

"We played ball every day, from March right on through to the first snowfall. When he was ten years old that stupid son of a bitch could hit the ball harder and run faster than any fifteen-year-old. And now what? He's sitting in a bucket of shit because of some watered-down millionaire bitch who I wouldn't of humped with your nose."

"I agree, Mr. Tippen," Tinker said, having listened to this diatribe—spoken with increasing fervor—most patiently.

"That goddamned bitch was ruining him," Tippen said. "Giving him all sorts of fancy notions.

What the hell was he doing in New York? Sitting in nightclubs. Drinking booze. A few weeks before *spring training*? With a chance to make the Dodgers?" Tippen's voice rumbled loudly at this last. He raised one huge fist and shook it frustratedly in the air, his eyes turning to ice for a moment.

"Stupid kid," he said bitterly. "Do you know where his only brains are? In his arms and legs. And do you know who put them there?"

"You did."

"I had him squeezing hard rubber balls from the time he was five years old. And I made him run in heavy boots, so that when he put spikes on he could fly. He could run so fast people said his feet never touched the ground."

"I know," Tinker said. "I've seen him play."

"So he's thrown it all over for a social girl with an ass on her like a ten-year-old boy. We've got women around here, they've got *asses*. What the hell did he have to stay in New York for? He was up here for Christmas. I told him then that if he didn't cut out of there and come home I was going to come down there and drag him back by the collar. I told him that if he wanted to live like a degenerate at least wait until he was a star."

"May I come in, Mr. Tippen?" Tinker asked.

Grudgingly, the big man stepped aside and Tinker entered. To his surprise the interior was quite neat and tidy, maintained with a certain homespun pride. The living room furniture was worn but sturdy, with lace doilies on the armrests of the chairs and sofa. But what most struck Tinker was the room's obeisance to baseball, or, more specifically, to the Brooklyn Dodgers. The wall was covered with framed glossies of Brooklyn baseball icons dating back to World War I era stars Nap

Rucker and Zack Wheat, and on up through Dazzy Vance, Babe Herman, Burleigh Grimes, Van Lingle Mungo, Babe Phelps, Whitlow Wyatt, on up to the current stars. There were Dodger flags and pennants, an aerial photo of Ebbets Field that was at least four feet across and two high, and pictures of every manager going back to Wilbert Robinson. A pair of umbrella stands were jammed with bats, and a brass bowl on an end table held a pile of autographed baseballs.

When Tinker looked at Tippen he saw that the big man had been watching him with an almost grim smile of pride.

A heavyset woman came thumping down the stairs. When Tinker had full sight of her he thought of an icebox on legs. She had curly brown hair, a pair of shoulders like an epauletted doorman, a huge unsupported bosom that bobbled around under her print dress. Her round, fleshy face appeared stubbornly humorless. Tinker could not help idly wondering if sex between the two outsized Tippens was an engineering possibility.

"Elsie," Tippen said, "this is a guy from a New York newspaper."

"*Daily News*, Mrs. Tippen," Tinker said. "My name is Joe Tinker."

Mrs. Tippen looked at him as if he had spoken in a foreign language, then turned to her husband.

"What does he want?" she asked.

"Wants to talk about Harvey."

Mrs. Tippen looked sternly at Tinker.

"What is there to talk about?" she asked. "That boy's gone and broke his father's heart."

"Harvey's in serious trouble, Mrs. Tippen."

"His own doing," she said curtly. "His father

gets a hand on him, that boy will really know what trouble's all about."

"We brought him up straight," Tippen said. "How can a boy go wrong when all he's ever been taught or ever dreamed about is baseball?"

"New York City," Elsie Tippen muttered.

"I don't think Harvey did it," Tinker said.

Elsie Tippen's face changed for a moment, softened.

"We don't know about that," she said. "But guilty or no, he's our boy and we'll stand with him."

"Are you satisfied with the legal representation he's getting?" Tinker asked.

"The man is the Dodgers' lawyer," Tippen said. "I'm sure they know what they're doing. Harvey's a Dodger; they take care of their own."

"We don't know any lawyers," Mrs. Tippen said. "And couldn't buy one if we did."

A few minutes later Tinker was back outside. He hadn't been offered a chair, much less a cup of coffee.

Tippen was walking to the car with him.

"So," Tippen said, "what do you think's going to happen to him?"

"It's too early to tell. Don't believe everything you read in the papers."

"That's a hell of a thing, coming from you."

Tinker supposed it was.

Tippen paused, standing amid his harvest of rejected and abandoned. He picked up a length of heavy, rusted iron pipe and pounded it several times into his palm. If the impact stung, and Tinker imagined it must, the man didn't show it. Tippen was staring into space, muttering. Then he suddenly wheeled, raised the pipe into the air, and with horrific force brought it smashing down upon an ancient stove, cleaving a frightening groove into its surface.

"Damn that kid!" Tippen said in a lethal whisper. He slid a pair of seething eyes into their corners and studied Tinker, who was standing stock-still, staring back, holding his breath. When Tippen spoke again it was in a voice that sounded dulled and flattened with malign influences. "I think that girl got what she deserved," he said. "Don't you?"

Tinker thought it best to agree.

On his way back, Tinker stopped at Harvey's old high school, hoping the coach might be able to contribute some warm colors to the portrait Tinker was trying to paint. School was just letting out as he parked Harry Knackers's faithful Plymouth at the curb under a leafless oak tree that had a trunk as thick as a barrel. Entering the school, he found coach Ted Cliffie in an empty gymnasium. The gym was small, with two basketball hoops on one wall, a set of parallel bars, a couple of chinning bars, a pair of bristly climbing ropes hanging from ceiling rings, and a few hard padded mats.

"I do a little of everything around here," Cliffie said. He was a trimly built man who wore his black hair in a brush cut and had a thin mustache. He walked with precise little steps, his hands in the pockets of his baggy cardigan. "You know how it is in a small town. I teach phys ed and coach the teams. Baseball and basketball. The parents don't want football."

They wandered around the gym as they talked, Cliffie booting aside an idle basketball as they went.

"Harvey was the best athlete we ever had here," the coach said. "A nice kid, though it was all from the shoulders down with him, if you know what I mean. To be honest, I wasn't surprised that he got into trouble over a woman. I've never seen anybody with the biomagnetism that he had. He was only sixteen or so, but every girl in school had a crush on him. I think even a few of our lady teachers did too. And supposedly he was having affairs with about half a dozen women in town, some of them married. I understand he's insatiable," Cliffie said, somewhat ruefully, Tinker thought.

"Being a star athlete didn't hurt, I guess," Tinker said.

"He played basketball brilliantly, but it was his baseball game that really caught your eye. He played with genuine fervor. In fact, a bit too much for a kid, I thought. You want them to be competitive, but Harvey was driven. Then I figured it out. It was fear."

"Fear?"

They paused at one of the ropes.

"Can you climb one of these?" Cliffie asked.

"I did in the Marines," Tinker said.

"Marines, huh?" the coach asked, sizing him up for a second. "Yes, fear. He was terrified of his father. You met Harvey senior, so you know what I mean. That man used to come to every game, every practice, exhorting the kid, sometimes threatening him. Of course nobody had the guts to tell him to shut up. There's no reasoning with him."

"The old man a frustrated athlete?"

"No, I don't think it's that. He's just got a romance with baseball and with the Brooklyn Dodgers in particular. You know how their fans are."

"I know them well," Tinker said.

"Well, that goddamned father epitomizes the furthest limits of partisanship. He's a Dodger fan *in extremis*. There's something mystical about his obsession with that team. So you can imagine what must be in his head now: he's got a son who's about to make the team, and all of a sudden the kid's accused of murder."

"He's focused everything on Harvey."

"I'll tell you one story that'll sum it up," the coach said. "It was in Harvey's junior year. We were playing a team from Torrington. It's the bottom of the ninth, we're down a couple of runs, it's two out, the bases are loaded, and Harvey's at the plate. The count goes full. Everybody is yelling, but all you can hear is Tippen senior, bellowing like ten men, sitting right behind our bench, naturally. The pitcher winds up and delivers. You know what the bastard throws? On three-and-two? A change-up. Now, most sandlot hitters thrive on those things. They wait for them. With a lousy hitter you can get murdered, but a good hitter is dug in looking for your best pitch and you can get him out by changing speeds. Right? Harvey is a good hitter and he's frozen by that pitch. The ball floats right on by him and the umpire yells strike three. End of game. The next thing we know there's this roar and his father is jumping over the bench, scattering players left and right, and heading like a mad bull for home plate. I figured he was going to tear the umpire apart. But no. He was after Harvey for striking out, and Harvey knew it. The kid took one look at him and dropped the bat and took off like a shot down the left field line, with the old man after him. It was like something out of a Charlie Chaplin movie. I heard that Harvey was afraid to go home and spent the night at a friend's house. That father's a lunatic. He's going to die of apoplexy."

Christ, Tinker thought as he prepared to drive back. *No wonder Harvey felt safer in jail.*

18

Tinker dropped the story on Scott's desk the next morning, then sat down and waited for the boss to read it. He didn't have to watch Scott's face as the editor sat back in his swivel chair and carefully read, chin in hand. Tinker knew the story was good. You always knew when it was good. He glanced at the expensive topcoat and silk scarf and tweed jacket on the coat rack. There were a few framed photos on the walls, of Scott with various *News* executives, with Ruth, with Dempsey, with Runyon, and the one Tinker knew Scott prized above all others: standing at a long-ago dinner together with Ring Lardner.

Scott put the pages down on the desk.

"Good story," he said. "I wouldn't change a word. The son carrying the father's dream right up to the edge of fulfillment, and then tragedy. Very nice."

"I had to tone the father down a bit."

"Really?"

"He's a zealot. A maniac. Everybody in town is afraid of him."

"Thinks he's John L. Sullivan, huh?"

Tinker smiled. The reference was a giveaway to a man's time and orientation. When Scott, born in the late 1890s, had grown up, the aura of the old bareknuckle champion was still compelling. A later generation invariably referred to Dempsey when seeking a metaphor for the invincible. For Tinker and his contemporaries, undoubtedly Louis would always be the man to smash all others.

"Well," Scott said, "that about wraps it up."

"I'd like to stay on it," Tinker said.

"There's nothing left to stay on. It's a police story now. The kid has signed a confession."

"He was browbeaten into that, Scotty. Everybody knows it. They painted pictures of the electric chair and frightened him into signing."

"I don't know anything about that, Joe. All I do know is there's nothing left in it for us."

"I've been talking to people, Scotty. This kid didn't do it."

"Then let the cops take care of it."

"The cops have put him into this mess."

"Then let his lawyer handle it."

"Bollinger supplied the lawyer. All Bollinger wants is to get the thing off the front pages."

"But the kid's a hell of a prospect," Scott said. "They'd do anything to save him, if they could."

"Bollinger feels that guilty or innocent, the kid's tainted."

"I'm afraid we've exhausted our mandate, Joe."

"Scotty, if I could just sort of poke around behind the scenes, informally . . ."

"You're heading for Florida in a few days."

"Send somebody else. Temporarily. Give me a couple of weeks."

"You're serious, aren't you?"

"Very."

"Well, Joe, so am I. I'm not sending anyone else. I'm sending you. You cover the Brooklyn Dodgers for this newspaper, you do it exceedingly well, and you're going to Florida."

"My heart's not gonna be in it," Tinker said morosely.

"It will. Just wait until you're down there and you pick up a paper and read about six inches of snow in New York, while you're feeling that hot sunshine on the back of your neck and listening to the crack of the bat. It's a time of return for you, Joe. Don't forget that. Just remember where you were a year ago."

Iwo Jima, Tinker thought. That's where he was. Fighting for some goddamned airstrip, with rifle and machine-gun fire from mountain fortifications spinning up the dust around him. No thanks. He would rather not remember.

"Get down there and enjoy yourself," Scott said. "You've earned it."

Several times during the morning he considered dialing Rita's extension and inviting her to lunch, but didn't. A similar impulse to meet for a drink after work was also rejected. He would have been on the defensive and there was no call for that. He felt he had been judged too harshly. Screwing Juliana Overman (and how much could he have enjoyed it out on that cold terrace?) had been an impromptu thing, unplanned and thereby insignificant (according to Tinker's moral calculus, anyway). If he had made a mistake, it was in trying to be too honest with Rita, a notion that only enhanced his sense of wounded innocence.

He left the *News* building at about five-thirty and headed out into the chilly evening. He walked through the commuter crowds storming the entrances of Grand Central and continued west on

Forty-Second to Times Square. With his hands in
his topcoat pockets and a cigarette set in the corner
of his mouth, Tinker advanced into the New York
night, his plans formulating slowly in his mind.
When he got to Times Square it was already glittering and blazing like an orgy of whimsical rainbows. Canopies of light burned brightly on the
marquees of the Paramount, the Capitol, Loew's
State, Criterion, Palace, Strand. No secrets here.
Everything wide open, offering gaudy welcome to
the gullible and shrewd alike, ready to swallow
and disgorge. It had certainly swallowed young
Harvey Tippen, who had understandably preferred the rainbows to a dreary country town covered with dead snow.

He flagged a taxi and directed the driver uptown
to Riverside and Seventy-Fourth. Since he had already been given the chill for seeing Juliana, he
figured there was no harm in seeing her again. If
later on he decided to bare some contrition this
would help make it more genuine. And maybe he
could learn something that would help Harvey.
But most of all he was just feeling roguish.

The doorman was not on duty and Tinker
walked right on through. He took the self-service
elevator up to the penthouse, wondering just how
he would be greeted. He had to admit that women
of this pedigree were alien to him; there was no
way he could have foreseen the events of his last
visit and he didn't know what to expect now.

The elevator opened to a small corridor. There
were two doors; one the front entrance, the other
a service door leading to the kitchen. When Tinker
got to the front door he found it slightly ajar. He
could hear the radio playing within, a big band
familiar.

Tentatively he pushed the door aside, wondering if he should have telephoned ahead. Given this woman's whims, he didn't want to walk in and find some guy's moon flying up and down on the hearthrug. He stepped into the living room; the lights were on but it was empty.

"Mrs. Overman?" he said.

The radio went silent for a moment, then another number began, which a corner of his mind registered as Glenn Miller. He moved to the center of the living room, head cocked, listening. The interior of the apartment was dark. He called her name again. Then he walked to the mantelpiece where the radio was and turned it off. The fireplace was filled with cold gray ashes. He turned around and faced the large, silent, well-lighted room, staring at each piece of furniture as if to make sure no one was sitting in it. The shelf that shut the liquor cabinet was down.

The drapes were drawn back across the terrace door, and he wondered if perhaps some chilblain sex might be taking place out there. He walked toward his own moving reflection in the glass, slid the door aside, and stepped out into the cold. The wind was humming in cadences, swirling about in the corners. The bricks were still out there; otherwise the terrace was bare. With a puzzled expression he looked around for several moments, then stepped back inside, sliding the door shut behind him. Again he confronted the living room, feeling the eerie ambiance of a place where you had expected to find someone and had not.

Both bedroom doors were open and he went to each, speaking her name into the darkness. He hadn't thought of looking in the kitchen; somehow he felt it would be the last place one would find

Juliana Overman. The kitchen was along a hall-way, an open door on the right. Deciding to be thorough, he went and had a look.

There was just enough light from the living room to show her lying there, facedown, and enough light to see that she was nude from the waist down. He didn't bother speaking her name. His hand felt along the wall for the switch and he turned it on, his eyes remaining fixed upon her. She was wearing a yellow blouse, nothing else. Her hands lay at her sides, fingers glittering with rings. Her full white buttocks were sagging slightly to the sides. Her brown slacks had been bunched up and thrown in a corner. He made a forward movement, then stopped. Best not to touch any-thing. The whole thing had changed now.

He went to the telephone and made the call, then went out into the corridor and waited by the door.

19

She was strangled," Selman said.

"You mean it wasn't—"

"No."

They were standing outside on Juliana Overman's terrace. The wind had died down. Beyond the Hudson's running currents the Jersey shore threw out both scatterings and clusters of light.

Selman peeled the cellophane from a cigar, crumbled the crackly paper in his fist, and threw it out into the night. Then he lit the cigar. Behind them the apartment was full of the usual activity —a free-form choreography of policemen, photographers, forensic people. By leaning over the ledge and peering straight down, Tinker could see the roof of the ambulance that was parked at the curb waiting to carry Juliana's body downtown.

"You seem disappointed," Selman said. "You were hoping for another broken neck, weren't you? That would have helped Harvey, wouldn't it?"

"Of course," Tinker said.

"What were you doing here?"

"I was here the other night, running an interview. We'd gotten on and I thought I'd just drop in." Tinker shrugged. "I'm on the outs with my girlfriend at the moment."

"This is a bit off your reservation, isn't it?"

"Roger, are you telling me I lack style?" Tinker said, glancing across his shoulder at Selman.

The terrace door was pushed aside by a uniformed officer.

"Lieutenant," he said. "We found the doorman. He says somebody called him about the smell of smoke in the basement and when he went down to investigate he got clobbered. Rapped him real hard on the back of the neck, then tied up his hands and feet. One of our guys found him. He's just come to."

"How long ago was he hit?"

"He says about an hour or so."

"Which is about how long she's been dead," Selman said to Tinker. Then to the officer, "I don't suppose he got a look at the guy."

"No, sir."

"That would be too easy," Selman muttered. "He wasn't called on the building's intercom, was he?"

"No," said the officer, still standing in the doorway. "There's a phone in the concierge room. It came in on that."

"He didn't ask who it was?"

"No, sir."

"All right," Selman said. "Tell him I'll be down in a little while to talk to him." When the officer had gone Selman turned around and leaned on the edge, staring off into space, cigar angled in the corner of his mouth.

"You'd've thought the doorman would've been suspicious," Tinker said.

"These guys are trained to obey," Selman said. After some long, thoughtful moments, during which he puffed several voluminous exhalations of smoke into the cold air, he said, "It's the same guy, Joe."

Tinker waited.

"The strangulation was supposed to make us think otherwise," Selman said. "Then he pulled her clothes off to make it look like a sex crime."

"In the kitchen?"

"An empty ice bucket was on the table. She'd probably gone in there to fill it up. He followed her in and killed her."

"So it was somebody she knew."

"Had to be."

"What does that do for Harvey?"

"For the moment, nothing. All I've got is a hunch."

"Then you're going to stay on it," Tinker said.

"I'll do what I can."

"How do you figure it ties in with Gloria?"

"Well, if we knew that . . ."

"They were friends," Tinker said. "Same crowd, same lifestyles . . ."

"Look, Joe, what I'm thinking is unofficial. I could be wrong. So I don't want you to say anything to anybody."

"What kind of statement are you going to make? I mean to the papers."

"They'll ask if there's a connection between the murders and I'll say we can't find any."

"They're going to speculate."

"Let them speculate. The whole thing is different. Different way of killing, a sexual assault . . ."

"You could say the place was ransacked."

Selman smiled and put his arm around Tinker's shoulders.

"No, Joe," he said indulgently. "Wouldn't the guy who did it know that wasn't true? And he's the one we're trying to fool, isn't he?"

"So I'm not a detective," Tinker said.

They went back inside. There were seven or eight men in the apartment now, passing through the living room to the bedrooms to the kitchen, where Juliana still lay with her face on the floor and her can exposed.

Selman stood in the middle of the living room, arms folded, gazing at the front door, rocking gently back and forth on his heels. The large, sausage-thick cigar didn't look right in his youthful face.

"He kayos the doorman," he said to Tinker, "then takes the elevator up here. He knocks on the door and she lets him in. Surprised to see him, probably. If he had phoned to let her know he was coming over, there was the chance she might inform the doorman that Mr. So-and-so was expected and to let him on up. So he comes in, asks for a drink. She goes to mix it, sees she's out of ice, and goes into the kitchen to get some. He follows her in and strangles her right there. She was dead when she hit the floor, the way her arms are lying. Then he rips off her pants to make it look like something else, to mislead your neighborhood copper. Then he takes the elevator back down and walks out. We're going to have to question everyone in the building, see if they saw anything."

"Why'd he leave the door open?" Tinker asked.

"I don't know, Joe," Selman said. "Maybe to make sure she was found. And you probably didn't miss him by much."

"I always wanted to die in a penthouse," Tinker said. "Someplace with a roof under my feet."

20

It certainly was not the way Juliana would have liked to make the front pages. For some papers she was the "Second Society Gal Murder Victim," while for others the killing was a "Macabre Coincidence." It had to be a coincidence because the police already had a signed confession from Harvey. Detective Roger Selman, the investigating officer, was quoted as saying there was no apparent connection between the murders of Gloria Manley and her maid and Juliana Overman. The only one to squirt any doubt was Tony Marino, whose story in the *News* carried a quote from an unnamed source in the D.A.'s office "wondering aloud about the validity of Harvey Tippen's confession." Tony left the potentially explosive quote stand without comment. As he read the story over his morning coffee in a restaurant downstairs from the *News* offices, Tinker allowed some grudging respect for his colleague.

Tinker went upstairs, stopping off at the city room. He found Tony at the water cooler.

"What about that quote about the validity of the confession?" Tinker asked.

The water cooler belched as Tony filled a paper cup.

"What about it?" he asked, draining the cup

empty, then crushing it and dropping it into the wastebasket.

"Is it true or did you make it up?"

"Joseph," Tony said with a pained expression.

"Does the source believe the confession was coerced?"

"That was the implication."

"What's he going to do about it?"

"Joe, this guy is as junior as you can get in that office."

"Then he's not going to do anything."

"He *can't* do anything. He says they're satisfied that the statement was obtained without coercion."

"Are you?"

"I have mixed feelings. And what the hell were *you* doing up there?"

"Looking for information."

"And getting your name in the wrong end of the paper."

When he got to his desk Tinker found a white envelope with his name typed on the front. Inside were a pair of tickets to Florida and back. The date of departure was three days away. When he looked up he saw Jimmy Edgers jerking his thumb toward Scott's office.

"Wants you," Jimmy said. "Wear your most contrite face and walk soft."

When he walked into his boss's office Tinker was greeted with a deep, despairing sigh.

"All right," Scott said from behind the desk. "What the hell were you doing there?"

"I'd interviewed her a few days ago. I went back to get a few more questions answered."

"Contrary to my instructions."

"That woman knew a hell of a lot."

"All of which I'm sure she'd already confided to the police. Joe, you deliberately went against what I'd told you, in addition to the fact that you might have got yourself killed."

"I like the order in which you put that."

Speaking from behind a jabbing finger, Scott said, "If you weren't heading south in a couple of days I might be of a mind to suspend you. For your own good. For *my* own good. Now, I've got a nice safe story for you. I want you to call a bunch of Dodger players and talk to them about how they're getting ready to depart for spring training. Human interest stuff. Kissing the kiddies goodbye, that sort of thing."

Tinker pondered it for a moment.

"I'll have to do it from home," he said.

"Why?"

"I've got all their private numbers in my book there."

"Get them from information."

"Scotty, most of these guys are unlisted."

"I never know when you're bullshitting me. All right. I'd rather not know. Go home and do the story. I want it back here by closing time."

"It's a good idea for a story, Scotty."

"Get out of here," Scott said, and Tinker left as he had come in, hearing a deep, despairing sigh.

Norah Gregg was neither as rich as her late cousin nor as attractive, though not as rich didn't mean poverty. She lived in a small apartment on Park Avenue in the Sixties, which was a nice neighborhood to visit and an even nicer one to be from. Her gray-facade four-story building, which Tinker guessed had once been some mogul's townhouse, was like a fallen hyphen, hemmed in on either side by a pair of towering fortress-of-wealth residential buildings that were guarded by be-capped and white-gloved doormen.

When he was buzzed in from the sidewalk, Tinker pushed aside the heavy barred door, was buzzed through a second door, and then mounted a thickly carpeted staircase that rose up into what he told himself was affluent silence, the kind of silence you don't break by whistling. Norah Gregg's apartment was on the second floor.

"We lived near each other but didn't get to-gether that often," Norah said, "but we still felt our kinship very deeply. It was a small family; we were each only children. My mother was Mr. Man-ley's sister. My parents are dead. Even though I was the older one, Gloria was always like a big sister to me. I loved her very much. I'm going to miss her."

Norah spoke in a voice soft with regrets. She was nothing at all like her late, glamorous cousin. In her small oval face, made owlish by her dark-rimmed glasses, and her short, stubby body, Tinker could see the dowdy matron of the future. She sat rather earnestly on the edge of a black crushed velvet sofa as if at a job interview, her knees pressed together, her hands clasped in her lap.

"The papers have written some terribly mis-leading things about her," she said. "But Gloria wasn't like that at all. She was kindly and gen-erous. But she had a vibrant nature and liked to enjoy herself. Why shouldn't she? People liked her. She was very beautiful. At the cemetery I couldn't believe that she was being put into that hole in the ground and that I was standing there.

She was always the one who had all the fun, you see, all the admirers."

Did he, Tinker wondered, detect an ever-so-muffled note of grim satisfaction there?

"I intend to write a sympathetic story about her," Tinker said.

"She was only twenty years old. It doesn't seem fair. Why would that man want to kill her?"

"Do you think he did?"

"According to the papers he's admitted it."

"She gave him a bad time that night, didn't she?"

"She could be like that at times, but that wasn't reason enough to take her life."

"No, it wasn't," Tinker said.

"And now poor Juliana. I can't believe these things are really happening."

The living room where they were sitting was small and elegantly furnished. There was one bedroom, the door half open. The kitchen wasn't large either. Altogether, the place was about the same size as Tinker's, the difference being the address and the rent, and the fact that this place didn't feel lived in; it was as antiseptic as a hotel room. A good hotel, of course.

"Did Gloria have any enemies that you knew of?" Tinker asked.

"No," Norah said gravely, shaking her head. "But she led such a fast life, met so many different people. You could go to one of her parties and meet a hundred people, and then at the next party meet a hundred different people."

Great, Tinker thought. *The list of suspects is the Manhattan directory.*

"Not that I went that often," Norah said. "Gloria knew that I didn't like large parties. Sometimes I think she didn't know half the people herself. They just kept coming and going, all night long."

"What happened that night when the party at El Morocco broke up?"

"Nothing. We all went home. Gloria said she wanted to go downtown for a sandwich. The rest of us went home, except for Juliana and that man."

"Harvey Tippen."

"Yes."

"There was Frank Serrano, Brandon Pfund, Bobby Pilleter, Vernon Slate, and yourself, right?"

"Yes. We all said good night on the sidewalk and parted. Mr. Slate took me home."

"He did?"

"We walked to the corner and hailed a cab. It was very late and he wanted to make sure I got home all right."

"And the others?"

"I don't know what they did. Went home, I suppose."

"And Mr. Slate saw you to the front door?"

At that point a tall, slickly handsome man emerged from the bedroom. He had a thin, straight mustache and a full head of black hair so shiny Tinker wanted to ask him what he'd done with the sardines. He was wearing a three-piece navy blue suit. Tinker clocked him in at around forty-five years old. At first glance he seemed smooth as alabaster; at second glance you saw that he bit his nails.

"Why so many questions about that night, Mr. Tinker?" he asked in a voice crossed by suspicion and curiosity. He advanced halfway across the small living room and stopped. "I understood you were here to do a story about Gloria."

Norah had turned at the man's entrance and

smiled for the first time, a childlike admiration in her face.

"Mr. Tinker," she said, "this is Vernon Slate. He's our family's lawyer."

Tinker rose and shook hands, at the same time receiving a most piercing appraisal and a lip twitch somewhere between a smile and a smirk. Tinker wondered if Norah was aware of the instant, cordial dislike between the two men. Tinker, with his open, friendly personality, seldom disliked anybody, and never this quickly. The fact that his feeling was patently reciprocated made him feel better about it, as though he had achieved some emotional checkmate.

"I didn't think the interview called for the presence of a lawyer," Tinker said amiably, resuming his seat as Slate sat down next to Norah, who was visibly more relaxed now. The lawyer leaned back comfortably, crossing his legs. The guy, Tinker thought, seemed a bit at home here.

"I'm not just Miss Gregg's attorney; I'm also her friend."

Norah smiled shyly at Tinker, as though some sweet secret had slipped out.

"What does everyone's movements have to do with a sympathetic story about Miss Manley?" Slate asked.

Tinker sat back in his cushiony armchair and pretended to be as much at ease as the lawyer.

"Just trying to see the whole picture," he said.

"You sound investigative."

Tinker laughed. "I don't mean to be," he said. "After all, that aspect of the case is wrapped up."

"Yes, it is. Frankly, when Norah called and told me you had telephoned for an interview I told her not to see you."

"A lawyerly reflex?" Tinker asked, smiling.

Slate reached over and took one of Norah's hands in his and held it as he spoke.

"Miss Gregg has been through a nightmarish experience," he said. "She's trying to put it in the past. And she's been doing very well."

"Thanks to Vernon," Norah said.

"Norah is a very kind person," Slate said, "but this sort of discussion only undermines her recovery."

"I'm trying to be eulogistic about her cousin," Tinker said.

Norah gave him an odd, triumphant smile. From the moment Slate had taken her hand in his the change in her had been apparent. She no longer seemed timid; it was as if there had been a transfusion of confidence.

"We appreciate that," Slate said.

"How long have you been the family lawyer, Mr. Slate?"

"My father handled the family's affairs for years, and now I do. What has that to do with anything?"

Now Tinker showed an abashed smile.

"You know how newspapermen are, Mr. Slate," he said. "The whole picture. We interview everybody in sight. We ask a thousand questions, then print a half dozen answers. Our editors insist on thoroughness."

"Well, I think you've had your thousand questions," Slate said.

"Not quite," Tinker said, patting his knees for a moment, then getting to his feet. "But I wouldn't want to upset Miss Gregg any more than is necessary."

Norah Gregg's eyes had risen with Tinker. Staring up at him, she said softly, "You haven't upset me, Mr. Tinker."

Slate escorted the visitor downstairs to the street door. Tinker didn't think the man was being polite, just making sure that he left.

"I'd rather not have her badgered any further," Slate said as they walked down a staircase so thickly carpeted it silenced every footstep.

"You seemed more upset than she," Tinker said.

"That's her breeding. Don't let it fool you."

"It didn't fool me. I got the idea she has some very ambivalent feelings about her cousin's death."

"I beg your pardon," Slate said coldly.

"Human nature, Mr. Slate. The great corrective that prevents too much grief. If not for human nature, grief could break us. Gloria was everything that Miss Gregg is not and never can be: beautiful, stylish, sensual, immensely popular. Miss Gregg had to envy and resent it just a little, don't you think?"

"That's the most cynical recitation I've ever heard," Slate said. They were at the front door now.

"I think part of her is glad that Gloria's dead."

"Good-bye, Mr. Tinker," Slate said, reaching out and pulling the heavy door open.

"Who stands to inherit Gloria's money?"

"Good-bye, Mr. Tinker."

"Are you married?"

"That question has distasteful implications. Good-bye, Mr. Tinker."

"Good-bye, Vernon," Tinker said, stepping outside into the chilly Park Avenue sunlight.

Tinker walked east to Lexington, satisfied that he had added another suspect to his list. Motive:

greed, which was one of the best of them all. It had been sitting right in front of him: the drab little cousin, who was probably going to inherit it all now; the lawyer, who was certainly familiar with the will, and who had ingratiated himself with the drab little cousin. Money sure did strange things to people, though Tinker didn't know which was more appalling: killing for it, or marrying that unappealing little beanbag for it. But why would Slate have then gone and murdered Juliana? Selman suspected the murders had been committed by the same man. But if Selman was wrong, then there was a chance that Harvey was guilty after all, a possibility Tinker was so far steadfastly refusing to accept.

He walked into a bar on Lexington in the Fifties that was the saloon equivalent of a railroad apartment—long and narrow. He slipped into the phone booth at the rear, dropped a nickel into the slot, and dialed the paper. When the switchboard operator came on he asked her for Sports. Fred Mason answered and Tinker asked for a favor. Since he, Tinker, did not feel it necessary to return to the office, would Fred act as rewrite? Fred would. And so Tinker dictated his story on how half a dozen Brooklyn Dodgers were preparing for their departures to spring training. One guy was buying a set of brand-new luggage. Another was having his car tuned up. Another was putting in his last working day as an insurance salesman. Another was racing to finish wallpapering his kid's room. Tinker made up quotes, a joke or two. All bullshit, but nobody would ever know. The story would take up some space in tomorrow's paper and then be forgotten.

21

After telephoning his cleverly (he felt) fabricated story in to the paper, Tinker left the bar and began walking straight down Lexington to Forty-Sixth Street, where Bobby Pilleter lived. There were any number of descriptions for Gloria's thirty-five-year-old former lover: sportsman, man of the world, playboy, gigolo. A hustler by any other name. You always found characters like this wherever the wealthy or the celebrated gathered; sometimes they were on the periphery, sometimes further inside the group, but never at the heart of things, always provisional and disposable.

Pilleter had agreed to see him, though grudgingly, saying that the interview wouldn't "be the biggest thrill of the day." Tinker claimed to be gathering material for one of the paper's regular Sunday features, Justice, a series that dealt with notable American crimes. Pilleter told him to come by at five-thirty.

Pilleter lived in a sturdy five-story brick building just off Lexington. It was a sturdily respectable-looking building, but because it was so close to Third Avenue and the El it had an appearance of genteel shabbiness. Tinker stepped into the small vestibule, the front door swinging slowly shut behind him on what seemed a very tired old spring.

Tinker was a man to study the names on the bells of a building he was in for the first time. He had always done it and had yet to come across any interesting surprises. He reached out his finger now and pressed the dime-size white enamel bell under Pilleter's name.

Pilleter's apartment was on the fifth floor and Tinker was glad of the elevator; the walk downtown had tired him. When he stepped out of the elevator he found Pilleter waiting for him, standing in front of an open door at the end of the corridor, wearing a white T-shirt and dark slacks, arms folded, an expression of moody appraisal on his face, as though he might yet change his mind and shut the door before Tinker got there.

Tinker was aware of being intently studied as he walked along the corridor; in fact, he felt like he was being visually frisked. He was used to speculation about his professional visits; Pilleter's thoughts seemed to be centered on what harm his visitor might be capable of, what might lie behind seemingly innocuous questions.

Then, as he neared the tall, yellow-haired, athletically muscled Pilleter, Tinker said, "Hey, I know you."

Pilleter smiled.

Of course, when Tinker saw him at Shor's or Leon and Eddie's or walking through the Garden lobby on fight night, Pilleter was expensively dressed, often in a tuxedo, always looking like a man who was passing from one party or event to another, and of course never alone. His female companions always exuded wealth or glamour, often both, the breed running from lithe debutantes to hand-retooled matrons. Pilleter's suave manners and engaging charm never faltered, whether he was too old for the lady on his arm or too young. Like a good actor, he always looked like he belonged wherever he was, adapting to life's every changing minute, a gift of adaptability that Tinker imagined had to derive from a total absence of scruple or sincerity. But Tinker allowed a grudging appreciation as he shook hands, for the guy had acquired his style by observation and practice—the hard way.

Pilleter's living room was large and uncluttered, but what was there was tasteful: a sofa, a couple of armchairs, a low glass-topped coffee table with a cut-glass decanter in the middle. A pair of goose-necked lamps hung on opposite walls, capable of swiveling light in any direction. A baby grand stood near the window, on it the only bit of show Tinker saw in the room—a framed picture of Gershwin, and although he didn't get close enough to read it, he could see a scrawled inscription.

"I thought the name was vaguely familiar," Pilleter said when they were sitting opposite each other in the armchairs, drinks in hand. Christ, Tinker thought, but the guy had an extraordinarily common handsomeness; he could have been anything—a cowboy or a bandleader or a fighter pilot or a floorwalker at Macy's. "I'll bet we've met a half dozen times," Pilleter said, "or at least rubbed shoulders. I guess we're on the same circuit."

"Not quite," Tinker said. He was still wearing his topcoat; Pilleter hadn't asked him to remove it.

"Oh, come on, newsie, don't begrudge me my fun. We're both up from pumpernickel sandwiches, trying to make a go of it."

"When was the last time you ate pumpernickel?"

"A long time ago and never again. Where are you from, Joe?"

"Right here."

"I should have guessed. You have a New York face."

"And you?"

"You might better ask where I'm not from," Pilleter said, flashing one of those toothpaste-endorsement smiles that certain of his women friends paid to have brighten their evenings. "I've been on the go since I was fifteen. I've been in Honolulu, Hong Kong, Bombay, Baghdad, Cairo . . ."

"Paris, London, Rome . . ." Tinker said, continuing the litany.

"Not to mention Havana and Rio."

"Where'd you start from?"

"St. Louis. But don't ask me anything about it."

"What'd you do during the war?"

"Would you believe that this handsome brute of a man was 4F? Heart murmur," Pilleter said, tapping his chest for a moment.

Tinker had been expecting some tale of blazing heroics, which he had been prepared not to believe. He was slightly disappointed.

"So I fought the war from New York," Pilleter said.

"Don't feel sorry."

"But in a way I am. You know, newsie, I'm a son of a bitch in a lot of ways, but I am patriotic as hell. So I tried to do my bit. I persuaded quite a few wealthy ladies to throw lavish parties on behalf of the war effort. I'll bet we sold a few hundred thousand dollars' worth of war bonds. I may not have been in the front lines, but I contributed a hell of a lot more than some draftee who spent those years behind a desk in Fort Riley, Kansas. Listen, you're a sportswriter, aren't you? So how come you're doing this story?"

"The paper is expanding my beat," Tinker said. "Eventually I'll be going into general reporting."

"Do you want to do that? I can remember somebody one night at Dempsey's pointing you out and saying, 'See that guy there? That's Joe Tinker. Best sportswriter in New York.' I was impressed."

"I guess they put me on this one because of the Harvey Tippen angle."

Tinker glanced out the window. He could see snow falling in the dusk, not a lot, just a scattering. Against the concrete and glass across the street it looked confused.

"He's a hell of a ballplayer," Tinker said absently, as if giving voice to an idle thought.

"I'm afraid he's played his last game," Pilleter said.

Tinker had been around many athletes, including prizefighters, who were the best-conditioned men he had ever seen. But he had never seen a man in better physical shape than this guy. Pilleter's T-shirt was stretched taut across his chest, and when he sat down there was not a bit of roll-up at his beltline. Tinker wondered whether the guy worked out or if this was what screwing women of every age did for you.

"If you ask me," Pilleter said, "that kid's being railroaded."

"You think so?"

"The cops probably beat the shit out of him or scared him into signing that statement. Christ, in my time I've been picked up for a few things and

I can tell you it's scary as hell when you're in there alone with them. I can imagine what it's like when they're talking about murder. That must really freeze your juices."

"What were you picked up for?"

Pilleter screwed up the corner of one eye, as if measuring Tinker.

"It's not for publication."

"Okay," Tinker said.

"I mean, I never robbed any banks. But you know how it is when you're on the road, when you're a kid. Vagrancy. Petty theft. Brawling. Doing things you have to do in order to survive. I've been in American jails, Italian jails, French jails, and God knows where else."

"How recently?"

Pilleter laughed. "You're a canny bastard. The last time the name of Bobby Pilleter appeared on a rap sheet was when I was twenty. So, who've you spoken to?"

"Everybody who was at El Morocco that night."

"You just about squeezed in Juliana then."

"Yes."

"Try and figure that one out. I don't care what the cops say, it was the same guy."

"For what reason?"

"Why do you kill somebody, Joe? For gain, for revenge, for security. Was there a robbery done at Juliana's place? According to the papers you were there. Was there?"

"I don't know."

"All right, so you've been told to keep your mouth shut. If it wasn't robbery, then maybe revenge. Sounds unlikely, but you never know. Or maybe it was for somebody's personal security:

Juliana knew something they didn't want her to tell."

"Like who killed Gloria."

"That would do it," Pilleter said flippantly.

"How well did you know her?"

"Juliana? Not very. She was Gloria's friend. She was an attractive woman, but a bit feathery upstairs. You know how some of these wealthy babes are. Sometimes I think money paralyzes the intellect."

"Funny thing for you to say."

"Why? Because I exploit them? I do what I do, buddy. I don't twist anybody's arm, and when they keep calling and wanting to see me again, then I *know* I'm doing the right thing."

"It's your business."

"And I'm good at it. And when the time is ripe I'll marry one of them and retire. Tell me what I'm doing wrong. You've seen me out with these women. Don't they always look happy? What am I doing wrong?"

"It *seems* wrong," Tinker said, "but I don't know if it is."

"If you come down to it, your candy store bookmaker is a more objectionable character than I am. *He's* breaking the law, I'm not."

"Did Gloria give you money?"

"She was a very generous kid. Yes, she did. We were together for a few weeks last summer. Spent some time in Saratoga, celebrating the end of the war. Then we came back to the city. The whole thing didn't last very long, but it was nice while it did."

"Surely she didn't have to pay for companionship."

"No, she didn't. We were together because we

wanted to be. I took money from her because frankly I couldn't afford the places she wanted to go to."

"What happened?"

"Exactly what we expected. We had some good times, then went our separate ways, and remained good friends. She was a mature kid for her age. Very sophisticated. You know her father's a fairy, don't you? Well, it never bothered her in the least. She said he was old enough to make his choices and that was that. Compare that to her cousin. I take it you've met Norah Gregg."

"This afternoon," Tinker said.

"Quite a difference, huh?"

"Slate was there. The lawyer."

"From what I understand he's always there. Gloria told me they were planning to get married. She said that Slate had officiated at Norah's grand opening."

"Grand opening?"

"Norah was a virgin until recently. I suppose it's understandable, looking at her. But she's rich. And you think *I* do things for money?"

"How rich is she?"

"She's got it all now, buddy. Under the terms of their grandfather's will—Grandpa made the family fortune, you know—it's all going to end up with Norah. The old boy apparently didn't trust his own kids, so he left the bulk of it to Gloria, who was his favorite, and the rest to Norah. This is what Gloria told me. She was going to inherit on her twenty-first birthday."

"Which unfortunately she never reached."

"So the shekels all go to Norah," Pilleter said with a wink of the eye.

"Vernon Slate obviously knows this."

"Family lawyer. He's got to know it. Want another drink?"

"No thanks," Tinker said. It was dark outside now, the lights in the building across the street looking much sharper. The snow seemed to have lost interest and stopped.

"So Slate is marrying a fortune," Tinker said.

"He's welcome to it," Pilleter said. "If he wants to sleep with that little sack of lemons, then he's welcome to all of it. Do I look less reprehensible now, newsie?"

"I never said you were reprehensible," Tinker said.

"You got enough?"

"A few more questions. Why? You pressed for time?"

"Soon. I'm taking a distinguished middle-aged woman with a ski-jump bosom to dinner."

"You know, there are a lot of crass questions I could ask. I mean off the record."

"But you're too much the gentleman. Come on, wrap it up."

"What happened at El Morocco that night?"

"Nothing. It all happened later."

"I understand Gloria created an ugly scene."

"It wasn't so ugly," Pilleter said, "as far as those things go."

"What provoked it?"

"His existence provoked it. Harvey Tippen's. She wanted to be rid of him. She'd been giving him hints but that simpleton didn't know it. I didn't like what she was doing and told her so."

"Then what?"

"The party soon broke up. It was late. Time to go home."

"You all left together?"

"That's right. Then Gloria got the bright idea that she wanted a corned beef sandwich. On the Lower East Side, no less."

"Did she ask anybody to join her?"

"Well, I guess she did, in a general way. Sort of, 'I'm game for a corned beef sandwich. Who wants to come?' Words to that effect. The only ones to take her up on it were Juliana and that nitwit. So off they went and that was that."

"Where did you go?"

"Home. Here. Where else do you go at that hour?"

"Somebody didn't go straight home," Tinker said.

"Don't tell me you think one of them did it? Come on, Joe, I know you're looking for a story, but be realistic."

"There are motives."

"I know what you're talking about," Pilleter said. "Gloria told me all about it, how she set those two bozos up."

"Which bozos?"

"Frank Serrano and Brandon—forgive me, Brandy—Pfund."

"Set them up?"

"She never had any intention of backing Pfund's play. She made a bet with me that she could get Serrano to bend over for Pfund. She was annoyed by this great masculine, great lover image he tried to present. She and Juliana plotted the whole thing. She told Pfund she'd put up the money for the play and that Serrano would do anything to be in it. Then she told Serrano that Pfund wanted to hire him but that Frank would have to compromise his manhood to get the job. Pfund believed he had to cast Serrano or it was no go. But it was all a gag. Or as Gloria put it, a 'goof.' "

"Then she never had any intention of backing the play."

"Of course not. It was all a gag. The joke of the week."

"Did those guys find out about it?"

"I'm sure they did. Gloria and Juliana were a couple of babbling brooks. And anyway, what was the fun of pulling a gag like that if you couldn't tell anyone?"

"So they each had a motive," Tinker said.

"Motive your ass," Pilleter said. "Why should Pfund be upset? Sure, he was disappointed, probably indignant, but what did he lose by it? And if Serrano was mad at anybody it should have been Pfund. Don't go talking like that about a fairy director and a self-important bit actor. Slate was better motivated, if it comes to that."

"What about you?" Tinker asked with a wry smile.

"Sure," Pilleter said. "Why not me? Dig deeply enough into anyone and you'll find a motive for anything. Hell, I've been accused of everything else in my time. All right, add a murder."

"Two," Tinker said, holding up two fingers.

"Yes. Alas, poor Gloria. Isn't that how Shakespeare has it? Anyway, newsie, you're overlooking one tiny possibility: maybe the cops have in their bumbling way got the right guy. The way I read it, there's a good possibility of that. A guy dismisses a cab and walks home forty blocks at that hour of the night. A guy who suddenly can't produce the clothes he was wearing? I know you're sympathetic toward him—and so am I—but if you're going to write this story you have to be objective."

"Well, if Harvey did it then there are two murderers."

"Juliana, huh? Well, this is getting to be too much for my ill-educated brain. I'll leave it to you. Anyway, you've got to scram now. I've got to shower and shave and turn suave."

"For tonight's performance, eh?" Tinker said, getting to his feet.

"Laugh all you want, buddy boy, but when you're downtown eating your hot dogs and beans later I'll be feasting in one of Manhattan's finest restaurants."

"With somebody else picking up the tab?"

"What other way is there?" Pilleter said, spreading his arms and feigning great innocence. He got to his feet and reached out to Tinker. "I hope I was of some help," he said as they shook hands. "If I can be of further service, call. Maybe we ought to get drunk together some time."

"You make that sound like a compliment," Tinker said.

"It is," Pilleter said, walking him to the door. "I'm very choosy who I get drunk with."

22

Harry Knackers's arthritic 1937 Plymouth did not have heat, nor did it have a radio, and the absence of these amenities made Tinker's drive up to the Catskills even bleaker. He drove along the river to Newburgh, then headed west into Sullivan County, finding himself alone on a winding road for long, lonesome stretches. Small, winter-grim towns came and went, with little in between but empty road hemmed in by leafless hardwood trees. A sign informed him he was passing through the Shawangunk Mountains, an uprising of earth and rock that didn't impress him. Nor did the Catskills impress him very much, as mountains went. They lacked the singular look and character of the Greens, Whites, or Adirondacks, not to mention those real worthy-of-the-name mountains out west, which he had seen from a troop train during the war.

The Catskills looked better in summer, of course, when he had been up here before the war to cover fighters who had set up training camps at one or another of the hotels. But now the mountains looked shabby under large patches of snow, their trees gray and stark. He passed frozen lakes with boarded-up bungalows standing around the edges, their tiny piers fixed in ice.

Large roadside billboards advertising the resort hotels began appearing. Recreation. Swimming Pool. Kosher Cuisine. Radio in Every Room. Whole Family. The peeling, weather-scruffed depictions of summer warmth and frolic looked somehow lunatic in the winter setting. The hotels were all silent and empty now, pools drained and filled with dead leaves, tennis courts covered with snow, canoes stacked in padlocked boathouses. Tinker's Jewish friends vacationed here, the Italians went to the Poconos, the Irish down to the Jersey Shore. That was the way it seemed.

The day had started out sunny but grown increasingly gray, as if the sun only lit the Catskills during "the season." He passed through Monroe and Middletown and Wurstboro and Monticello and on up toward Liberty, where he would turn off for Neversink. It was in that area that he had been told he would find Brandon Pfund.

The Broadway producer had no Broadway play to produce, and so he had accepted the job as director of a summer playhouse, where he would stage six different shows in July and August. For a guy who had been expecting to ride Gloria's money to a Broadway opening, this had to be a most deflating comedown.

Tinker had been told that Pfund had driven up here yesterday to check out the theater, to see what repairs and maintenance might be needed, and to ascertain the limits of the facilities before determining what touring companies to book.

Nothing clammed up tighter than a resort town in the off-season, and when Tinker pulled into Liberty there was hardly a soul to be seen or a car parked anywhere. When he turned off the Plymouth's ignition the engine stopped with a flat finality that made him wonder if it would ever start up again.

He stepped out into the pure mountain cold, smelling the pleasing aroma of a nearby wood fire, and walked across some hard-packed snow to a large bar that advertised itself as an inn. This was where, he had been told, Pfund was staying. Quite a dropoff from El Morocco, Tinker thought as he looked at the front door and then up at the two stories of windows above, the latter having the woeful look of some tenements he knew around Ninth Avenue in the Forties, except that these were wood frame and seemed nearer collapse.

A few locals in heavy jackets and plaid caps with dangling earflaps were inside wiling away the time, which at this time of year they probably reckoned not in days but months. From them he learned that "Mister Puh-Fund" was working up at the barn.

"The barn?" Tinker asked.

"Where they give the shows," he was told.

Tinker received directions, downed the straight bourbon he had been thinking about for the last half hour, and left. Harry Knackers's Plymouth muttered churlishly about it, but started up again.

About a mile out of town he saw the sign at the side of the road. Nailed to an upright post, it was about twice the length and width of an ordinary bookshelf, with serrated edges to give it, Tinker imagined, a native look. In letters that looked like they had been scorched into the wood, it read MOHAWK PLAYHOUSE, and underneath was a directional arrow.

Tinker turned off onto a wide, unpaved road that ran alternately smooth and bumpy. Parts of it were snow-covered and he could see tire tracks in it. On either side was the landscape he had become drearily accustomed to, nasty-looking gray bramble and frozen dumbstruck trees, some of them shattered into hoary lifelessness by long-ago bolts of lightning, and behind it all the misty shoulders of the Catskills. Live up here long enough and you could get to believe the earth was shaped like a soup bowl.

The road ballooned out and became the parking lot for the Mohawk Playhouse, a lot that looked like it could accommodate a few hundred cars. There was only one here now, a black Packard parked near a small refreshment stand adjacent to the theater. The stand, which no doubt sold plenty of orange juice under the stars during intermissions, was boarded up now.

Getting out of his car and looking at the Mohawk Playhouse, Tinker could see why the locals referred to it as "the barn," for that was probably what it had been in its original incarnation. It was a large, bulky building with a peaked roof. Though its original conformations had apparently undergone some restructuring, it still retained a good deal of its rustic origins, which Tinker supposed was part of a summer theater's appeal. An elevated boardwalk, the kind you saw in movies set in Old West towns, ran the length of the theater's front.

Tinker stepped up onto the boardwalk, opened the front door, and entered the lobby. There were a pair of ticket windows on one side, a large wooden bench against the wall in the center, and restroom doors on the other side, differentiated by signs that said "Pa" and "Ma." Another doorway led straight to the theater's center aisle. A fluted wooden door, closed during performances, was shoved to one side now.

He entered a theater that was dark except for the stage, which was lit from above and empty. He went slowly down the aisle, which had a very slight gradient, unlike some New York theaters that seemed to dip like ski slopes. Rows of empty seats stretched out on either side. There was no balcony, though there would have been room for one. The gutting of the place had left behind a high ceiling supported by a complex network of crisscrossing beams.

Tinker was almost to the foot of the stage when Brandon Pfund walked out from the wings. He was wearing a bright red turtleneck and dark corduroy slacks. He was holding several sheets of paper, which he studied for a moment, and then directed his gaze straight up. When he looked down again he saw Tinker.

"Hello?" Pfund asked, removing a pair of horn-rimmed glasses. "Can I help you?"

"Mr. Pfund," Tinker said.

"Say, I know you. You're the fellow that works for Winchell. What the hell are you doing here?"

"Just a few follow-up questions," Tinker said, trying to remember what name he had given Pfund at El Morocco.

"You came all the way up here for that?"

"You know how Walter is. Compulsive. You see, I'm heading down to Florida in a day or so . . ."

"Lucky you."

"Right. So I figured I'd get this wrapped up. I wasn't sure how long you'd be up here."

"I'm going back tomorrow morning, thank God. This place is bad enough in the summer, when it's at its best; now, it's not fit for convicts. I just came up for a few days to check out the theater. I'm going to be producing plays here this summer." Pfund said this latter in a neutral voice, giving a piece of information he was too honest to be proud of and too professional to disparage.

"Quite a knockdown from Broadway."

"Broadway will still be there. And anyway, it's the same crowd. Who do you think the Broadway audience is? It's the same people who come up here for the summer."

"Except here they come to the theater in their underwear."

"What do you want, anyway?" Pfund asked, a note of irritability in his voice now. "Flicker, that was your name, wasn't it?"

Right, Tinker thought. That was it. He climbed up onto the stage. The boards were hollow under his feet.

"It's a whole different world up here, isn't it?" he said.

"That's the point of it," Pfund said curtly.

"And you can feel it," Tinker said, gazing out at the legions of empty seats that swept back into darkness. "A command post."

"I have work to do. Tell me what you want."

Pfund replaced his glasses. A turtleneck was wrong for him; his double chin rolled up on the high collar.

"You knew weeks ago that Miss Manley wasn't going to back your play," Tinker said.

"You came all the way up here to ask me that?"

"I came all the way up here to tell you that. When we spoke in El Morocco you implied she had still been considering putting up the money."

"So?"

"So you'd found out several weeks before that it was all a lark with her, some grand practical joke."

"Who told you that?" Pfund's eyes became stern behind their dark-rimmed lenses.

"You must have been pretty ticked off."

"I wasn't happy about it. I'd been made a fool of."

"And the two women who plotted the stupid joke are dead."

"That's right. And I'm not in mourning for either one of them, if you must know. God knows who else's life they played games with. Gloria was a spoiled, callous little bitch."

"Who got what she deserved."

"If this was an audition, Mr. Flicker, I'd have to tell you that melodrama is not your forte. But since you work for a man who is known for his influence and his ruthlessness, I suppose I have to put up with your questions."

"So you knew weeks ago that her interest in your play was a sham."

"So I knew," Pfund said impatiently. "But I still hadn't given up hope. A nitwit like Gloria could have changed her mind back again. A producer sometimes has to take a lot of crap."

"Same as an actor."

"What does that mean?" Pfund asked warily.

"Frank Serrano."

"What has that got to do with it? Look, you're overstepping your bounds here."

"When did he find out it was all a joke?"

"I don't know."

"Probably after you did," Tinker said.

Pfund stared thoughtfully at him.

"What do you want to know?" Pfund asked.

"You took advantage of the guy."

"Did I? How little you know about the theater."

"Did it really have that much to do with the theater?" Tinker asked.

"Oh yes, quite," Pfund said with what Tinker interpreted as a superior little smile. "What do you think happens when one actor or actress is the same as the next, when so many of them can handle the same role? Do you know how many of them are out there? How do you choose one over the other?"

"So you were doing Serrano a favor?" Tinker said.

Pfund gave him a sour, weary smile.

"You're looking into a world you obviously know nothing about, Flicker," he said. "People you can't begin to understand. Hopes and dreams and aspirations that have so little to do with reality it's pathetic. All they want is to be allowed to step out onto a stage. How they get there is irrelevant."

"Do you think Frank Serrano believes that?"

"Frank Serrano *knows* that. Nobody held a gun to his head. What's so shocking, Flicker? You've heard of young actresses screwing producers and directors, haven't you? And sometimes not even for jobs but just for opportunities. And you probably never thought twice about it, because you thought it was perfectly *normal*, didn't you?" Pfund said, emphasizing the word with some disdain. "Probably made you wish you were head of production somewhere yourself. Well, once you accept that you have to accept all the rest of it. If you're going to look into the den of iniquity, don't do it from the doorway and don't do it selectively; go inside and see it all. Have a good look."

"You just wanted to make sure you got your share, huh?"

"I was living my life. My personal life. What are you after—an explanation or a *mea culpa*? Well, you won't get either. One I can't give and the other I won't."

"Some people would say you took advantage."

"And gave advantage. Or intended to. Don't forget that."

"A business deal," Tinker said dryly.

"If you like."

"Even after you knew there was going to be no backing, no play?"

Pfund's wry smile made Tinker feel dismally naive.

"I just don't understand you people," he said. He meant Gloria and Juliana and Bobby Pilleter and Vernon Slate as well as Pfund, who evidently thought the remark was meant for him alone.

"Then don't try," Pfund said.

Tinker thought about clarifying his remark, but instead asked Pfund if somewhere in this large, drafty barn there wasn't something to drink.

He followed Pfund from the stage into the wings, then into a narrow lighted corridor that was a warren of small dressing rooms, each with its door open. A pile of props was pushed into one corner; Tinker spotted a two-wheeled bicycle, a colorfully striped beach ball, several unattached telephones, a bird cage, a folded-up ironing board, a baseball bat, a few croquet mallets, and some odds and ends of furniture.

"The place is a shithouse," Pfund said when they walked into his brightly lit office. The furniture looked like it might have been culled from the Tippen front yard, the several venerable easy chairs appearing cold and uninviting, the sofa a Victorian monstrosity of purple crushed velvet, the rolltop desk exuding a Dickensian air.

Pfund handed Tinker a bottle of Canadian Club and the visitor sat down on one of the abysmally uncomfortable chairs, trying to arrange himself around the broken springs.

"There are no glasses," Pfund said. "I wasn't expecting company."

The bottle was about half gone. Tinker unscrewed the cap. He had been taught that it was impolite to wipe the bottletop with your hand and he didn't do so now. He took a gulp and handed it back to Pfund, who similarly drank without touching the bottle's mouth.

"Yes," Pfund said as if beginning some elaborate disquisition, "I'm one of 'them.' You can live with it easier in the theater than anywhere else. As long as you don't misstep, you're accepted. When Noel Coward and Cole Porter are queer, it's all right for you to be, within reason. That's one of the things I love about the theater—you can pretty much be yourself. There's an awful lot of compassion and understanding, and even though a lot of it is phony, some of it is genuine, more than you'll find anywhere else."

Pfund offered the bottle back but Tinker shook his head. Pfund took another swallow. A certain mellowness had replaced his previous tension.

"It was pretty rough in high school," he said. "I was 'The Pansy.' I wasn't overt about it, of course, but kids find out. Instincts are very keen at that age, which makes kids the most evil bastards in the world, when you take into account the long-term damage they can inflict. I guess I found out about myself when I was twelve or thirteen. You get a sense of yourself, of who you are. I don't think I understood all the implications. The girls liked me. There's an irony. They gravitated to me because I was courteous and a gentleman, which meant I wasn't always reaching for their brand-new little titties like the other boys."

Pfund was standing with his back to a wall that was covered with framed, autographed glossies of performers who had played the Mohawk Playhouse through the years. There were some very familiar faces. Pfund lifted the bottle of CC to his thick lips and drank again. He shut his eyes while he swallowed, then exhaled in obvious gratification. He wanted to talk and seemed to be collaborating with the whiskey in order to do it.

"The first time," he said, "was when I was about twelve. The gym teacher asked me to stay after school and help him clean up the place. How the hell he knew, I don't know. I wasn't an effeminate kid or anything like that. We went into his office and he locked the door and he told me about his wife being ill and that he wasn't allowed to have relations with her. I didn't know what the hell he was saying. I thought 'relations' were people. But then he drops his pants and his shorts and sits down on a chair and waves his knees apart and says, 'You know what to do, Brandon.' Well, I didn't know what to do. But I did it anyway."

"Did you tell anybody?" Tinker asked.

"Don't be naive. Anyway, college was a little better. You're away from all the bastards that know you. College is different. It's the beginning of the outside world. You catch the eye of somebody. You know. They know. It's the optical equivalent of the Masonic handshake. As long as you're discreet, it's okay. Like the army."

"The army?" Tinker's voice had risen with involuntary surprise.

Pfund laughed sardonically.

"They'll sniff you out there quicker than anywhere else," he said. "And I could sniff them out. You'd never guess how many brass-knuckled NCOs with medals and combat ribbons like to go the other way. And majors and colonels. Once *those* bastards find out about you, you have no choice."

"It's hard to believe," Tinker said.

"You mean hard to accept," Pfund said, an edge in his voice. "Well, that's too bad. Look, why don't you go into town and pick up some sandwiches and come back and I'll tell you some stories about sweet Miss Manley."

"And Juliana?"

"Whatever I can tell you. I have no qualms about speaking ill of the dead."

Tinker accepted Pfund's five-dollar bill to cover lunch and left. Once more, to his pleasant surprise, Harry Knackers's Plymouth turned over its engine on command and Tinker aimed it back toward town.

He found a bus-shaped diner at the far end of Main Street, one of those unadorned places where the food was basic and good enough. It had a small sliding door, sawdust on its tile floor, stools only, and a counterman who seemed annoyed by your presence. There were no other customers when Tinker walked in.

Pfund wanted a fried egg sandwich and that took some time. Tinker had a cup of coffee while he waited, drinking from one of those thick-rimmed white cups that seemed endemic to these places, watching the aproned counterman put to-

gether the ham and Swiss on rye he had asked
for.

"How's the winter been?" Tinker asked.

"Cold," the counterman said.

"You a Dodger fan?"

"Yankees."

Tinker never knew what to say to a Yankee fan.
They had all those pennants and world champi-
onships, they had Ruth, Gehrig, DiMaggio. There
was no point in talking baseball unless you could
argue, and you couldn't do that with a Yankee
fan. It would be like arguing with somebody who
had unspeakable amounts of money.

He left the diner with a paper sack containing
the sandwiches and two containers of coffee and
with a vague recollection of the counterman having muttered something that might or might not
have been "thank you." A soft rain had blown in
on an icy wind, making the dreary Main Street
stores and the weathered clapboard houses on the
side streets seem even grayer and bleaker.

He wasn't quite sure what to make of Pfund.
Tinker didn't know any homosexuals, nor did he
have any opinions about them; but evidently
they—or at least Pfund—were capable of nurtur-
ing resentments for a long time, and like some
things that were stored for too long in the dark
could turn dangerously combustible. He tried to
imagine childhood confusion and shame and
gibes, the bitter festering rage. It was bad enough
to have to live in a world that mocked or despised
your preferences and to have to hide those preferences and pretend to be something you weren't;
and then to have someone manipulate all of that
for the sake of a crude practical joke—well, Tinker

could imagine a short fuse beginning to glow with red-hot coals.

But in the army? Well, he supposed it was possible. After all, that branch had had millions of men under arms during the war. Anything was possible. Anyway, you couldn't always tell; look at Pfund, he wasn't pale or limp-wristed. But surely not in the Marines, although, uncomfortably, he remembered a certain drill instructor at Parris Island who had looked at him funny. No, Tinker thought. That's got to be my imagination. Not in the Marines. Never.

When he returned to the Mohawk Playhouse the stage lights were still on. Illuminated in an otherwise dark building, the bare stage rendered a somewhat poignant portrait. Tinker thought it might be a good idea to find a table and a couple of chairs and eat lunch right there in the middle of the stage. When he stepped up onto the boards and paused to gaze out at the sweep of empty seats he had to admit that there was indeed a certain magic to all of this. Then he walked off into the wings, calling Pfund's name.

Backstage, the lights were on in the dressing room corridor, and the doors swung back on dark rooms. It felt chillier in here than before and he soon saw why—a door at the end of a short corridor running perpendicular to this one was partially open, enough for Tinker to see a long sliver of daylight. He paused, staring inquiringly at it.

"Pfund?" he called out.

There was no answer and Tinker was suddenly aware of the silence around him, as if it had crowded upon him and smothered his voice. He looked toward the office at the end of the corridor.

"Pfund?"

Now the silence felt as though it were thickening around him, extending back down the corridor and across the stage and through the rows of empty seats and up into the dark drafty rafters of the cross-beamed ceiling, into every angle and corner of the old barn. It had a poised, watchful quality, like malice in recession.

He walked toward the office, entered it, and for the second time in a few days Tinker found someone stretched out dead in front of him. Either he was getting good at this or else it was so patently obvious, but the moment he saw Pfund, Tinker had no doubt that he was staring at a corpse.

Brandon Pfund was lying on his back in front of the rolltop desk. One side of his head seemed broken open; at least that was the appearance given by the blood, and there was a lot of it. Gleaming, the blood looked as though it was pulsating as it seeped thickly down the side of Pfund's face, onto his neck and under the collar of his turtleneck sweater. His right hand was rolled into a soft fist. His horn-rimmed glasses lay several feet away, and near them a baseball bat, the barrel streaked with several long, bloody smears.

Tinker stepped closer, the bag of food still in hand. Pfund's eyes were open, stunned, glazed surfaces staring into eternity. His lips were peeled back over a macabre twisted grin; the blows to the head had jarred loose a set of upper dentures.

There was no indication that there had been a struggle. Whoever had done it had probably come in through the stage door, lifted the bat from the pile of props, and come in here and nailed Pfund before the producer knew what hit him. There were indications of other blows to the head and face, but that first shot against the right side of the head must have been a killer.

Tinker backed away, throwing the bag of food onto a chair, then turned and hurried out into the corridor. He picked up a telephone, banged on the receiver several times before realizing the instrument was a prop, and threw it angrily against the wall. He ran back along the corridor, through the wings, across the stage, leaped into the aisle, and continued running, the skirts of his topcoat flapping around his knees, the rows of empty seats blurring around him.

When he got outside he was startled to hear the growling sound of an automobile starting. The sound was coming from behind the building. A quick look over his shoulder told him that Pfund's Packard was still there. Tinker jumped off of the elevated boardwalk and began running across the frozen ground toward the rear of the building, a cold, steady rain striking him in the face.

Suddenly a large gray sedan came roaring around the building, snow spraying up from its sharply wheeling tires. Tinker caught a glimpse of a man behind the wheel, a fedora pulled low over his eyes, his shoulders bunched high in a black overcoat, suggesting a posture of rigid tension. Tinker stopped in midstride and began crisscrossing his hands frantically in front of his face in the universal stop gesture. But then he saw that not only was this car not going to stop, but it also was not going to make any attempt to avoid flattening him. In fact, as Tinker began moving out of the way he realized that the car's bearing was moving with him. Running toward the playhouse, hearing the car barreling down upon him, Tinker left his feet and hurled himself laterally through

the air, crashing upon and then right on through
the boardwalk amid crisp sounds of splitting wood
and landing on the cold irregular earth of the Catskill Mountains. A moment later he heard the crash,
and when he got to his feet he saw that the sedan
had plowed in full smoking fury into the side of
Harry Knackers's Plymouth. As Tinker climbed
out of the large hole he had created in the boardwalk he saw the sedan jolt back in gear-grinding
reverse and that billowing gray smoke was coming
from both cars. The sedan lurched forward, but
without control, it appeared. It cleared the building but then pursued an erratic course, collided
with a huge snow-streaked boulder, mounted it
for a moment, and then tipped up, raised itself for
a moment against the gray sky with spinning
wheels, and came thudding down on its roof.

Tinker had a quick, despairing look at the red
flames bobbing antically inside the Plymouth, then
raced toward the sedan, which was belching
smoke through its broken, upside-down hood.

Crouching and looking through the cracked and
blood-splattered windshield of the upended car,
Tinker saw Frank Serrano lying there in an awkward sprawl, his battered, bleeding face flat
against the passenger-side window and his legs
twisted grotesquely back over the top of the driver's seat. The floor mat had come up as the car
went over and all the dirt under it had spilled
down on Serrano, flecking his badly gashed face.

Tinker called out to him several times, but Serrano's eyes were frozen in the same flat, sightless
gaze as Pfund's.

Tinker straightened up and looked at the Plymouth. The inside was filled with a rosy, foolishly
cheerful glow. For several moments he watched it

with a rapt incredulity, as if bearing witness to something blasphemous.

The explosion stunned him, its suddenness so unexpected and so startling he stumbled backward and then tipped over as a hot swift wind rushed at him. He fell back into the snow and lay rigid, staring puzzledly up into a gloomy gray sky that was dropping a slow, soundless rain on his face.

When he sat up, Tinker leaned back on his arms, his disoriented look suggesting a man just roused from deep sleep. Parts of Harry Knackers's 1937 Plymouth had blown right through the walls of the Mohawk Playhouse. Unsteadily Tinker got to his feet, one arm crooked in front of his face against the waves of heat gusting from the burning wreckage.

He ran into the theater and saw that the lobby was already afire, smoke curling out through the box office windows, while some red-hot metal from the recent Plymouth had lodged itself in the walls. Realizing that this place was not going to be standing much longer and that there was nothing that he could do about it, Tinker headed backstage, again going down the aisle, this time at full speed, taking the stage at a single bound and continuing through the wings. When he got to the office he was brought up short by the sight of Pfund, as if somehow he hadn't expected the body to still be there. "Goddammit," he said. But he was going to have to do this.

Bending down, he took Pfund's ankles in his hands and, looking back over his shoulder, began dragging the body along the floor. He swung the body around the desk and bumped it through the doorway and out into the corridor, Pfund's smashed head leaving a smeary trail of blood after

it, his eternally fixed eyes making him look as
though he had chosen to endure this indignity
with stately calm.

Tinker kicked open the stage door and backed
out into the slow rain. He dragged the body along
the snow-topped ground, Pfund's arms stretched
back over his head now, turtleneck and undershirt
pulled up and exposing some rubbery white belly.
When he had gone what he felt would be a safe
distance from the now doomed playhouse, Tinker
gently let the inert, out-pointing feet to the
ground. He paused for a moment to straighten his
aching back. Then he returned to the playhouse
and retrieved the murder weapon, which he
picked up and held gingerly by the knob as he
scuttled once more from the building and across
the snow. He lay the bat down carefully, almost
ceremoniously, next to the body.

Now he braced himself for one final necessity,
which he felt particularly squeamish about. The
last available car was Pfund's Packard, and the
keys were going to have to be fished from the
dead man's pockets. Tinker reminded himself that
he had seen enough corpses these past few years,
but corpses in wartime were somehow different;
in wartime you were shielded from finer sensibilities by the cold grimness of your own survival.
And anyway, you never had to pick their pockets.

He knelt and patted one pocket, then the other.
The second yielded a light tinkling. Either the keys
or some loose change. As carefully as any light-
fingered crowd-working dip, he slid his fingers
inside the pocket, found the keys, and lifted them
out.

When he got to Pfund's car he could see the
flames roaring out of the front of the Mohawk

Playhouse, throwing billowing clouds of black and gray smoke up into the cold air. Serrano's car was still smoking though not afire, while the 1937 Plymouth was a goner. Then he got into the Packard, turned the key in the ignition, and started for town to tell his tale.

23

I should have let them keep you up there," Selman said.

"Why?" Tinker asked irritably. "What did I do?"

"I don't know what you did, Joe, but you left behind two corpses, two wrecked automobiles, and one landmark burned to the ground."

"Landmark my ass. It was a converted barn."

"To those people it was a landmark," Selman said indifferently.

"What did you tell them exactly?"

"That you were a reporter covering the case for your paper and doing some unofficial snooping for the NYPD. Two lies in one sentence."

"You didn't actually use the word 'snooping,' did you?"

They were sitting in a coffee shop on Second Avenue just off Forty-Ninth. Their booth had cracked red leather seats, the white Formica tabletop showing the rings of past glass bottoms. The starving Tinker had just finished a sandwich and a Danish, Selman just coffee. It was almost ten o'clock at night. Tinker had stepped off a Greyhound bus an hour ago, called Selman, and met him here.

"They're going to want you back up there for further questioning."

"Good," Tinker said. "Then I can legitimately postpone going to Florida."

"I thought you wanted to go."

"No. *You* wanted me to go. I'm staying here until Harvey is cleared."

"Has it occurred to you that the murderer might be lying on a slab up in Sullivan County?"

"I don't think either one of them did it."

"Then why did you go charging up there?"

Tinker sipped his coffee, then sighed, looking up at the fluorescent lighting for a moment. In a quiet, near-empty place fluorescent lighting seemed depressing.

"I wanted to find out if Pfund definitely knew that Gloria had been playing games with him. And he did. That gave him a motive, Roger. Both of those guys had very strong motives."

"And now they're both dead. You spoke to Juliana Overman, who might still have provided some important information, and a day or so later she's dead."

"It proves I was on to something," Tinker said defensively.

"You know the guy I'd really like to get? The one who pegged a shot at you."

"Yeah?"

"Yeah. For missing."

"Thank you, Roger," Tinker muttered.

"You're forgetting something, Joe. This case is officially closed."

"Not for me it isn't. And you're not comfortable with that either."

"Not entirely," Selman said. "What else did you get out of Pfund?"

"Mostly he talked about being queer. It sounded sad."

"What else?"

"He sure didn't like Gloria. And neither did Serrano."

"Apparently Serrano didn't like you either."

"The son of a bitch tried to pancake me."

"Then we would have had three stiffs in addition to two wrecked automobiles and one destroyed landmark."

"Between the actor and the producer," Tinker said, "I'd pick the actor, if I was picking."

"Why?"

"He had more rage in him. This was one infuriated guy."

"Why?" Selman asked.

"You didn't know? Pfund had auditioned him, in bed. Serrano allowed it in order to get a part in the show Gloria was allegedly backing, which she never had any intention of backing. The whole thing was some sort of sordid joke, cooked up by Gloria and Juliana."

"And Serrano found out about it."

"Gossip runs through that world like water through a tap."

"That certainly could have set him off against Gloria *and* Juliana, as well as Pfund."

"Did he have an alibi for Juliana's murder?"

"We were never able to get hold of him for questioning."

"Christ, I don't know," Tinker said wearily. "It beats the shit out of me. These people, the way they live . . . I thought I was so worldly-wise."

"There are a lot of morally sinister people out there, Joe. Each with their own private cesspool."

"If Serrano did it, you can hardly blame him. Christ, he must've hated those people. You take away a guy's self-respect . . ."

"He gave it away, Joe. Anyway, he was no Bambi in the woods. We ran a check on him. He was a pretty nasty bit of business. He'd been in some trouble in Philly before the war, enlisted in the army early in '42 and was dishonorably discharged eight months later for brawling and one thing and another. That's when he came to New York and became an actor. I guess he started brooding about what had been done to him, found out where Pfund was, maybe even knew the theater, and stole a car and went up there to settle it."

"Stole the car?"

"This guy had been around, Joe."

"Jesus," Tinker said, "given his history and his disposition, he could've been the one."

"He certainly didn't spare Pfund. We know that much, anyway."

"It was a mess. A baseball bat, Roger."

"Why would he throw a shot at you?"

Tinker, staring down into the dregs of his coffee, looked up at Selman.

"He wouldn't have," Tinker said. "I hadn't even met him then."

"So you're back to Harvey."

"Roger, are you playing games with me?"

"No, Joe," Selman said, smiling and shaking his head. "I'm just thinking like a cop."

"What about that guy Buxton? You get any more out of him?"

"He claims he was asleep in bed with his wife at the time the murders were committed."

"Does she back him up?"

"Not really. She was asleep. She says she thinks he was there. Anyway, you saw Buxton; do you think he's capable of murder? And why would he kill Juliana?"

"Maybe you're dealing with two killers after all."

"No," Selman said firmly. "I've been operating under the premise that there's one killer. I'm one hundred percent convinced of it."

"What about that lawyer?"

"Slate? Very strong motive there," Selman said reflectively, moving his spoon around through his empty cup. "Seems he's got financial problems. Some bad investments."

"And he's going to marry the cousin who's the beneficiary of Gloria's death."

"A hell of a motive," Selman said. "But we can't place him in the house at the time of the murders. And when Juliana was killed, he was with Norah Gregg."

"You've never accepted the possibility of a burglary that went spectacularly wrong, have you?"

"There's no evidence of that. And anyway, the case is closed."

"Not in your mind it isn't."

Selman smiled ruefully. "Come on," he said. "Let's get out of here."

They stood outside on the sidewalk for a few moments, watching the flow of Second Avenue traffic, then began walking, each with hands in pants pockets, shoving aside their open topcoats.

"I'm supposed to be on a train for Clearwater tomorrow," Tinker said.

"You'd better tell your boss you're not going, that you have some unfinished business with the Sullivan County constabulary."

"God," Tinker said, trying to imagine Scott's reaction.

"And you're going to have to explain to your friend about his car."

"Fuck him and his car."

They crossed the street at Fiftieth and began heading west.

"I guess I'll grab a cab and go home," Tinker said. "This has been a day."

"You're going home?"

"Aren't you?"

"I thought I'd go over to the Manley house and have one more go-around. Maybe we overlooked something."

"I'm going with you," Tinker said.

"Instinct told me you'd say that," Selman said.

24

The heat had been turned down in the Manley house and Tinker and Selman found the place uninvitingly chilly. There was an air of conspiracy between stillness and darkness, while the chill felt as though it was in some corner preserving the grisly echoes of what had happened here.

They walked through the vestibule to the living room, where Selman turned on a lamp that seemed to cast more shadows than light. The heavy draperies that were swept across the windows gave the room a feeling of being totally shut off. Either there was no traffic on East Fiftieth Street right now or else the sounds weren't getting through.

"That's the mother," Selman said, pointing to a shadow-dimmed portrait over the fireplace. Done in oils, it was a head and shoulders depiction of a strikingly attractive woman in her late thirties. "She was a knockout, huh?"

"Very formidable," Tinker said, staring up at the compelling black eyes and full, smugly set lips.

"Doesn't look like her daughter at all, does she?"

"More beautiful, more sensual," Tinker said. "And at the same time she looks like she could have operated a Gatling gun, if necessary."

"They say she screwed herself to death."

"She must have had two-way arteries: cold blood going in one direction, hot in the other."

There were two large sofas and a half dozen armchairs in the large, carpeted room. A pair of rosewood end tables stood at the end of each sofa, each holding a thin lamp with wide hand-painted shades. A mahogany hutch was buried in the shadows of one corner, its shelves displaying a set of bone china. A chandelier hung in the ceiling gloom like a giant tiara. The andirons in the fireplace were stacked with fresh logs.

"That's where she was found," Selman said, pointing to an area of the carpet.

The spot looked no different from any other, though Tinker's intent, scrutinizing stare suggested that it might.

"By her father," he said.

"He was going to have lunch with her that afternoon."

"I don't suppose he's been of any help?"

"No," Selman said. "All we've gotten out of him is a litany of self-reproach. Some of it probably justified."

Tinker looked around, feeling an odd sense of helplessness, as if there was a direction for him to reach out to but he did not know which.

They went into the corridor and stood at the foot of the stairs.

"She knew the guy," Selman said. "There's no doubt of it in my mind. The nutbuster in this case is that she was in the habit of giving keys to her lovers. And the lady was promiscuous."

"Did Harvey have a key?"

"No, as a matter of fact. I guess she never took him that seriously. But he was with her that night.

As an assistant D.A. has said to me, 'He was the last one to see her alive.' You know what the translation of that is? 'He was the first one to see her dead.' "

"But nobody saw Harvey go inside," Tinker said.

"That's correct. We found the cabbie who dropped them off. He says that when he drove away Harvey was standing on the sidewalk looking up at the front door. Even in that simple statement there's an insinuation."

"You're saying the D.A. honestly believes the kid is guilty?"

"He may have had to talk himself into it, but, yes, that's what he believes. And with the signed statement in hand he's gone from believing to knowing."

Tinker looked up to where the flight of stairs disappeared into darkness.

"Jesus, Roger," he whispered, "it's spooky, isn't it?"

"A place like this holds a murder for a long time," Selman said.

"There's an aura."

"It'll take more than new people and fresh paint to get rid of it."

Shoulder to shoulder they began mounting the stairs, Tinker riding his hand along the polished mahogany banister.

"We figure," Selman said, "she was up in her room—the lights were still on the next day—heard something downstairs, and came down to investigate. She went into the living room and he killed her. The maid probably heard something, maybe a scream, came out to see what was going on, saw enough, and ran back to her room. That's where he got her. Then he probably went out the back window."

At the head of the stairs Selman turned on the hall light. A table holding a cut glass bowl stood against one wall, over it a set of small framed landscapes.

"Guest rooms," Selman said, pointing to three closed doors.

Gloria's bedroom door was open. Selman entered first and turned on the bedside lamp.

"This was how we found it," he said, "with this light on and the bathroom light on. Her jacket and purse were on the bed. She couldn't have been in here for more than a few minutes."

Tinker stared at the king-sized bed with its heavy spread and three pillows in glossy red slips. A well-executed painting of an exquisite chestnut stallion hung over the cushioned headboard.

"That's her jewel box," Selman said, pointing to the vanity table, where a chair with a padded seat was pushed in. "As far as we can tell, nothing was taken."

"Was there any jewelry on the body?"

"What she was wearing that night. Diamond earrings, a ring set with a ruby worth about three years of your salary. Does that take care of your burglar theory?"

"He still could have panicked and run. Or been interrupted by the maid."

"No, Joe. If it was a burglar he would in all likelihood have come in through the back window."

"And killed the maid first."

"Right."

"What's bothering you, Roger?"

Selman sat down on the bed.

"Because it was someone she knew," he said. "And I don't think we've got him."

"And the best brain on the NYPD can't get him."

"Maybe the best brain isn't working on it."

"The problem is, nobody's working on it. Your buddies have closed the case."

"It keeps nibbling at me, Joe. It just keeps on nibbling."

Tinker looked around the large bedroom. Gloria Manley was still a presence here, from the lineup of various-sized bottles and jars of creams and lotions on the vanity to a small teddy bear sitting in a corner chair to the long racks of stylish clothing hanging emptily in the open closet to the bed no one had slept in since her death.

Leaving Selman brooding in the bedroom, Tinker returned downstairs. He followed the corridor to the sitting room, where he paused in the doorway and looked in. Already beginning to feel the intruder, he did not put on the light but went on to the kitchen. Here he did turn the switch and open the large, immaculate kitchen to a glow of overhead light. There was a table and four chairs, more than a dozen cabinets lining the walls, and a long butcher-block slab mounted on cast-iron legs standing in the center.

He walked into the well-stocked pantry, which had doors at either end. Passing through, he entered a small corridor that led to the dining room at one end and the maid's room at the other. He walked toward the closed door of what had been Maria Espardo's room. He put his hand on the knob and turned it slowly, opening the door as discreetly as he could, as though there were someone sleeping within. Before entering he groped along the wall for the light switch, pushed it up, and illuminated a floor lamp standing near the bed.

He took a few steps in and paused. So here was where Gloria and probably all who had preceded her in ownership had tucked away the help. It had the look of a room in a second-rate hotel, neat, modest, and functional. No matter how long you lived here, you would always be a transient.

The bed was unmade, the cover thrown back, probably as it was when Maria Espardo rose from it for the last time. The hard wood floor was bare except for a shag rug at the side of the bed. Tinker went to the window and with his fingers parted several of the Venetian blind slats and peered out into the yard and at the backs of the houses on Fifty-First Street. Some lights were on, but all of the blinds were drawn.

He turned from the window, folded his arms, and moved his eyes around the room. Then he went to the bureau. An unframed painting of a crucified Christ was tacked to the wall above it. On the bureau's surface were a pair of candles in tall holders, a plaster Virgin Mary between them. There were also a prayer book and a paperback Spanish-English dictionary.

Folding his arms again, Tinker stared intently at the bilingual dictionary. The red and white cover was creased and curled slightly up from the body of pages beneath it. His flat, inquiring scrutiny went on for several minutes. Finally he unfolded his arms and reached out and picked up the book, pressing it tightly between his thumb and fingers.

He returned upstairs to where Selman was still sitting on the edge of Gloria Manley's bed. Walking into the room, he said, "We've been stupid."

Selman looked at him.

"Maria Espardo did go to *a* church that night," Tinker said.

He threw the book onto the bed next to Selman. The cop contemplated it for several moments, then allowed a thin smile and, without looking up, said, "Tomorrow, Joe. We'll start tomorrow."

25

After agreeing to meet the following morning, Tinker and Selman parted. Tinker headed crosstown, picking up the Sixth Avenue subway at Forty-Seventh and riding downtown.

His mind was a welter of conflicting thoughts as he sat back on the hard yellow wicker seat as the subway ran through its underground tunnel. He barely took notice as the train lurched to a halt at Forty-Second and people sauntered in and out, and then again at Thirty-Fourth, few people at this stop at that time of night, and then fewer still at Twenty-Third.

The excitement he had felt when first realizing the implications of the Spanish-English dictionary had now settled as he considered his plan of action. Between Forty-Seventh and Forty-Second Streets he was buoyant and optimistic; between Forty-Second and Thirty-Fourth he could feel his optimism being tempered; between Thirty-Fourth and Twenty-Third he began wondering just how helpful his hypothesis was going to prove, and by the time the train pulled into the Fourteenth Street station and he got to his feet, Tinker realized that the odds against his accomplishing anything to help Harvey Tippen were extremely intimidating.

Tinker didn't realize how tired he was until he

was climbing the stairs to the street. He felt a deep enervating weariness, and not just from this day, which by itself had been enough to wrinkle granite, but by all of the days since he had decided that Harvey was innocent.

Emerging at street level, he began walking not north to Sixteenth and home but east toward Fifth Avenue. Because of the presence of Hearn's and S. Klein's with their racks and racks of cut-rate women's fashions, Fourteenth Street was almost manic with activity during the day, but at this midnight hour the street was nearly empty.

He called Rita from an all-night coffee shop near a newspaper kiosk at Fourteenth and Fifth.

"Did I wake you?" he asked.

"No," she said. "Where are you?"

"Practically on your doorstep."

"You sound like hell."

"I've had a few glimpses of it lately."

"Then you'd better come over," she said and hung up.

Five minutes later she buzzed him into the converted townhouse on Twelfth Street where she had one of six apartments. He went up the staircase to the second floor, where he found her waiting in the doorway. She was wearing a maroon bathrobe over pink silk pajamas.

"You weren't in bed yet, were you?" he asked as she closed the door behind him.

"I was heading in that direction," she said coolly.

They went into the living room. She waited for him to choose a place to sit, and when he chose the sofa she took a chair across from him.

"Somebody tried to kill me today," he said.

"I know," she said, crossing her legs. "In the Catskill Mountains."

"How did you know that?"

"I think everyone at 220 East Forty-Second Street knows," she said, reciting the address of the *Daily News*. "Some sheriff or somebody from Sullivan County called to check on you."

"Called who?"

"It eventually reached the executive suite. It had to do with you and two dead people, Joe. This was a bit over the head of Sports."

"Then Scotty knows," Tinker said dejectedly.

"From what I hear, if you show up at the office tomorrow there might well be another attempt on your life."

"Shit," he said, closing his eyes and rubbing his face for a moment.

"Anyway, there's no point in showing up. You've been suspended. We got word about four o'clock. The Guild has been informed."

"I'm not surprised," he said. "I've done the exact opposite of everything I was told to do. But all in a good cause. God, but Scotty must be ticked off."

"I don't know, but people were heading upstairs to see if lava was actually flowing out of the sports department."

"I was supposed to be on the train tomorrow. Heading for Clearwater."

"What are you going to do?"

"Oh," he said with exaggerated nonchalance, "I've got things to do."

"You could try to patch it up."

"Not yet."

"Who tried to kill you?"

"An unemployed actor. Don't ask me any more. The whole thing is a blur in my mind."

"That woman whose body you found—"

"Juliana Overman."

"Was she the one . . ."

"Yes."

"I'm sorry."

"It wasn't like that at all," he said. "Let's not get into that again. Where's your husband these days?"

"Safely in Jersey City."

"Not so safe; he followed me the last time I left here."

"I know; he told me the whole story."

"He almost got us both killed. What are you smiling at?"

"I'm sorry," she said, unable to control her mischievous smile. "He won't do it again."

"He should have followed me today. He would've gotten an eyeful. Listen, can I stay here tonight?"

She squinted one eye almost shut.

"Under what circumstances?"

"All I want is a hot shower and a good night's sleep."

"I'll join you in the shower," she said. "We can discuss the rest later."

26

Rita was already gone when Tinker opened his eyes the next morning. He put on her maroon robe and went into the kitchen, reheated the coffee she had left on the stove, gulped a cup, and then returned to the bedroom to get dressed. She had stretched his jockey shorts over a chair and left a ripe red lipstick imprint flush on the lower portion and a note that read SEE YOU TONIGHT.

He returned to his apartment, schemes, plots, and ideas running through his mind as he hurried through the bright forty-degree morning sunshine. Upstairs, he changed his clothes and had just finished shaving when the telephone rang. He hesitated for a moment before answering. The last person he needed in his ear right now was Scott. When he lifted the receiver and brought it to his ear he answered in a high-pitched voice.

"Hello?"

"Joe? Is that you? What the hell's wrong with you?" It was Selman.

"Nothing, nothing," Tinker said, descending a few octaves. "I thought it might be Scott. Where are you?"

"I'm in the station house. How soon can you meet me?"

"Where?"

"How about just inside the main entrance of the Forty-Second Street Library."

"Twenty minutes," Tinker said.

Selman had not been idle, not last night nor this morning. Both logic and intuition had locked onto Tinker's suggestion, and while he had not done any legwork he had been on the telephone. And had got some results.

"I think it's the first thing about this case that makes any sense," Selman said when Tinker showed up. They were walking in one of the library's wide, marble-floored, high-ceilinged corridors, past framed lithographs depicting nineteenth-century New York scenes, one of which showed the fortresslike reservoir that had stood on the tract of land now occupied by the library.

"The church is a few blocks over, in the East Thirties," Selman said. "It's where she would have gone."

"She would have gone there for confession, when you stop to think about it," Tinker said.

"She would have had to. The place we originally went to was okay for Mass, but otherwise . . ."

"She needed a Spanish-speaking priest."

They left the library through the Fifth Avenue exit, reentering the bright morning sunshine, back onto the sidewalks of the city of perpetual motion. Fifth Avenue's two-way traffic was ceaseless at that hour, the doubledecker buses riding like ships of state among the automobiles and taxis.

"You've spoken to him?" Tinker asked.

"I reached him last night. He's expecting us."

"How much have you told him?"

"Just that it's a police matter."

Tinker was hard put to keep up with Selman's

quick, seemingly anxiety-ridden strides. Selman was like a hunter closing upon a long-elusive prey, impatient, uneasy, irritable, shouting profanely back at an irate cabbie who berated them for crossing the avenue against the light. They timed and dodged the oncoming traffic like a couple of urban toreros, hopped onto the sidewalk, and began heading east.

When Tinker was introduced to Father Alfonso he had to smile. Of course, Tinker thought. A distressed Maria Espardo, with her chancy command of English, would not have gone to Father Michael Martin O'Shea to unburden herself; she would have come here, not just for a church or for a particular priest, but for the comfort and support of her own native tongue.

The life's experience in Father Alfonso's face made him of indeterminate age. His intensely black eyes were younger than the rest of his gaunt, swarthy face with its sharply etched lines across his forehead and along his cheeks and at the corners of his mouth. He had a full crop of black curly hair that seemed to roll back across his head. His mouth was wide, full-lipped, his nose long and delicately thin.

They met in the vestry. Filled with liturgical objects and with vestments hanging on the wall from wooden pegs, the small, cramped room also contained several stiff-backed wooden chairs. Wearing a black cassock, Father Alfonso asked his visitors to sit. He remained standing.

After thanking the priest for taking the time to see them, Selman came to the point. Tinker watched the priest's face; it was as if Selman's every word was being absorbed and digested syllable by syllable.

"Maria Espardo," Father Alfonso said quietly. "Yes, I remember. She came here some time ago. A week. Maybe ten days. It was late. I remember it was quite late."

Since they had been looking for a Spanish-speaking priest, Tinker expected to hear a voice hued by accent, but he heard no such tones or intonations in Father Alfonso's carefully measured responses.

"She apologized for coming in at that hour," the priest said with a faint smile, as if such an apology had been ingenuous.

"We understand it might have been around eleven or eleven-thirty," Selman said. He was sitting on the edge of his chair, leaning forward, as if anxious to get his words to Father Alfonso as quickly as possible.

"I think it was around that time."

"And she was in some distress?"

"I would say it was more like agitation."

"Did you know her, Father?" Tinker asked.

"No. She did say she came here for confession, though she attended Mass at a church closer to her home. Is she in some difficulty?"

"She's dead," Selman said.

"I see," the priest said softly.

"She was one of the women murdered last week in that house on Fiftieth Street."

"Ah," the priest said, nodding. "Yes."

"You didn't know?" Selman asked.

"I heard, of course. I prefer not to read those stories. I find them too disturbing."

Now Father Alfonso drew up a chair and sat down opposite Selman and Tinker. There were several moments of silence while the priest's face reflected what appeared a communing, a profound privacy. Then he said, "How can I help you?"

"We have to know what she told you," Selman said. "It could be of the utmost importance."

"Oh," the priest said with a wry smile, "it was quite a little story."

"Are you able to tell us?" Selman asked. "I mean, without violating any ecclesiastical ethics."

"It wasn't told in the confessional, if that's what you mean. She came to me with a dilemma. She needed advice."

Tinker, trying to hold his silence, was unable to.

"Was she in danger?" he asked. "Did she say that?"

"She didn't say it, but I sensed that she felt she was."

"Then she knew something," Selman said. "Had some information."

"Had it thrust upon her, it seems," the priest said. "And, it also seems, to her misfortune. One more victim, gentlemen. One more victim."

Father Alfonso went on, his voice alternately flattened with grief and remote with melancholy, as though being filtered through layers of emotion.

"I suppose it is inescapable," he said, "that our war—Spain's war—is so dwarfed by what came after that if people remember it it is simply as a prelude. But for those people who were there, who found themselves surrounded by it, it became their defining experience. Maria Espardo's family came from a village about fifty miles south of Madrid. Unfortunately for this village, it was located near an important main road as well as some bridges; consequently it suffered from heavy air bombardments. Maria's father, mother, and younger sister

were killed. How many millions of people in our
world today have similar stories to tell?" Father
Alfonso smiled sadly, philosophically, for a moment. Then he went on.

"The bombs that killed Maria's family were
dropped by Fascist planes. This motivated her
older brother Francisco to join the fight against
them. About a year later she learned that he had
been taken prisoner and was being held in a stockade about seventy-five miles away. Taking her life
in her hands, she went there—walking most of
the way—to try and see him. Some of the guards
must have taken pity on her, because when she
got there they allowed her to talk to him through
a wire fence. The boy tried to reassure her that he
was being treated satisfactorily and was all right.
He told her he was one of the lucky ones. The
unlucky ones in that particular stockade were cap-
tives from the international brigades, most especially the Americans, the ones who called themselves the Abraham Lincoln Brigade. The stockade
commander seemed to have a special resentment
of them and subjected them to extremely harsh
interrogations, and sometimes worse. There was
a dreaded basement room and those who were
taken there were only seen again as *fiambres*—literally, cold meats or corpses. The prisoners told tales
of men sitting on a chair in this room and being
questioned while behind them stood an American
of cruel strength, a man who never spoke, who
only stood and listened and waited. When the
interrogator was satisfied he would nod to this
man, who then stepped forward, took them in
hand, and with a single twist cracked their necks."

"Did the brother know the name of this man?"
Selman asked.

"No," the priest said. "The man apparently was some sort of renegade or adventurer—Spain was fertile ground for that type in those years, wasn't it? This one aligned himself with the Fascists and seemed to have some grudge against these particular countrymen of his. But Maria saw him once. She had stayed in a nearby village to be near her brother. She was working in an outdoor market and one afternoon a car drove in and stopped. The door opened and the American and two officers got out and bought a few items from her stall. When they were gone someone told her that that had been 'the bad Americano' from the stockade. She had sensed who he was, she said, because when he appeared everyone fell silent and averted their eyes."

"So she had a good look at him," Tinker said.

"A very good look," the priest said. "She said she would never forget him. 'An evil man with a kindly face.' That was how she described him."

"And then she saw him again," Tinker said. "In New York."

"Maria's brother died in the stockade," the priest said. "How, she never knew. She resolved to get away from Spain and after much travail she came here."

"And saw him again," Tinker said. "In the home of her employer, the night she died."

"That is correct."

"Did she name him?" Selman asked.

"No," the priest said, shaking his head. "Nor did I ask. She said she walked into the room carrying a tray of drinks, saw him, and was so shocked she dropped the whole thing on the floor. You can imagine how petrified she must have been."

"What about him?" Tinker asked. "He must have known she knew him."

"She said he stared at her for as long as she was in the room. I think he must have understood he had been recognized."

"Did she tell this to anyone besides you?" Selman asked.

"No," the priest said. "She wouldn't have. She was too terrified. That's why she came here. She didn't know what to do. She *couldn't* have known what to do. I don't think we can begin to imagine what she must have been feeling."

"And what did you tell her, Father?" Selman asked.

"I kept asking her if she was absolutely certain of her memory, but she said there was no doubt. She said if she'd had any doubt, then the way he looked at her would have dispelled it. And if you had seen her face and heard her voice you would have believed she had no doubt. We sat together, right here in this room, for nearly an hour. I tried to comfort and reassure her; that was my first concern. What did I tell her?" Father Alfonso gave a little grunt of a laugh. "We are asked far more questions, Lieutenant, than we have answers for. I told her to go home and think about this and then come back the next day and we would try and decide what to do. I had every intention of helping her, but I wanted time to think it through and perhaps take some advice." After a pause, the priest asked quietly, "Do you think I failed her?"

Selman didn't answer.

"What did you think when she didn't return?" Tinker asked.

"I didn't know what to think," Father Alfonso said.

"You never connected her with the murders?"

The priest shook his head.

"I didn't even know about them until a few days afterward," he said. "And then when I heard the police had arrested someone . . ."

"The police made a mistake," Tinker said. And then added, "Most of them, anyway."

"There are two things I never do," Selman said when they had left the church and were standing outside on the sidewalk. "I never drink when I'm on duty and I never drink this early. Come on. Let's go."

The bar on Third Avenue was virtually empty when they walked in. The bartender looked up from rinsing some glasses when they entered, then dried his hands with the bar towel, rolled down his sleeves, and walked toward them. He dropped a pair of round hard cardboard coasters that said "Schaefer Beer" in front of them.

"Two beers," Selman said.

When the two white-capped glasses had been placed before them and the bartender had returned to his washing, Selman said, "Did you ever write a story, Joe, and when you got to the end realized you'd been focusing on the wrong person?"

Tinker lifted his glass, drank, and felt the cold beer run down into an empty stomach. It didn't feel good.

"The whole time," Selman said, "I've been concentrating on the wrong victim. I missed the primary victim. Well, now we can start to turn it around. The first thing we have to do is find out which one of them was in Spain in 1937 or thereabouts. There'll be ways of doing that. Once we've established that we'll at least be narrowed down. But then, Jesus, what'll we have? What can you hang on the nine-year-old memory of a dead woman? How much weight is that going to carry? And this time we won't be dealing with a simpleton like Harvey Tippen, but somebody who's probably as tough as steel. What are you so quiet about?"

Tinker had taken just the single swallow of beer.

"For the moment," he said, "do nothing. I've got some people to see and some calls to make. I'll be in touch later."

Selman stared at him curiously. "Yes?" he asked.

"Maybe," Tinker said.

27

Tinker arrived ahead of time at the bar at Madison and Sixty-Fourth, with the window table he had requested waiting for him. The outside view was across to the west side of the avenue to a row of stores now closed for the night, their awnings rolled down at angles. The largest of the stores, a purveyor of expensive men's fashions, had a wide double-door entrance.

Tinker waved off an approaching waiter.

"My friend will be here shortly," he said, then glanced at his watch: 7:45.

The place was illuminated by small pink and blue bulbs that created a surfeit of "atmosphere." The brightest lights came from behind the bar, where the array of labeled bottles resembled a display of medals and awards. The bar and its gold foot rail were polished, while the bar stools had padded red leather seats and backs. A piano stood on a small platform near a rear wall; the pianist came on at nine o'clock to play and sing "ballads and old favorites" (so said the framed placard hanging outside in an illuminated glass box).

No one was sitting at the bar, and a few tables were occupied by couples facing each other over candles burning in pink or blue jars, like people waiting for a séance to begin.

At five minutes to eight a taxi pulled up outside. Tinker watched the passenger door swing open and a moment later Bobby Pilleter stepped out onto the sidewalk, throwing the door shut behind him. Last seen by Tinker wearing a white T-shirt and slacks, Pilleter was resplendent in a double-breasted black overcoat and black homburg. He was wearing gray kid gloves. He no doubt had plans for later in the evening.

There was an expression of amused disdain in Pilleter's face when he entered and surveyed the place. Tinker was amused by Pilleter's amusement. It was simple: by Tinker's standards the place was elegant, by Pilleter's, slightly gauche.

Pilleter removed his hat and then his gloves, which he slapped into the hat, and then his coat, checking them with the cloakroom woman. Then he looked around, finally finding Tinker, who had been waiting to be discovered.

"I hope you don't approve of this place, Tinker," Pilleter said, joining him at the table.

"Why?"

"Too strenuous an attempt to create 'atmosphere.' You don't do it by turning down all the lights and illuminating a few colored bulbs. That's the same kind of thinking that believes it's elegant to have a washroom attendant."

"Isn't it?"

"It isn't," Pilleter said. "It's a very subtle error of judgment. A fine point, but a telling one. You'll see a washroom attendant at the Hotel Astor, for instance, but never at the Pierre or St. Moritz."

"I guess you would know about those things," Tinker said as the waiter came over and took their order. Tinker asked for bourbon neat, Pilleter for a light scotch and water.

"You look like you're ready for a night out," Tinker said when the drinks had arrived.

"I'm picking up a lady at nine-thirty and we're going to a party at the Essex House."

"A rich lady?" Tinker asked.

Pilleter studied him with distinct lack of amusement. "Very," he said.

"I'm not implying any disapproval," Tinker said with what he hoped was an ingenuous smile. "I guess I'm envious. I'd probably do the same as you, if I had your style."

"You said you had something interesting to tell me."

"Intriguing."

"What?"

"Not interesting; intriguing."

Pilleter lifted his glass and sipped, staring at Tinker over the rim. In his newly revised appraisal of the man, Tinker was now noting things he hadn't before. Under that neatly combed and parted yellow hair, which made him look so much younger than the older women he escorted, was a pair of extremely shrewd and watchful eyes, their calculation right there on the surface. And the man had a stuttering smile; first a terse movement at the corners of his mouth, and then the full keyboard, with all the sincerity of a professional greeter's. Yes, a man looked different when you believed he was a murderer. No matter how casual, his gestures, inflections, expressions all seemed ulterior and suggestive. You wondered that murder did not somehow, in some way, show in a man's face, leave a mark somewhere. Some people, apparently, were poisoned by what they did, but others not. How had Maria Espardo described him? *"An evil man with a kindly face."* Tinker saw it differently: a weak man with a false face.

"You never told me you'd been in Spain," Tinker said.

"That was because I never have been," Pilleter said, putting down his glass.

"You couldn't have forgotten it. It wasn't that long ago."

Tinker got the first part of the smile only, the slight twitch at the corners of the mouth.

"When was it?" Tinker asked. "Thirty-six, -seven, -eight?"

"It never was. Anyway, there was a war going on there then. Who would have wanted to go?"

"Oh, some people went."

"That's right, some did."

"The Abraham Lincoln Brigade, for instance."

"Political idealists," Pilleter said disparagingly. "A bunch of blockheads fighting on the wrong side."

"The wrong side?" Tinker asked.

"The losing side," Pilleter said pointedly.

"Losing made it wrong?"

"Is there another way of looking at it?"

"That's cynical."

"Realistic. Anyway, it has nothing to do with me. I don't give a damn about politics."

"Only money."

"That's right," Pilleter said.

"What's more political than money?"

Pilleter laughed. "Now who's being cynical?"

Tinker glanced out the window. Several men had gathered in the doorway of the clothing store across the street. They were wearing dark overcoats or lumber jackets.

"I want to give you my version of some recent

events," Tinker said, looking back to his companion.

Pilleter lifted his arm and consulted with his watch for a moment.

"Make it the *Reader's Digest* version," he said. "I've got to leave soon."

"I'll keep it to the point, since you know it anyway."

"If I know what it is, why are you going to tell it to me?"

"Just to let you know that *I* know."

Pilleter leaned back in his chair, the expression on his face so bland that Tinker could not tell whether the man had any idea of what was coming.

"I don't know why you were in Spain during the civil war and I don't know why you were doing what you were."

"Then what the hell *do* you know, Tinker?" Pilleter asked on a note of peevish impatience.

"That somehow you were on the side of the Fascists. I don't know why. Maybe for money. Maybe it was just your nature. Maybe just for the hell of it."

"Speaking noncommittally, there is such a thing as political principle, you know."

"I fail to see the principle involved in breaking men's necks. Particularly when those necks belonged to your countrymen—who were fighting in service of *their* political principles."

"The Abraham Lincoln Brigade," Pilleter said coldly, "were a bunch of naive simpletons who did more harm than good. Anyway," Pilleter added with a mocking smile, "so I heard, never having been in Spain myself."

"Maria Espardo saw you in Spain," Tinker said.

"She knew who you were. You had made quite an impression on her, which is not surprising, since she had been told what you were doing in that stockade. Her brother died there, you know. I'm sure she wondered how. No wonder she never forgot you. And then she saw you again, in Gloria Manley's living room. She was frightened out of her wits. You spotted it, didn't you? I guess it was obvious. She was so shaken she dropped a tray of drinks."

Pilleter was sitting back in his chair, the fingers of one hand moving thoughtfully at the point of his chin, his staring eyes fixed almost clinically upon Tinker, who felt he could read the thinking behind those eyes.

"My neck doesn't break that easily, Bobby," he said.

"That's a natural conceit," Pilleter said without change of expression.

"Anyway, you must have started thinking right then and there about what to do. Then, when you were all coming out of El Morocco later on and Gloria announced she was going downtown, you saw an opportunity. Get over to the house, let yourself in, take care of Maria, and get out. But you didn't take Gloria's unpredictable nature into account. She'd changed her mind about going downtown and come home instead. So after you'd wrung Maria's neck you come out and are suddenly faced with Gloria, who must have heard something and come downstairs. You really had no choice. Poor Gloria. She probably spent the last seconds of her life puzzled and incredulous. Why was her good friend and former lover doing this to her? Then you went back to Maria's room, raised the window to make it look like a burglary

—a bungled burglary—and left, either through the window or out the front door, we aren't sure which."

"We?" Pilleter asked quietly, raising one pale eyebrow.

"You'd taken a hell of a chance," Tinker said, "but you were an experienced man. Anyway, what choice had you? If Maria told someone, you'd be run out of your social circle, lose your entrée to the wealthy and foolish. You'd lose whatever golden hen you were hoping to eventually land. Not to mention the likelihood of some other, more brutal penalties."

Pilleter smiled unconvincingly.

"You're not a newspaperman," he said, "you're a writer of fiction. A teller of fables. Aesop in a cheap suit."

"You probably figured you were back in the sunlight when they picked up Harvey and squeezed him into signing a statement. But," Tinker said, "one thing was still nagging you. Maria had whispered something in Spanish to Juliana as you were all leaving Gloria's place. Now what could that have been, Bobby?"

As Pilleter slowly reached forward for his drink, Tinker couldn't help but think, *Jesus, but the son of a bitch has big hands.* Pilleter drank slowly, his eyes never leaving Tinker's face. The waiter came near, sensed the tension, and backed off.

"You called Juliana the night I was there," Tinker said. "When she told you she was talking to the press you came over and waited downstairs. You must have been pretty concerned. When I came out you recognized me. You couldn't be sure she hadn't told me anything, so you followed me downtown, followed me out of the subway, and pegged a shot at me."

"Somebody shot at you, did they?" Pilleter asked, replacing his glass on the table.

"You knew she hadn't told the police about you because they had questioned her before they did you, and they never mentioned it to you. You weren't sure what she had told me. But you couldn't take any chances, because if she hadn't said anything yet, she would sooner or later. So you went up to see her and put her away. Since Harvey was sitting in jail you had to make it seem the murders were not connected; so instead of your usual method you strangled her. Totally unnecessary, Bobby. Maria had never told her anything, had only whispered her thanks to Juliana for having been kind to her, for helping her to clean up the mess."

"So if Maria never told anybody anything," Pilleter said, "then you're making this all up."

"I never said she didn't tell anybody. You're a miserable son of a bitch, aren't you? But not so goddamned clever. When we were talking the other night—when you probably realized that Juliana hadn't told me anything—and I said something about two murders at Gloria's, you said, 'Yes. Alas, poor Gloria.' Well now, everybody's focus had been on Gloria, but to you the prime victim had been Maria. Only for you was Gloria the afterthought."

Pilleter showed a faint, sneering smile.

"And then," Tinker said, "you said something about me being downtown eating my hot dogs and beans while you would be feasting in one of Manhattan's finest restaurants. Downtown? I thought about that later and asked myself: how does this guy know I live downtown?"

"Speaking of feasting," Pilleter said, again consulting with his wristwatch, "I *do* have an appointment."

"Forget it."

"Forget it?" Pilleter asked, lifting an inquiring eyebrow.

"You can't just walk away from this, Bobby. A good friend of mine is sitting in jail."

"That's because he confessed," Pilleter said with simple logic.

"If he can do it, then so can you."

Pilleter laughed uncomfortably. "I have nothing to confess to," he said.

"Sure you do; we've just been talking about it."

"So you worked the whole thing out all by yourself. Very ingenious. What are you going to do with it?"

"Did I say I'd worked it out by myself?" Tinker asked. For the first time he picked up his drink, sipped for a moment, wiped his lips with his tongue, then put the glass back down. He glanced out of the window. There were now eight or ten men standing in the doorway of the clothing store.

"I suppose you're a clever guy, Tinker," Pilleter said. "Probably not as dumb as you look. But you have nothing. Nothing. You've woven a tale. Most interesting. But where are you going to take it? Who's going to believe it?"

"The police."

"Give me one reason why they should."

"Because you're going to tell them it's true," Tinker said.

Pilleter studied him for a moment, then laughed mirthlessly.

"I take it back," he said. "You *are* as dumb as you look."

"You'd be better off telling it to the police," Tinker said, adding, with a nod toward the men who had gathered across the street, "than to them."

Pilleter's eyes flashed to the knot of men in the doorway, then back to Tinker. "Who are they?" he asked.

"Friends of mine. Some bitter, some sweet. But all with long memories."

With evident reluctance, Pilleter asked, "Of what?"

"Spain. They were all there, the same time as you were. You might even have bumped into a few of them. You almost surely bumped into some of their friends. They'd like to ask you about their friends."

"Who are they?" Pilleter asked tersely.

"They were with the Brigade. There are hundreds of them in this city, Bobby. They're having a reunion tonight. In your honor."

"What the hell have you done, Tinker?" Pilleter demanded.

It looked as though the surge of fear and anxiety had aged Pilleter's face by a decade; or maybe it was a flood of memories that were suddenly pouring through his mind in shrieks: of frightened helpless men sitting, backs to him, in chairs with their hands bound behind them; of fingernails cracked from whatever it was that imprisoned men did against the earthen walls of fetid cells; of leaden questions put in heavily accented English; of men who were lost and trembling in their terror, or who were profanely defiant, or who tried to recite their rights, and who were now haunting him like risen ghosts; of those malign glances and nods from the interrogators that told him it was time to take hold with his hands and dispatch this one.

He wanted to tell Tinker that there had been a reason for it, and maybe once there had been, but it was as forgotten now as it had become back in Spain, where the only reason for doing it today was because you had done it yesterday.

"They know who you are," Tinker said.

"There was a war going on," Pilleter said angrily, leaning forward. "Things happen in war. For Christ's sake, you know that. In war everybody is a victim. Look, I was living in Spain when that thing broke out. I was just a kid, and I was scared. I wasn't on anybody's side. But then little by little I got sucked in. It's a whirlpool; you get too close and down you go." Pilleter whispered, pointing across the street, "Those bastards. They weren't soldiers, they were idealists, a bunch of politically naive fools who listened to too much Union Square bullshit and then went and pushed themselves where they weren't wanted. They did more harm than good, screwing up actions in the fields, costing lives. They were embarrassing, and I spoke out against them. A lot of Americans did. And I got . . . involved."

Pilleter sat back, staring sullenly through the window at the men, who were standing motionless in one dark, shapeless knot.

"What do you want?" he asked tonelessly.

"You walk out of here with me," Tinker said, "and you have a chance."

"Men who've gone through war come out of it a little crazy. There's no craziness like it. It never goes away. You never know when it's going to break loose."

"You stick with me and you'll be all right."

"One at a time," Pilleter said, still staring across the street, "they weren't so tough."

"Those are the survivors," Tinker said. "They're tough."

"So," Pilleter said, pushing his chair back from the table and standing up, "it's come to this: I'm putting my life in the hands of a fool."

Tinker got to his feet. Together they began heading for the door.

"My blood will be on your hands," Pilleter said melodramatically.

"Your blood," Tinker said, "will be all over Madison Avenue if you don't stay close to me."

Together they went to the door. Tinker opened it. Pilleter paused for a moment, then they stepped outside. They were out on the sidewalk when Tinker realized that Pilleter had left behind his coat and hat, and the thought flashed through Tinker's mind: *He's going to run for it*. He took a firm grip on Pilleter's arm and looked along the avenue, where a police car opened its headlights and began rolling along the curb toward them.

"Hey!"

The shout came from behind them. They spun around to see their waiter standing in the doorway, his previous professional civility replaced by an irate expression and posture as he waved a piece of paper at them.

"You forgot something," he said.

Tinker hesitated, then felt Pilleter draw away and a moment later took a solidly crashing fist against the side of his face that sent him reeling;

the struggle to keep his balance was futile and he collapsed to the sidewalk, legs flying up in front of him, aware that Pilleter was running—he could hear leather heels rapping on Madison Avenue.

As he sat momentarily dazed, Tinker's refocusing eyes found themselves fixed on the piece of paper being waved in his face, and he looked up into the waiter's stern face and heard him demanding, "What the hell is going on here?"

Tinker got to his feet and yelled to the men across the avenue, but they were already moving, first in a single dark flow and then their dark shapeless mass breaking apart into individual running figures.

Pilleter had plunged recklessly into Madison Avenue's rolling traffic. Tinker watched aghast as there were abrupt outbursts of horns and a hysterical screeching of brakes as Pilleter darted through the vehicles as if he were indestructible. *Jesus*, Tinker thought as he watched breathlessly, *if the son of a bitch is plowed under . . .*

But Pilleter made it across, running into Sixty-Fourth Street, heading for Fifth Avenue as the men ran along the west side of the avenue to cut him off.

Tinker rushed through the momentarily stalled traffic, crossed the avenue, and became the rear element in the chase down Sixty-Fourth Street. He could see the terrified Pilleter outdistancing his pursuers into the night, racing toward Fifth Avenue and the park that lay just beyond. Running in the middle of the street, Tinker soon began passing the men, gasping, angry. Two men broke out of the pack and began gaining on Pilleter. Up ahead Tinker could see heavy traffic on Fifth Avenue, thinking, *If he tries to get through that he's dead*.

A male pedestrian coming from the opposite direction stood flush in Pilleter's path.

"Stop that man!" a voice roared.

The pedestrian froze for a moment, then jumped aside and ran up to the top of a brownstone stoop.

Pilleter was brought down by a flying tackle a few feet from the corner. As Tinker closed in on the two men who now had their quarry pinned to the sidewalk, he stopped and whirled around, holding his arms up.

"Wait! Wait!" he shouted to the others. "Stay there."

The men seemed only too willing to obey, pulling up short, panting, their chests heaving as they strung out on the sidewalk and in the middle of the street.

Tinker advanced to where Pilleter was stretched on the ground with Roger Selman sitting on his chest and the other man crouched over him.

"Bobby," Tinker said, "these two men are policemen. Tell them what you have to tell them and do it now and do it fast, otherwise we're walking away from it and you're on your own."

Gasping, breathing with difficulty, Pilleter said, "Keep those other bastards away from me." He lifted his head from the sidewalk and glared into the darkness where the street full of men were looming, motionless.

"We'll keep them away," Selman said.

Pilleter lay his head back down on the concrete, inhaled deeply, closed his eyes, and in resignation expelled the air he had gulped.

"What do you want?" he asked, his voice sounding almost indifferent.

"Who killed Gloria Manley?" Selman asked.

Christ, Tinker thought, she was still first on the list.

"I did," Pilleter said.

"And?"

"And the maid."

"Why?"

"She recognized me."

"From where?"

"Spain," Pilleter said. With his eyes closed and in a voice so mild, he sounded as though he was talking in his sleep.

As the police car rolled up to the scene, Tinker, feeling suddenly exhausted, turned and drifted back to where the others had reunited into a group. Maurie the Educated Cabbie was standing in the front.

"I want to thank you all," Tinker said.

"Who is that guy, anyway?" Maurie asked.

"You'll read all about it in tomorrow's *Daily News*," Tinker said. "It'll be an exclusive." He smiled affectionately at the curious, still slightly puzzled faces watching him. "You guys were great," he said. "I'm going to see that you all get a ball autographed by the Brooklyn Dodgers and two tickets for Ebbets Field on Opening Day."

One of the cabbies stepped forward.

"I'm a Giants fan," he said.

It was three o'clock in the morning when Selman finally walked out of the station house. A light snow had begun falling, crowding softly through the streetlights and leaving white streaks on the empty East Side streets and across the tops of the patrol cars parked out front. Pausing in front of the double doors at the head of the steps as he belted his trench coat, Selman looked up at what seemed like a gently descending sky. He snapped up his collar and began going down the steps. When he reached the sidewalk he looked to his left as someone carrying a large black umbrella turned the corner. A tired smile played on the cop's lips for a moment.

"I was hoping to catch you," Tinker said, approaching.

"Do you really need that thing?" Selman asked, indicating the umbrella.

"I've never owned one," Tinker said, looking up into the inside of his protective cover. "Actually, I don't own this one either. I took it from Scott's office."

"I take it you've been reinstated."

"With honors. They're running the story on page three. So, how'd your end go?"

"Pilleter kept asking where those guys were. God, I wouldn't want his conscience."

"So everything is all sealed up."

"Except for a few departmental details, like how and why Harvey Tippen happened to confess."

"I hope that'll be seen to," Tinker said.

"Public relations will be working overtime."

"How did you like Tinker's irregulars?"

"Your cabbies? Good bunch of guys. When we were standing in that doorway and they found out I was a cop all they did was bitch about unjust tickets and unfair traffic regulations."

"Anyway, we gave the lie to one good old New York canard."

"Which one?" Selman asked.

"That you can never get a cop or a cabbie when you need one. Here, Roger," Tinker said, handing him the umbrella.

"Thank you," Selman said with mock sincerity. Then he turned and began walking away.

28

As the East Coast Champion began pulling slowly out of Pennsylvania Station, Tinker sat back in his coach seat, head rolled to one side, staring through the window at the dark tunnel. The start-up was so gentle the platform looked like it was sliding past a stationary train. Yes, Scott had taken him back, not grudgingly but sardonically, and with too many reasons: for a job well done, for Tinker's basic talent, because at least he would not have to look at his ace reporter for six weeks, and because of Tinker's agility. Agility? Yes, Scott said: you broke every rule and disobeyed every order and ignored every request—and still landed on your feet. But the handshake was warm and the glint in the eye warily affectionate.

Tinker rolled his head aside and contemplated his seat mate.

"And you, you son of a bitch," he said, "what have *you* got to say?"

"I already said thanks," Harvey said, a sudden wounded look in his face.

"No, no," Tinker said, raising an admonishing finger. "I want more than that. And either I get it or when this train stops at Newark I'm throwing your ass out onto the platform."

"I already said."

"What you already said almost got you sent up the river. I want to know what you didn't say and why. What did you really do with that suit of clothes?"

"Like I said, I threw it away. After that night with Gloria I never wanted to see her again. Wanted nothing to do with her. So I threw it away, because she'd bought it for me."

"That was your way of becoming independent?"

"Yeah," Harvey said with an emphatic nod.

"But you didn't walk home that night, did you?"

"Well, no."

"Cough up, Harvey."

"I'd better not."

"Harvey—"

"You gotta promise never to tell."

"Look, kiddo, because of you I almost lost my job, my girl, and my life. So now that the story is over I feel that my curiosity is entitled to be satisfied."

The train was picking up speed now, still gliding through the tunnel darkness.

"I was supposed to meet her in Toots Shor's that night," Harvey said.

"Gloria?"

"Right. But she didn't show. So while I was sitting there this woman comes up to me and whispers in my ear that she'd like to see me later. I said sure. I always tell 'em that."

"Because you're a gentleman."

"Yes. I had no idea of seeing her because I was seeing Gloria. Which I did, later. But then we had that to-do at that nightclub—which was all her fault—and I told her I wasn't going to see her anymore, which was what she wanted anyway, and I guess I was feeling sort of blue. So I picked up the invite and dropped in on the woman."

"At three-thirty in the morning?"

"I called first."

"And you spent the night with her?"

"I left at about nine-thirty in the morning."

"Who was she?"

"You won't tell?"

Tinker crossed his heart.

"Edena," Harvey whispered. "Bollinger's wife."

"You screwed the boss's wife?"

"She liked me."

"Oh my God."

"So you can see why I couldn't tell anybody," Harvey said. "What chance would I have ever had with the Dodgers?"

"What chance would you have had in Sing Sing?"

"I would have been safer there."

"Safer?"

"Joe, if I would have cost me my career because of a woman my father would have killed me."

"You mean to say you were more afraid of your father than of going to jail?"

"He's crazy, Joe. I know it's not nice to say about your own father, but he's a wild man. A fanatic. His whole life has been aimed toward me making the Dodgers."

The train finally cleared the tunnel and suddenly the coach car was bathed in bright morning sunlight.

Tinker settled back in his seat and closed his eyes.

"I appreciate what you did, Joe," Harvey said.

"I just hope you're the ballplayer everybody says you are, Harvey," Tinker said. "Otherwise it was all for naught."